LiT
Part I – The Dark Ignites
2024 Edition

I0654256

Maxwell F. Hurley

LiT
Part I – The Dark Ignites
2024 Edition

FICTION4ALL

DEDICATION

This book is dedicated to my wife, Sena and our son,
Ethyn

A special thank you to Matt Weber and Jonah Geib

Prologue

In the absence of Lite, the Dark reigns. The war over the fate of the newly conceived primates rages to this day. In an effort to protect humanity, God gave His children a gift of free will to save them from the Dark. Free will allows humans to accept the Lite into their souls to save them from Dark rule. To ensure the new inhabitants of earth receive the correct amount of Lite, the Conduit of Lite is sent as a distributor.

The balance between the Lite and the Dark is difficult to maintain. An overabundance of Lite takes away free will for His children's entrance into Heaven. If the scale tips to evil, the Dark will reign over the primates in Hell, both on Earth and in the afterlife. To gain control and power, the Dark created Infiltrators, a raw form of the Dark whose only job is to kill and possess the willing primates to become Demons.

Throughout time, to hold the Dark back, God has asked particularly special people to accept the role as Lite Sentries. These selfless humans willingly accept the roles to hunt and destroy any Infiltrator or Demon sent by the Dark in an attempt to offset the balance. Now, the balance again is starting to sway, so God again must ask someone to be Lit...

Introduction

As the alarm went off, Mole's first thought of the day was wondering if anyone ever truly enjoyed the sound. It didn't matter what joyous song or soothing tone a person put to wake up to; if a person was in a deep sleep, any noise that woke them up would be nails on a chalkboard. He rubbed his eyes cautiously, trying not to get that hard, crusty substance that forms near the corner into his eyes. Naturally, the first thing Mole did was open his weather app on his phone to see what kind of bike ride he was getting himself into. He often wondered why he would put this on himself. Even though it was his last year in high school, he thought he wanted to do something no one in his class ever did.

He had a feeling of guilt mixed with humor entering his tired mind as it said, "You've already done that." Then a small amount of shame came about because it was something he should not be making light of. This goal he set for himself was something different though; this was something his mom and himself could be proud of.

His senior year was just coming to an endpoint as spring was beginning; this was causing a bit of anxiety. This goal he and his parole officer, Joseph, decided to take on helped him work through his temptations. He wanted to prove to himself that he could set a goal to stick to it. So far, he was doing pretty well at it. No one really knew what he was doing. His classmates just thought he wasn't allowed to drive a car since he ran into that tree. Now he knew the Jack Daniels and Wild Turkey he was chugging down that night didn't make matters any better, but that tree came out of nowhere.

He went into the closet to try to find out what he wanted to wear. Too little clothing and it turned into a miserable cold ride where he knew he wouldn't be able to warm up for the rest of the day. Put too much on and he was unbearably hot. He decided to put on a light jacket with biking shorts to venture out for his quick 30-mile bike ride. His mom bought him this jacket when she saw how serious he was in his commitment. She even had his name embroidered on it "Kale Moler." Even though everyone called him "Mole" as a nickname, he was glad she put his real name on the jacket.

He quietly walked into the kitchen to make himself an English muffin with peanut butter. He didn't want to wake his mom up because she got called into the restaurant late last night. His English muffin popped up from inside the toaster. A small burn was on his fingertips due to the heat from the muffin coming out, but he needed it at that temperature otherwise the peanut butter wouldn't spread as easy. After all the mornings of trying different breakfasts before his training started, he found it was the easiest food on his stomach.

Mole looked at his watch. "Crap," he thought.

He had to get moving because Alex was supposed to be picking him up for school. Speaking of Alex, Mole got a sinister smile on his face as he dialed Alex's phone number. Even though he was running a little behind, he had time to mess with Alex. He dialed her phone.

A very tired, drawn out, "What?" answered on the other side.

"Don't forget to pick me up at 7:30," Mole decided to remind his best friend.

"Huh, what? Mole! Why the hell are you calling me at…four in the morning?"

Mole snickered, almost choking on his breakfast. "Oh, were you sleeping? My bad." He just heard what he could only relate to as a growl as she hung up. Once again, he glanced down at his phone. He was even further behind on time, but it was so worth it.

The wind was brisk which was surprising for this time of year, but it didn't bother him. He actually liked it being a bit cooler out for his training regime. It felt to him that he got a better workout in these temperatures. His body wasn't getting overheated, and it was just the right temperature for him not to sweat too much. The only thing he didn't like was that the heat from his body and cool air temperature made his riding goggles fog during the ride. A couple of times at the stop signs, he had to wipe them off.

He liked the town at this time of day. It was quiet, peaceful, and he knew he was a little bit safer from getting hit by a car than during the day or evening time frame. The ride was dark, with dawn just a hint away. It was a clear sky but for some reason the trees on the side of the road were particularly darker than usual. His mom kept on telling him not to wear headphones on his bike rides, but he had a hard time riding without them.

Joseph agreed as well because the race didn't allow them anyway. "Train the way you race," he kept on reminding him. He knew this, but the music gave him a doorway to think about everything going in his life; he thought about movies, school, his family, and of course, girls. *Who is the lucky one going to be? Who was going to end up with whom? Is Alex ever going to find a guy that lasts more than a couple of weekend nights?* He had all these questions, with no answers in sight. Even though there were no answers over that next hill, he just felt good thinking about it while he was on his bike.

A vibration from his GPS watch let him know he just passed another five miles. Those little notifications were minor motivators for him to keep on going. There was no doubt that he was making good time. It was a game he played, "Morning Mental Math," as he computed how long it would take for him to complete his ride at the current speed. It was always a good feeling when he would get faster than he originally thought. It was amazing how much more he could do compared to where he was at the end of last summer. The time on his watch was telling him he needed to start thinking about heading home. There was another 30 minutes of riding before he had to start heading back to the house.

Mole looked up from his phone which was attached to his bicycle to realize he was about to go down Reaper Hill. This hill was just under a mile down to return with an immediate incline up for the same distance. This hill was always Mole's challenge; no matter what, once he was at the top he needed to take a small break. The interesting thing about this hill was in the spring, the bottom of the hill accumulated water. When he was younger, he used to go playing in the pool of water regardless of how cold it was. It was amazing how immune children are to the elements.

Mole decided to get a quick glance down at his GPS to see what speed he was at; he usually topped out at forty-five miles per hour before he started chickening out. This morning was something different though. It was pretty cold, and the air was stinging his face as the tears from his eyes were drying on his cheek. He decided to start slowing down on the ride because his vision was starting to blur from his eyes watering.

Mole tightly gripped the handlebars on his bike when he noticed something on the bottom of the hill. Was that a black figure running across the road? He started to slow down. If it was a bear, it was big and very rare to see. The black figure took off into the woods. Mole slowed down near the bottom of the hill. He wanted to see if it was a bear.

Why? he thought to himself, there was no way he could get enough speed on his bike to outrun it.

He was slowly moving, hoping he had enough momentum to get up the hill if the bear decided to come after him. The sound of breaking branches caught Mole's attention to the other side of the road. Something big was coming. He turned to see two glowing blue eyes rushing in his direction. His bike started to veer onto the gravel on the side of the road.

Mole lost control of his bike, causing him to fall into the ditch. Mole groaned as he looked to see his legs tangled within his bike as it laid on top of him.

"Ah, man." He just laid there looking at the stars. "That sucked." He looked around to see if he broke anything or was gushing blood. He untangled himself and stood up, wiping himself off of the evidence of his recent venture.

A deep growl froze him. He was hoping what he saw wasn't real, but he looked up to a dark large mass with blue eyes jumping in his direction.

"Oh, sh—"

It jumped in his direction, knocking him back down onto the ground. It was like a wall pushing him over. Whatever it was it didn't stop and just sprinted into the woods.

"Ow," he said softly.

A shadow of a man came up to him extending his hand. "I saw that crash. Are you okay?"

"Yah, thanks," Mole said as he looked at his bike. Mole extended his hand allowing the man to help him up. "Did you see that...thing that ran into me?"

The man shook his head no. The man, who was quite large, picked up his bike. "Looks like it's still functional." He adjusted the chain to make sure it still functioned. He carried the bike onto the road in the direction of Mole's house. "I think you should go home and make sure you're okay."

Mole didn't find any fault in that logic. He needed to get home in time for school. "No argument there." Mole hopped onto his bike. "Thanks again." Mole clipped his shoes onto his bike pedals and headed off into the direction of his house.

"Enjoy the morning," the man said, walking in the opposite direction. He continued to head towards the hill, whistling loudly as if he didn't care in the world.

Mole shook it off and headed back to the house. Mole couldn't believe he saw a bear, let alone two of them, on the bottom of Reaper Hill. "No one at school will believe me."

Chapter 1

Alex liked to lie in bed with the cool air hitting her face from the window being open throughout the night. The fresh air had a soothing effect on her to help her sleep at night. For some reason, she was having some trouble sleeping at night lately. Plus, having Mole wake her up at four in the morning didn't help matters. Her dad constantly nagged her about opening the window when they spend money on central air.

Now, don't get her wrong, she loved central air on those hot nights, but nothing beat those crisp cool nights to clear her head in the morning. She opened her eyes to watch a small bird looking in her direction. The bird sang her a small little song before flying off for its adventures for the day. She reluctantly glanced over at her clock to realize she didn't have much time to shower, get dressed, and get out the door before she had to pick up Sara. Then on top of it all, she had to go pick up Mole before heading out to school.

She stumbled over to her mirror where she looked at her unwashed face from last night. She rubbed her face before looking in the mirror, trying to wake up. Her dad said she looked like Alice Cooper in the mornings with her eyeliner smeared. It was just another thing he could get on her case about.

She looked again in the mirror. "Who is Alice Cooper?" She picked up her phone to look up who she was. To her surprise it was a guy, a very old guy. She compared her phone with the reflection in the mirror, without ever admitting it to her father he kind of had a point.

Her dark eyeliner was smeared on her very pale skin. Her brown eyes were accompanied by a surrounding redness. Her woven braided black hair was put into a bun with multiple strands hanging out to the side. There were times she was annoyed with her hair weave, but the eight hours she spent putting it in with Sara far outweighed the minor aggravations managing it. She took out the elastic band keeping it together and it dropped down to the small of her back. She turned around, looking at the length of her hair.

"Alex." Her mom softly knocked to her bedroom door. "You need to get moving."

"I'm up, Mom," she let her mom know as she took off her pajama bottoms and hopped in a small path to her bathroom. She had to maneuver around an obstacle of clothes scattered throughout her room.

"ALEX!" Her dad's deep, loud voice yelled from their bedroom. "You need to get moving. Your car is blocking mine and I've got court."

Her dad's voice startled her as she tripped on her boots lying on the ground. "Oh shoot!" she said on the way down to ground tumbling onto her floor. She took a quick second to regain her composure. "Damn that hurt."

Alex realized her pants were down at the bottom of her feet as her bare butt was pointed at the ceiling. Luckily, she landed next to her mini-fridge. She pushed some of her clothes out of the way so she could open it up to get one of her Apollo energy drinks. The can was a bit colder than she suspected. She tried being fancy and opened it with one hand. That didn't work out so well as it slipped out of her hands. She quickly picked it up and opened to a stream of foam over the edge of the can onto her clothes. "Son of a ...."

"Language," her mother said on the other side of her closed door. Her mom slightly peeked in on her daughter lying half naked on the ground drinking an energy drink. "Rough morning?"

Alex took a chug of her energy drink. She got up and went into her bathroom. "No more than usual. I'm just getting into the shower." Her mom decided to enter the bedroom of despair. Alex was in the middle of washing her hair when she heard her mom walking around her room picking up her clothes. She popped her head out of the shower. "Mom, what are you doing?"

"Trying to find your floor."

Alex rolled her eyes as she went back to finish her shower. The water was the perfect temperature, where she regretted shutting it off. She was looking for a towel to wrap herself in and found one on the floor. The smell from it wasn't that bad. Alex shrugged it off as she went to dry herself off.

"No," her mom handed her a clean towel. She sat down on the toilet, surveying the bathroom. "You really need to clean this bathroom."

Alex didn't hesitate to use the clean towel. It was soft and the fresh smell of clean laundry put a smile on her face. She liked this one a lot better. Alex considered her mom's suggestion for cleaning her bathroom for a little bit before shrugging it off as a suggestion. The taste of her Apollo drink was so good when she took another sip. She fluffed her woven hair, applied some dark make up to eyes as her mom was making small talk. The school backpack was ready, along with her phone, to head out the door. Her mom just stared at her with a caring smile.

Alex stopped to look around to see if anything was out of place. "What?" she asked, confused.

"You are so beautiful," she said with admiration. "I can't believe my baby girl is going to graduate this year." She came out of Alex's bathroom holding her dirty clothes. The room was extremely messy with clothes scattered among all of her stuff. Her mom was going to miss her when she leaves for college.

"Then she better actually start applying to college. I don't foresee one just dropping on your lap," Alex's dad grumpily chimed in from across the hall. "I bet you still haven't sent out any college applications," he sarcastically said.

Alex instantly gave a snarly look in the direction of her dad's voice and stuck out her tongue. She suddenly realized what she was doing and hesitated to look at her mom, who was raising her eyebrows at her. Her tongue retreated back in her mouth and rolled it around as if she was trying to get something out of her teeth.

Alex could only bring herself to say, "Ooops."

She never understood why her dad had been on her case so much regarding college. She knew she had to go, but she had no idea what field to go into. There weren't any interests of hers that would make money and any particular talents never presented themselves, so she just assumed college would be a waste of time. Her parents kept on saying that is what the first year was for, trying to find yourself.

"Try to get along with him, he's really going to miss you when you leave for college," her mom said as she hugged her only daughter. "Now get your boney butt to school."

Alex's dad came into the room holding his suit jacket in a garment bag. "Alex, I really need to get going." His eyes went from her boots to her to her woven hair. "What? No dog collar today?"

Alex snapped her fingers. "Thanks for the reminder, Dad."

"Really wish you would get out of this Goth stage you're into. The last time you hugged me I got eyeliner all over my shirt prior to court." He turned around to get ready to leave.

"I'm Industrial," Alex quickly corrected as she grabbed her small, studded collar off of her dresser. One last look in the mirror and she was ready for school. "And I don't look like some old guy who wears too much eyeliner."

He just looked at her and shifted to her room. "When you start getting interviews for college, how do you think you're going to come off?" He looked at his watch. "Damn, I have to go." He grabbed his briefcase from his bedroom. "Have a good day, honey." He kissed Alex's mom. Then he turned his attention to Alex. "I need you to move your car and try to think about your future and that whatever actions you do from here will affect your future." He did one last gaze at his watch. "I really gotta go. Come on, move your car, I gotta go. And have a good day at school."

Alex annoyingly nodded at her dad as he walked out of her room.

"And clean your room by this weekend or you're not getting the car."

She stuck her tongue out at him again.

Her mom shook her head with her eyes closed. "Why can't you try to get along with your dad? He kind of has a point about your room. It is a disaster."

Alex eyed around the room. There really wasn't a problem. Everything was placed where she knew she could find it. There was a system for her laundry. She knew exactly how long clothes could be on the ground before they started to have an odor.

"Ah, sh—" Alex stopped herself while her mother was staring at her. "Shoot, I have to go." She gave her mom a kiss on the cheek before heading out to pick up Sara and Mole.

***

"SARA!"

Sara came into the mudroom from completing her morning chores. The air was more brisk than usual for this time of year. She wasn't a real big fan of the cold but luckily, she was moving enough to keep warm. Her morning routine was down to the minute to get her chores done before leaving for school. Plus, there was a pretty good buffer as Alex would be running late before they had to be at school. Sara knew Daddy would be checking up on her soon. There wasn't much time to get into the bathroom to take a shower.

The loud knock on the bathroom door startled Sara. "Hurry up," her father yelled.

"Yes, Daddy," Sara replied.

She grabbed the neatly folded towels from the linen closet to dry off her hair. It was amazing how quickly it dried since she cut it. She was afraid it was too short and she looked like a boy, but Alex reassured her she looked amazing. Alex had tried to convince her to get weave like her, but there was no way she was going to comply with that.

Plus, Daddy would want nothing to do with it. He would probably take scissors to it. A quick cleaning of the bathroom had to be done before she could start on her bedroom. So much to do before she left for school. The closet had meticulously placed hangers arranged by type and then by color…light to dark. She gave a quick glance to make sure her shoes were placed neatly on her shoe rack.

A little tightening on the bed to ensure no wrinkles showed, and…perfect. She looked around for her backpack. Her heart was starting to race because she couldn't find it. It wasn't in its normal place. She was certain it was brought upstairs when she returned from school yesterday. A fearful sight when she opened her bedroom door to see daddy holding the bag.

He walked into her bedroom with might. Everywhere he walked he seemed to be a Goliath. "Good job on the bed." He then opened the closet, running his finger along her clothes. "Nice." Sara glanced down at her watch and met eyes with her dad. "Do you have somewhere to be?"

"Alex should be here soon," she said peering out the window, "…and…" She couldn't finish her sentence before he interrupted her.

"…and Alex doesn't run this household." Her dad thumped his chest. "I do."

Sara could only look at the floor nodding her head. "I know, Daddy."

She felt her dad lift her chin with his finger. "I'm just trying to teach you how to treat your husband when one decides to marry you." He looked around the room. "He will have the responsibility to take care of you; in return, you need to have a clean house for him to come home to."

"Yes, Daddy," Sara agreed. "I'm trying."

He handed her the book bag. "I don't want to find that bag in the kitchen again."

Sara heard Alex's car coming up the driveway with the music from her car penetrating through the house walls. With caution, she took the bag from her dad's hand. "Thank you, Daddy."

He motioned her for a kiss on the cheek. "Now go to school."

Sara walked outside to hop in Alex's car. She quickly gave her dog Buck a quick pat on the head and then jumped into the car.

Alex was chugging down her energy drink as she greeted Sara with a friendly wave. "And how is dear ol' 'Daddy'?" Alex said sarcastically.

"Oh, you know, the same," Sara said while looking at her bag for her cell phone.

Alex looked over at Sara's dad, who simply went by "Jim," and was looking out the window at the two girls. Alex wrinkled her nose at him with disgust. The two of them took off for Mole's house before heading to school.

***

"Are you getting ready for school, Kale?" Mole's mom asked him as he was finishing up his shower. "Alex should be here soon."

Mole rushed down the stairs. He did a quick glance out the window. "She isn't even close, Mom…I can't even hear her music." He grabbed his gym bag from sitting on the kitchen table chair.

Nerves were racing through his body as the Iron Man was coming close and his swim training was not where it should be. Joseph was able to make it to the local college pool to coach him to

24

improve his swim. The school had a pool, but he felt too self-conscious with his swimming while his classmates were there watching. He verified he had his swim and training watch in his workout bag.

"Mom, got anything to eat?" With a quick reflex, he caught a silver rectangle that was thrown at him. "A Pop-Tart? Really?"

"There, don't say I never made you breakfast," his mom replied back to him as she was looking at a new menu for the restaurant.

Mole opened it up and started to eat it. "Got OJ?" He quickly snatched a flying bottle of orange juice his mother threw at him. "I've got a quick question for you." He choked down his breakfast. "How is it that you own a restaurant, cook for hundreds of people a day…and I get Pop-Tarts and a bottle of Ocean Spray?"

"I don't cook. I pay other people to cook." She smirked back at him. She took a moment to put the menu down. Kale was joined by his mother as he was looking out the window to see if Alex was coming. "You know, Kale. You've accomplished so much since last summer." She brushed over his brown hair from his eyes. "But you're still a smart ass. But I wouldn't have you any other way."

"Thanks, Mom," Mole said, doing a final check into his gym bag.

She took a peek out the window, watching Alex come to the door. "Alex is here." Mole glanced over his shoulder as the doorbell rang. "Come in, Alex," Mole's mom yelled. Alex walked in with her friend Sara.

"Good morning, Ms. Moler," Alex said.

"Good morning, girls," she replied. "How are you this morning?"

"I'm fine, thank you," Sara answered.

Alex took a big chug of her Apollo energy drink. "Fantastic, I'm ready to carry the world on my shoulders," she said, pointing to the picture of Apollo carrying the world on his shoulders.

"You two are growing up more and more beautiful every day," Mole's mom, Kate, commented. "You each really have something special."

"Oh, what is that?" Alex was curious about that.

"You put up with him." She thumbed over to Mole who had half a Pop-Tart sticking out of his mouth.

"What?" Mole said with a full mouth.

"Are you all set for graduation?" Kate asked.

"As ready as ever." Alex took another drink. "I just haven't found my 'thing' yet."

"Thing?"

"You know, that feeling of what I'm supposed to do," Alex admitted to her.

"It will come." Kate gave Mole a hug. "Do you have money for lunch?" She held some money in her hand.

"I do." He quickly snatched the money from his mom's hand. "But I will also take this. I need to get something to eat between classes," Mole told her.

"You know, Mole, as much as you eat, I can't believe you have time for all that running and bike

26

riding you're doing," Alex observed. "That can't be good for you." She chugged down the rest of her energy drink.

Kale lifted up the garbage lid and Alex threw the can into the trash without hesitation. "Yeah, not really sure Apollo Energy Drink is on the Food Pyramid."

Alex waved her hand as if brushing him off. "You are nothing to me, little man."

"Alex, we need to get going before we are late." Sara frantically looked at her watch. "If I'm late again, Daddy is—"

Alex interrupted her, "I know. I know." She looked at her phone. "You ready, Mole?"

Mole nodded. He grabbed his gym bag and headed out the door.

"Aren't you forgetting something?" his mom yelled out at him.

Mole stopped and did a quick check of everything. "Not that I know of."

She got up and threw his school bag. "You may need that and tell Joseph that I will have my letter to him for the court by Friday?"

His facial expression dropped a little when she said that. "Thanks, Mom." He gave her a quick hug and headed out to the car.

"Your mom is the coolest," Alex said as she started up the car. "How come she never got married?"

Mole jumped in the backseat, sitting in the middle so he could talk to the both of them. "She had a couple of guys she saw now and then, but nothing serious. Probably just to get her some."

Sara turned quickly back at Mole. "That's your mother!"

Mole laughed. "She's human. She's got needs. As long as I don't hear it, see it, or know it's happening…I'm good." Mole got situated in the backseat finishing up his quick breakfast.

Sara turned back to face the windshield. "How is Joseph doing?"

Alex looked over at Sara grinning. "Or do you mean, 'how is Joseph's son doing'?" Alex pulled into the coffee shop just down the street from the school. "Yeah, I'll take a large double shot mocha. Want anything, Sara?"

"Daddy only gave me enough money for lunch today," she commented.

"And he won't even let you get a job." Mole reached into his wallet and pulled out the money his mom gave him. "The coffee is on me."

Alex looked back. "Do you want anything?"

Mole shook his head no.

Alex turned back into the speaker phone. "Make that two of them. That will be it."

"Please pull forward," the girl over the intercom said.

Mole face perked up. "She sounds cute." Alex pulled up the window and the attractive young lady handed the coffee over.

He jumped up and grabbed the money out of Alex's hand to write something on it. Sara tried to look to see what he was writing but couldn't make it out.

The coffee girl blushed and smiled when she read it. "That's sweet, but I think my boyfriend would be upset if we were to do that," she told him. "But I'll let you know if I'm able to." She handed them the coffee.

Mole was climbing over Alex to talk to the coffee shop girl. "I will be…"

Alex drove off for school before he could finish.

"Hey, I was laying down the groundwork." Mole laughed as he sat back in the seat. He opened up a water jug and started to drink. His attention was on his phone to study his intervals from his bike ride. "You will never believe what I saw this morning."

Sara looked back. "What was that?"

Mole grabbed a banana from his book bag. "I saw a bear run in front of me." He didn't want to admit it made him crash.

Sara looked at him in disbelief. "Really?"

Alex laughed. "Sure, Mole, a bear. Okay." She did a playful "Grrrrr."

Mole took it with a grain of salt. "I'm telling you, I saw it."

***

Osiah returned from his morning walk with Komptin. His body was chilled from being outside for so long. He really wasn't expecting to be out until daybreak but he also wasn't expecting to run into an Infiltrator either.

The first thing he saw when he entered the house was his favorite chair that was calling his name to come sit down. Osiah placed his jacket on a folding hanger set he bought on a late night infomercial. It saved so much space plus he got a complimentary hanging shoe rack with a purchase of ten. Komptin, a massive German Shepherd, laid down next to the fireplace falling instantly into a deep sleep. Sometimes Osiah thought God allowed Komptin to fall asleep instantly as a silent jab at him. Osiah sat down in the chair in the living room with hot cocoa with a bit of Bailey's Irish Cream.

He shut his eyes and tried to fall asleep as most people could do. "Nope." He looked down at his dog lying down by the fire, completely zonked out. "Show off," Osiah said, heading upstairs to take a shower.

After his shower, he came back downstairs to make himself breakfast with the instant breakfast maker he saw on TV a couple of weeks ago. Breakfast was a sandwich, which was dripping with cheese. The smell of egg and ham filled the kitchen. Upon finishing the sandwich, he found himself a bit hungry and he wanted something a little bit sweeter. Something sugary sounded particularly tasty.

A thump outside the door caught his attention. There wasn't anything he could see from outside the window. He didn't think anything of it. He wondered if his dog had heard to confirm if he had heard anything or not. Komptin who was now up had his ears perked. The dog's eyes flashed a glowing neon blue just before a sound of a knock on the door.

Osiah turned to the door and flew open. There stood the brightness of a protruding light that had a silhouette of a figure coming out from it. Osiah calmly sat down with his bowl of cereal. The light diminished and in walked a tall, light brown skinned man with a misty haze in the shape of wings and what looked like a halo of the same substance.

"Rise, rise in the presence of Malkaroy," he commanded.

Osiah continued to eat his cereal. He had to wipe some milk off of his beard. "You done?"

The light vanished and the misty wings and halo slowly vanished. "Osiah." Malkaroy sat down at the table. He swiped his hand across the table. He rubbed his hands on his pants with a facial expression of disgust. "How have you been?"

Osiah took a bite of his cereal. "I'm doing fine. Want anything to eat?"

Malkaroy stated, "I am not allowed many trips, I am not going to waste it on," he picked up a box with a leprechaun on it, "Lucky Charms."

"Don't knock it 'til you try it," Osiah said, taking a spoonful of cereal. "What brings you by? I haven't seen you since—" He looked at the calendar on the wall. "The forties."

Osiah took a moment to reminisce about how when Malkaroy and Osiah reached a mutual understanding of each other, he might even say they were close to being friends. Malkaroy got into a small altercation with a Host who kidnapped a primate and he swallowed his pride to ask Osiah for help since he was familiar with the circumstances. It didn't end as expected but Malkaroy always felt as if he needed to repay Osiah back.

Malkaroy started to run his fingers across the table. A small light stream followed his finger as he drew in the table top. "Yeah, that was an interesting time. I understand you had an interesting night." Osiah looked up at him. "You had a hunt last night?"

Komptin joined Osiah by his side. "I thought I was just going for a walk when Komptin alerted me to an Infiltrator. I think he was a scout though." He scratched Komptin's ears. "Whatever he was doing here, he didn't make it to daylight." He continued to eat his cereal. "The last one I came across was in the eighties when those kids accidently conjured one up. I thought they were focused on the Holy Land and the southern continent."

Malkaroy drew a neon blue dove on the table. "Actually, He was quite surprised to see that one was here; which He does not get often." Osiah went back to eating his cereal. "He has a proposition for you," Malkaroy put out to Osiah.

Osiah put his hands up. "Not interested," he said with a mouthful of cereal with milk dripping from his mouth into his lightly orange beard.

Malkaroy quickly replied, giving him a napkin. "But you do not even know what it is."

"I am not going to investigate this. I'm pretty sure they are going to find me on their own." Osiah got up and gave Komptin a leftover steak from the refrigerator.

Malkaroy drew a symbol of a sideways figure eight on the table. "There is a Lite Sentry coming into fruition."

Osiah stopped. He then continued to look in the refrigerator. "Really? Another one." Osiah closed the door. "That is going to tip the balance a little, isn't it?"

"No," Malkaroy said. "He's hoping it will put it back into alignment."

Osiah looked to Malkaroy who was petting Komptin. "Not interested. I'm not moving back there," Osiah said. "Plus getting Komptin through customs would be a nightmare." Osiah shut the refrigerator door. "It's hot, it's miserable, it's dirty."

Malkaroy showed his dwellings where Osiah had been living.

"Well, dirtier than here," Osiah omitted. "Plus, the people are fighting each other for something they don't even know why they are fighting."

"The Sentry is here, in this town," Malkaroy stated.

Osiah turned to look at Malkaroy. "Why not over in the Holy Land?"

Malkaroy replied, "Unknown. But this evolution has bred a new degree of Dark Infiltrators." Malkaroy got up from the table. "We need someone who knows the Dark Infiltrators and how they work. We would like you to train the Lite Sentry, to teach, to understand their power and ask if they will help us."

Osiah's curiosity peaked. "Can't believe a Lite Sentry is here? And of you course you just can't force them to do it."

Malkaroy replied, "Freewill is the essence of His will and gift to them."

"It will be the downfall of humanity and what lies after for them," Osiah replied. "I've never been so glad to know what lies for 'us' if we fall."

Malkaroy said, "Please have faith."

"What's the proposition part?" Osiah inquired. "Not that I'm interested, but what is it?"

The door opened and walked in Celestial. The beautiful blonde-haired angel walked through the door. Her presence could only be described by actual eyesight. Behind her were her two guardians assigned to her protection, two twins by the names of Ariel and Devine. The two of them were direct clones of each other; Ariel had neon green hair and Devine had bright purple.

"Celestial." Osiah stood up. "What…what are you doing here?"

Komptin walked over to Celestial as she knelt to greet him. Komptin placed his head on her knee as she petted him.

Ariel butted in, "We should not be here."

Devine interjected, "This place is filthy."

The two of them scanned over Osiah's residence.

"This is a mistake," they both said together.

Osiah annoyingly said, "Nice to see you again as well." He cautiously walked up to Celestial. "What are you doing here?"

Celestial grabbed Osiah's hand, helping her up ever so gently. "We need you to help us. This Lite Sentry has no idea what they are in for."

Malkaroy put his hand on Osiah's shoulder. "Osiah, you have been here long enough. You have punished yourself since first light. It is time to come home."

Osiah stated, "You know I can't, I shouldn't. My kind has never been through the doorway, well, not without repercussions."

"You have been here long enough," Malkaroy stated. "You know it is time."

"Mistake," Ariel and Devine reiterated.

"He just asks you to do this one last thing for Him," Celestial said.

Ariel and Devine started to get agitated. Celestial turned around, they both nodded in defeat.

Celestial gazed into Osiah's eyes. "Please."

Osiah reluctantly turned to Malkaroy, still holding onto Celestial's hand. "Why now? Why me? You think Sanah would be better suited to train the Sentry."

"The Sentry should be starting to feel the effects of her powers, she is going to need guidance. No one knows the Dark Infiltrators better than you do," Malkaroy informed him.

Osiah rolled his eyes as he sighed. "Sanah would be better off training her. I really don't want to go down that Dark path."

"You will not." Celestial grabbed his arm. "I know you."

"Wish I had your faith in me." Osiah looked down to Komptin, who in turn looked at him. Komptin flashed his eyes at Osiah, telling him he concurs. "Tell me what you know about her," Osiah reluctantly inquired.

Chapter 2

Alex didn't really enjoy her first morning class. Sara went off to her government class while Alex had to sit through mythology. It wasn't that they were joined at the hip, but Alex would have enjoyed sharing her first fifty-five minutes of pain with her. That way she could talk about it in detail throughout the day. Mole had already gone off to his first class of the day.

He was suffering through Algebra II, which always shocked her about him. After all he went through, he still managed to get through his classes with good grades. Alex was never much of a school scholastic. She maintained her grades but seeing the letter "C" on her tests and papers were not uncommon.

A small sense of relief came to her as she realized she still had five minutes before the bell rang. She opened her locker to get a new Apollo from her book bag. She assumed one more of these wouldn't hurt to have to get her to lunch. The preliminary bell rang, and she shut her locker door where Roger Somberson was leering at her. She was a bit startled but regained her composure quickly.

"What do you want?" she asked him, looking behind him for a way out of this conversation. Roger was a skinny little man with dark orange hair who liked to dress in dark clothes. He smelled like bad cigarettes combined with coffee breath. Alex heard rumors he was into some heavy drugs but never saw any hard evidence of the fact. He wore a medium length black leather coat with chains that rattled every time he walked.

Alex thought it was strange she didn't hear him coming up to her locker. She had heard some people in school talk about them dating because they were making out at a party the beginning of last summer. The sheer thought of dating him sent her stomach into a hurricane of nausea. His chains on his coat rattled as he leaned on the lockers next to her. She caught him eyeing her from head to toe.

"You didn't answer any of my texts," he grilled her.

Alex had to do a double take because she could have sworn he licked his lips at her. She scowled in disgust. "I was busy."

"Doing what?"

She looked up at him straight in the eye in a cold stare. "Cheerleading practice."

"You know Alex. I haven't forgotten about that night," he said grazing his finger across her arm. "If Sara wouldn't have walked in…I think that night would have turned into something to remember."

Alex went back to paying attention to her locker. "Am I ever going to stop paying for that night?" she said softly to herself. "Roger, get over yourself," she said, shutting her locker door. She felt him push her back to lockers. Her arm tingled as it was hit on the locker. "Roger, I was in a bad place and made a mistake by involving you the way I did. For that, I'm sorry, but this…" She started pointing her finger back and forth between her and him. "...is never going to happen."

Roger leaned over to her. "I know that you like it, hell, I know a bunch of guys that you toss to the wayside. We fit, we match." He took a look down the hall behind him. "I was there when Mole wasn't."

"Roger, knock it off," Alex said, pushing him off.

"What is it between the two of you? You must really like it to keep on going back to it," Roger said. Roger quickly looked behind to ensure no one was coming.

Alex rolled her eyes as the final bell for class ran. "Can I go to class now?" Alex felt a tingle in her arm as she pushed him away. She walked away rubbing her elbow.

"Oooo. You know I like you when you're feisty," Roger said rubbing his shoulder. He blew her a kiss as he seductively watched her walk away.

***

Anne was well on her way to graduation and fired up to start her next stage in life, college. She has been making this year the best, but she said that about every year. The goal was to make it better for the class below her to love it here as much as she has. She thought she was so fortunate for her class. The class was completely diverse. They had different religions, races, social classes, and certainly different viewpoints on how the world

39

works. She thought it would prepare her for the world, dealing with different people with various perspectives.

She looked around her mythology class when the bell rang to see Alex's seat was still empty. She could hear the teacher, Mr. Pologoski, ask, "Where is Ms. Johnson?"

Anne watched the overweight man get up from his desk to go shut the door. He used his foot to flip up the doorstop behind him. The door was closing when Alex snuck in the door before it shut. Her black weaved in hair almost got caught in the door.

"Well, good morning, Ms. Johnson. Nice of you to join us." He looked on his watch. "Are you all settled in?"

Alex gave him a thumb's up as she drank her energy drink. Anne had Mr. Pologoski for an English class last year so they both knew the rules. He didn't want food in the class, but drinks were okay as long as they weren't disruptive. Alex drinking her energy drink was more like an extension of her body. A person never saw her without one.

The slamming of Mr. Pologoski's hands on the keyboard caught the class's attention, well everyone but Alex. Anne chuckled to herself as she could see he was trying to withhold from swearing. "Ah, the hell with it. Ms. Johnson, you got a freebie. This new computer system that the IT geniuses decided to put in during the school break is directly sent from Hades." He got up from his desk and grabbed the textbook. "Well, good morning class, I hope you had a chance to finish reading the Odyssey, because we are going to dive into it. This is a classic story and I look forward to what your perceptions are regarding…" he stopped as he was interrupted by the speaker.

"All teachers, please ensure your attendance report is updated prior to the starting lecture."

Mr. Pologoski sighed as he leered at the speaker after putting his head down in disgust. "Class, apparently I need to go find I.T." He walked towards the door. "Be civil while I'm trying to figure this demonic creature out," he said, pointing to the computer.

The class started talking about various topics which were important to them when he left the classroom, but Anne was interested in what she could do in the Student Council. There was some good she could do for the school versus trying to build a resume for college. She was looking at her schedule she had on her phone. This Wednesday was the final volleyball game of the season.

"Alex," she tried to get her attention.

She never understood why Alex played volleyball. She didn't seem to care too much for it, almost like it was an obligation, but Anne couldn't get past the fact that Alex was really good. Such talent from such a tiny person.

"Alex," she said again.

Alex turned around.

"I think we should all meet at Marty's after the game to kindly celebrate our last game together."

Alex took a sip of her drink. "Sure, I don't think I have anything going on." It was Anne's turn to get a thumb's up from Alex. "Plus, Marty's got a great double cheeseburger."

Anne took out her phone and texted the rest of the team of her idea. She wanted to have a win for the school. Even though she wasn't the star on the team, which obviously went to Alex, she was placed as Team Captain. Anne didn't think Alex cared about the position at all.

Anne was shocked Alex was in on the idea. Alex was never one for social team meetings, something about Alex that seemed intrigued Anne. She didn't know a lot about Alex but was always opened to new findings in her classmates. All Anne understood about Alex was that she was into some sort of Goth, but not just Goth, Industrial Goth as Alex liked to put it. She was strong, fast in her emotions. That got her into plenty of fights throughout the year.

Sara and Mole were her best friends. Anne thought that was the most interesting thing about her. She was friends with two other people who were complete opposites of each other. Sara was quiet and reserved, Mole was loud, obnoxious, and for some reason, really into biking and running this past summer, but the three of them clicked. Anne liked that. "Hey Alex, how about coming to a student council meeting?" She couldn't resist asking.

"Don't push your luck." Alex winked at Anne, turning back to her mythology book.

***

Mole was feeling a bit antsy after school, so he decided to run all the way home. It wasn't the first time he had run home from school. It wound him down after being stuck behind a desk for seven hours. The run was just under an hour to complete. When he reached the driveway to his house, he stopped the watch. For being a fluke run, he was pretty happy with his runtime.

The normal ritual of heading over the kitchen to grab something to eat seemed as if it was on autopilot. His mom left him a note that dinner was in the fridge. Inside the refrigerator was an envelope with the words "Dinner" written on it. That gave him a small chuckle as he counted the money from inside.

Kale messaged his mom, "Thanks for cooking dinner. Going to Alex's V-ball game tonight. Be back around 8."

His mom answered back with a "Have fun."

He texted Sara to see if she was going to go to Alex's game tonight but didn't get a reply.

***

Sara went immediately home after school to get her chores done so she could go to Alex's game. The volleyball team was going to eat at Marty's. It was one of those unusual gatherings the class was going to do on a random night. Sara wanted to go.

She grabbed the Windex and went to town on getting those done before Daddy got home. Daddy loved glass. He said glass made a place look refined, but of course he didn't have to clean it. She hated glass. She despised it. The thought of smashing it into a million pieces had crossed her mind more than once. She especially hated the coffee table.

Her daddy's footprints were always on it. The grease from his boots was always difficult to get off. "Stupid glass," she thought. It was everywhere in the house. The kitchen table, the living room end tables, the coffee table was all glass.

She did a final inspection of the house before Daddy got home. She emptied the dishwasher and hand washed the remaining so there would be no dishes left over. She had about a half an hour before her daddy got home. She hoped everything was done. She did a final glance, and she ran upstairs to finish her homework. She was surprised that she didn't have that much. A thunderous noise of the semi-truck pulled into the driveway.

Sara placed her books in her book bag. She ran downstairs and heated up the dinner she made the night before for the two of them. Her daddy was yelling at the dog to shut up as he walked into the kitchen from the garage. The smell of diesel fuel was all over his flannel along with stains of grease. Sara just prayed he didn't get anything dirty before she left for the game.

"Hi, Daddy," she said, taking his coat and hanging it up in the closet. "How was your day?"

"Fine." He hung up his keys. Sara silently thanked God he took his boots off at the backdoor. "These Democrat Liberals are killing me with all these regulations. The price of keeping my truck on the road is getting more expensive." He looked at Sara. "Sometimes, I envy you as a woman. You don't have to worry about such things." He sat down at the table. "What's for dinner? I'm hungry."

"I just heated up dinner from the other night," she said, putting the heated plate on his placemat that she got for him.

"Took the easy route again, huh?" he said, playing with his leftovers.

Sara quickly went on the defense. "No, Daddy, just trying to not waste food."

The clock on the stove was getting close to Alex's game. Sara quickly ran through all her chores in her head to make sure she had them all done before saying, "Daddy, I got all my chores done."

He annoyingly glanced around the house. "Looks good. Animals fed? Is garbage good? Everything dusted and Windexed? Homework complete?"

"Yes," Sara answered back, looking around double-checking everything. The clock on the stove told her that Alex's game would start soon.

"Do you have somewhere to be?" he asked as he was playing with his food with a fork.

"I was hoping to go to the volleyball game." Sara was getting a sour pit in her stomach. "It's Alex's last game. I wanted to be there for her."

"Volleyball? Such a girly game. They better not be taking more money away from the football team to pay for that," he replied to her taking out his wallet. He handed her a little bit of money. "What is it, a couple of dollars to get in?"

"Five," Sara corrected.

"FIVE! For volleyball?" He gave her a ten-dollar bill. "I want a five back."

"Thank you, Daddy." She hugged him and went into the closet to grab her coat.

He got up from the table and opened the refrigerator. "How are you getting there?"

She stopped in her tracks. "I was hoping you could drive me. I'm sorry I didn't ask first."

"Really? I work all day and all I want to do is relax when I get home." He grabbed his keys. "Lucky it's the last game of the year. You need to find a ride home though." He picked up his plate. "I will just pick up something in the drive thru." He opened the garbage can to see it just under half full. "What's this? You told me the garbage was taken out."

Sara felt a lump in her throat as she put her coat back in the closet and shut the door. She knew she wasn't going anywhere. It was so quiet all was heard was her phone vibrating in her pocket. "I didn't think it was that full, plus garbage is coming tomorrow."

"Sara, I don't teach you to think and question me," He picked up the garbage bag. "Now come get this."

Sara went to grab the garbage bag as her dad pushed the bag into her, knocking her on the ground. The garbage spilled all over the kitchen floor. Sara could feel some of the morning coffee grounds in her hair. Then she felt sudden sharp pain from her daddy pulling her hair.

"Daddy," she said grabbing his hands that were gripped on her hair. Tears started clouding her vision as the pain of her hair getting pulled from the top of her head was intensifying.

"I work all day, you lied to me about your chores, just so you can go whore around with your little slut friend." He threw her into the table. "Pick this crap up while I go get something good to eat beside leftovers." He shook his head. "Damn it, Sara, when are you going to learn?" He put his coat on. "Give me your phone and the money I gave you," he demanded as he snapped his fingers at her.

Sara pulled the money back out of her pocket and handed it over with her cell phone.

"I'm sorry, Daddy," she said. "I will do better."

"I do this to teach you. You need to get it through that thick skull of yours. When you marry, you need to learn how to take care of a man's needs because he is the one who will provide for you."

Sara nodded. "I appreciate all that you do for me," Sara went into the kitchen cabinet to grab a new garbage bag.

"This better be cleaned by the time I get home," he commanded slamming the door.

Sara bent over picking up the garbage and noticed blood dripping onto the floor. She quickly grabbed some paper towels to clean up the mess. She went to the bathroom to grab a wet washcloth to try to stop her nose from bleeding.

***

Anne adjusted her knee pads sitting on the bench in front of her gym locker. Throughout her entire year, she observed how her teammates prepared for their game. It was interesting how everyone had their own little pre-game ritual. Anne herself just liked to double check everything and then recheck; Jennifer and Karen liked to volley the ball to one another while talking about the latest gossip, and then there was Alex. Alex's locker was on the other end of the bench from Anne's. Alex downed the last of an energy drink while she was listening to some loud music. Anne finished her final adjustment on her uniform and the coach called the team together for a quick meeting before the game time. Anne turned to Alex who was writing something in the palm of her hands with a blue permanent marker. Alex turned to Anne, gave her a quick wink and held up her hands to say "KILL" on them. Alex gave a smirk and got up to join the team. Anne knew right then and there they were going to win.

Anne gazed around the gym auditorium at the audience who was there to watch the game. Most of the audience were the parents of the players. A few of her teammates' boyfriends were in the stands talking not really paying attention to the game.

During the National Anthem she could see three boys sitting down in the upper bleachers. She could make out Roger, Paul, and Marcus. She didn't understand why they were here. At first she thought Roger was here to support Alex.

A rumor was flying around school that the two of them hooked up at some party last year. She could see them together; they seemed to be into the same interests. Anne didn't like it when she had those thoughts. People shouldn't judge by the physical appearance. It was something she wanted to try to work on. She wanted to give everyone a chance. Mole and his friend Dan were also sitting in the crowd, obviously here to support Alex.

The anthem completed and the game was about to get under way. Throughout the game the crowd was pretty low key. The only times the crowd really got involved is when Alex would get a good spike on the ball. She did it with such force, it would echo through the gym. The crowd reacted to massive hits as they echoed throughout the gym. If the other team got a chance to return the ball, Anne could see the pain from the sting of the ball on their arms.

It was nearing the end of the game and they were in no danger of losing. Westington's team was getting agitated at Alex because they couldn't block or hardly return the ball. Anne served the ball and Westington returned the ball with a spike aimed at Alex. Alex bumped the ball over to Anne who set the ball over to Kendra who spiked it for a point. One more point and the game was over. Anne served the ball, and it was returned quickly.

Kendra quickly bumped back to Anne to set up Alex perfectly for a spike. Alex jumped and nailed the ball at one of the opposing girl's feet. The girl lifted her feet out of the way out of a reaction of fear.

"Bitch," she mouthed over in Alex's direction.

Alex turned around to her teammates congratulating them in a celebration circle from the win. She joined the circle of girls celebrating. "What did she just call me?" She left the circle and started walking towards the other teams' players. Alex's fists were clenched heading in the direction of the girl on the other team.

Anne got in front of Alex to prevent her from doing anything rash. It was weird, but Anne never noticed how blue Alex's contacts were. "Please don't ruin this."

Alex succumbed to Anne's wish. "Okay, I'm hungry anyway." The two of them walked away but Alex still eyed the other girl.

Mole joined Alex by jumping over the railing. "Congrats!" he said, giving Alex a shoulder hug. "Hey, I'm hungry."

Dan was coming up behind him. "Yah, me too."

"Okay, we're all going to Marty's. Want me to give you a ride, Mole?" Alex asked.

"No. I got my bike."

Roger seemed to be coming out of the darkness at the end of the gym leading into the main part of the school. "I could use a ride," he said, walking in Alex's direction.

"Mole, where is Sara?" Alex asked him, looking in Roger's direction. Mole just shrugged his shoulders. "No, Roger, and I'm busy," Alex told him.

"Doing what?"

"Going to church." Alex paid attention to Mole and Dan who were commenting on how they were going to miss girls' volleyball, or more like watching them in their uniforms.

Roger looked at Mole, then back at Alex. "I could make you scream 'oh God'."

Mole stopped his conversation with Dan. Roger had gained Mole's full attention. "Get out of here, isn't there a baby goat out there that you need to sacrifice or something?"

Anne felt the air intensify. She thought it would be best to intervene. "Besides, she is giving me a ride." She looked over in Alex's direction. "Right?"

"Yep," Alex replied. "Let's go." Alex started walking towards the girls' locker room.

She stopped on the way to look up in the rafters. Something seemed to grab her attention. Anne just thought she saw a bird in the rafters. They got into the gym all the time.

Mole watched Roger's actions as he watched Alex walk away into the locker room. "Dude, take a hint."

Roger shot Mole an angry look and backed up as if he was ready to start a fight with Mole.

"Is there a problem here?" Dan quickly got in front of Mole. He was clearly overweight, but he had a country sense of morals to him. Which meant

51

Roger didn't have a chance to come out of this with a win. Anne watched Roger tuck his tail between his legs.

"Someday rodent. I guarantee she will be mine." Roger retreated out of the gym.

Mole kindly punched Dan in the shoulder. "Thanks, but why'd you do that?"

"Man, how do you think that phone call to Joseph would go after that fight?" Dan pointed out.

Mole had a realization on his face when he realized Dan saved him from something, but Anne couldn't figure out what it was. "Who's Joseph?"

Mole and Dan both looked at Anne out of worry. Then they looked at each other. "He's my Jiminy Cricket," Mole answered. "And someday I hope to be a real little boy." Mole put on his bike helmet from underneath his shoulders. "See you there Dan."

"See you there." Dan grabbed his keys from his coat pocket.

"He can't take anything serious," Anne commented. She didn't understand how anyone could be around Mole for more than five minutes because you could never have a serious conversation with him. Mole could only be handled in small doses. He had no school spirit, and he had a pretty bad reputation around town.

Dan shook his head. "Nope."

Anne turned to Dan. "Hey, have I talked to you about how you can support the student council for the benefit of the school?"

***

"Do you think she saw us?" asked a dark misty shadow figure. He floated off the rafter to join his master who was standing on the beam of the ceiling.

"You know that we cannot be seen unless we want to. But that seems to be the case, doesn't it?" Vandor commented as he watched the child primates leave the gymnasium floor.

Vandor stood on the rafter in his long black coat covering his black outfit. He peered down at the group of kids with his pure black eyes. Only a few strands of his long greasy hair came in front of his bone white face. His large hat tilted to the side as he looked behind him to see a bird on the rafter. Vandor assumed the bird caught her attention. He grabbed the bird and it screeched just before he bit the head off.

He held the bird as he jumped down to the floor. "Salamor," he commanded. Vandor walked over to where the girls were playing. He noticed some sweat pooled on the floor. He knelt down putting his finger into it. The smell had a sense of the Lite, so he tasted it with his black forked tongue. "Get down here, now."

Salamor floated gently down to his master's side. "To your command."

"There's a taste of a Lite Sentry?" Vandor looked in the direction of where the girls had left.

"That's a daring move if He did," Salamor insisted. "His feeble attempt to keep the balance."

"I didn't really anticipate this," Vandor turned to the shadows. "Go and find out which one it is. If it's the one I think it is, I think I may have plans for her." Vandor turned around biting into the rest of the bird. He looked up to the ceiling. "Bold but not smart."

***

Anne scraped the last of her dressing with the final piece of lettuce. It was so nice when the perfect amount of dressing matched the salad. The volleyball team was laughing, talking about plays, and talking about games passed.

To Anne's surprise, even Alex seemed to be enjoying herself. She even contributed to some of the stories as well. The girls' get together was officially interrupted by the members of the football team coming into Marty's in a sea of school colors of dark purple and white. Shawn Mansfield, who was the quarterback for the team came in and sat next to Anne. She scooted over to give him some room.

"Hello, Shawn." She organized her mess.

"What's going on ladies?" He looked over at Alex. "Long time, Alex."

"Shawn." Alex finished her double cheeseburger, not giving him a second thought.

"How can you eat like that and stay that skinny?" Shawn asked her. He gestured by putting his finger down his throat pretending to vomit.

Alex didn't even bother to acknowledge his actions. She dumped her Apollo drink into a cup with Mountain Dew.

"So, Anne, I was wondering if you wanted to go out to a movie?" Shawn inquired. "There's a good flick that I've been wanting to see."

Anne knew Shawn had a reputation. She had heard of many girls he seemed to go through. One time he actually said he "loved" a sophomore girl, slept with her, and then dumped her immediately afterwards. That poor girl took it hard, causing her to take some serious counseling. He did have a certain charm to him though. She did not want to submit to it.

Shawn was attractive and it wasn't that she wasn't attracted to him, but he was just after one thing. He grabbed the flower that Anne liked to place on the side of her hair. He smelled it. "Think about it." He got up, taking the flower with him.

***

Alex walked out of Marty's, running into Shawn who was on his way to join the group in the abandoned warehouse parking lot across the street where the class hung out. The cops didn't mind because they never caused any damage to it. Alex scoped the group before she found Mole talking to Dan with his bike on his side. She was kind of hoping Sara was there, but she was pretty sure her dad prevented her from coming out. Mole made eye contact with her. He gave her a nod of acknowledgement to make sure she was okay talking to Shawn. She returned a quick nod back and he went on to his business.

"Hey Alex, I wanted to talk to you really quick." Shawn came up walking close to her.

Alex spit out a piece of gum into a nearby trash can. "Yeah, what about?"

"Look, I would really appreciate it if you didn't talk about what happened a couple of weeks ago," he said while the two of them walked towards the class.

Alex sped up causing Shawn to walk behind her. "Shawn, you don't have to worry, it really wasn't that good to talk about."

***

Anne joined the group after she came back from using the restroom. She grabbed an apple from her purse as she walked up to her classmates. All of them were talking about events from the past four years.

Dan was trying to get a date for the upcoming weekend with no luck. Mole was just being obnoxious as usual making jokes about the school dance coming up. Shawn kept on giving Anne looks, waiting for an answer. Anne didn't want to hurt his feelings but also didn't want to go with him. Alex was talking to one of the other classmates, Jeff, and then saw the two of them walk off together. Anne wanted to see Mole's reaction as the two of them left together. All he did was watch where they went off to and then continued to talk to Dan.

Anne was looking for any type of jealousy, but it didn't seem like he cared. "So weird," she thought.

About a half an hour went by as the group of them was watching the volleyball team's opposing team get ready to get on their bus to leave Marty's. Alex came back from wherever she was with Jeff. He had a smile on his face and the group pretty much knew what went on between the two of them.

"Maybe Alex was dating Jeff now," Anne thought until she watched Alex go over to Mole. He towered over her as she leaned her back into him closing her eyes. He put his arms around her giving a quick squeeze without skipping a beat talking to Dan.

Jeff looked more confused than anyone. Anne just didn't understand it. What was it with Mole and Alex? It was such a weird relationship. Anne watched Shawn nonchalantly make his way over to her. She countered his advances by slowly making it over to Mole and Alex, mainly because Shawn wouldn't go near Alex tonight for some reason.

"You okay?" she overheard Mole ask Alex.

"Just a headache," Alex said, rubbing her eyes.

Kendra spoke up, "Hey, Alex, isn't that the girl who called you a bitch?"

Alex's eyes opened up. "Where?" Kendra pointed in the direction of the girl standing near the school bus waiting for the volleyball team to get on.

"Here we go." Mole sighed.

Alex got up from leaning on Mole to march towards the girl. The crowd began to follow Alex's approach to the girl because they all knew what was coming. Anne saw that the girl noticed Alex heading in her direction. In size comparison, the girl towered over Alex, but Alex was so petite, anybody towered over her.

"Hey," Alex shouted at the girl. "You got something to call me to my face?"

The girl confidently answered Alex. "Oh look, it's the Goth volley witch."

Without hesitation, Alex punched her once in the nose and then another across the face knocking the girl down in an instant. The crowds on both sides were stunned. No one knew what to do. Anne couldn't believe that came from her.

The second that happened, Alex didn't even break stride or emotion. "I'm Industrial." She picked up the girl from the ground and brushed the dirt off her jacket. She pulled out a napkin from her pocket and gently placed it on the girl's nose. Alex leaned in and kissed the Westington girl on the cheek. "Have a safe trip home. It was a good game."

As if nothing happened, Alex turned around and walked away. The crowd stood there, stunned, and it took a couple seconds before anybody said something.

"So, did everyone get that? Industrial." Mole got onto his bike. He said good-bye to Dan and then rode up to Alex who was heading towards her car.

Alex stopped and turned towards Anne. "Oh, did you need a ride home?"

"I'm good." Anne waved off the invite.

***

In the darkness of the shadows, Salamor was overseeing all that had transpired. He watched the skinny red-haired kid dressed in black watching ever so cautiously in the darkness. He just sat and stared at the future Lite Sentry. Salamor approached the boy who could not see him. He sensed the child's feelings were strong. There was envy and hate towards another in that group, strong sense of lust towards a girl, and rage, lots of rage.

Salamor felt as if a good amount of sin was upon this child. He could be molded into an instrument for the Dark; he could be the leader for the battlefront. Salamor needed to make sure his instincts were accurate. Another boy came up behind him smoking the gateway from the glass pipe.

"Hey Roger," the boy said, stumbling. "What are you doing man?"

Salamor started whispering in the ear of the would-be Dark leader. The boy's eyes became bloodshot and dark. Roger took a stick from the ground and hit his friend on the side of the head. The boy fell to the ground and Roger continued to kick him and jumped on top of him, continuing to punch him in the face. Salamor flew around him with pleasure at the sight of a potential Host.

"You may stop." Vandor walked out from the shadows. "What is your name, primate?"

59

"Roger," he said catching his breath looking down at the bloody corpse of Marcus. "Wow, what a rush!"

"Roger," Vandor walked to him stepping over a bleeding body. "What would you do for power? Enough power to do whatever—" He looked over in the direction of a young lady walking towards her car. "—or whomever you want?"

Roger fell to his knees. "To your command." Then from a slew of glowing red eyes came a single dark voice. A dark bearlike creature with glowing red eyes ran towards Roger. Roger opened his arms in acceptance. The creature knocked Roger back into the wall of the warehouse.

"Rise," Vandor commanded. "Roger, that's a primate name; from here on out, you will be called, Gron."

Gron acknowledged his new name with a sneer and flash of red in his eyes.

Chapter 3

Osiah used to enjoy their morning walks but lately they have been turned into hunting expeditions. He sometimes wondered if it was strange luck that he was in the same vicinity where the Infiltrators are starting to appear, or if he was drawing them to him, putting all the people in this town in danger. Osiah knew he was concealed from the Dark. The Dark couldn't find him by sensing his presence, but by chance if an Infiltrator had spotted him like the other night, Osiah had to make sure they didn't make it back to the Dark to report it to their master.

This time of the morning he normally would see a young man on his bike or run but today he was nowhere to be found on the chilly morning. Komptin was a bit more alert than normal today. The run in with the Infiltrator must have had him on edge. He felt something in the air, something he hasn't felt in quite some time. He was hoping what he was feeling wasn't true though. It felt as if someone got infiltrated last night; they are now a Host, or what the Lite calls them, Demons.

Osiah could sense it; it had been a while but the feeling in the air was unmistakable. "Stay alert, Komptin." His faithful companion looked up at him. "It would be nice to nip this before it even starts."

They continued to walk into the woods on their normal trail. Komptin started to bark as his eyes flashed neon blue. Osiah stopped on the trail and ignited a mystical purple fire glow around his closed hands. A flash of light radiated in front him where Celestial stood with Ariel and Devine. He shut his fists down and proceeded to walk ahead.

"Celestial," he approached her while trying to hide his smile.

She held out her hand and smiled. "Oh Osiah, how I have missed you. I apologize I had not visited sooner. I did not know how you would react to me."

He gently bumped her as they walked side by side in the woods. "Always with open arms." She smiled at him as she grabbed his arm. "I was hoping to take you somewhere nice."

Ariel chimed in as she stepped in mud. "At least this place is cleaner than the last place we met," she said, flinging the mud off her boots.

Devine had to get her voice in as well. "Are we trying to upgrade to a cleaner living arrangement?" she asked, flicking pine needles off her shoulder.

A bird landed on Celestial's shoulder and she generated a seed from her hand. She fed him a seed and the bird took off to their nest. "Have you approached the Lite Sentry?"

"No, not yet," Osiah replied. "A single man just can't approach a young teenage girl and say, 'come with me', that would not work in my favor, and then we would be in a world of trouble." He sat down on a fallen tree. "I'm working on it."

Ariel and Devine glanced at each other and rolled their eyes.

"Osiah, she must know what is in for her. Someone succumbed to Infiltration last night."

"I felt it." Osiah looked around.

"Vandor is the leading architect." She took a moment to wait for his reaction.

Osiah turned his attention to Celestial as he tightened his lips. "How do you know this?"

"A little bird told me." She looked to the woods. "This will make things more difficult."

Osiah nodded in agreement. "Just to make things more difficult."

Celestial extended her hand for Osiah to hold. "Walk with me." The two of them started to walk as the two of them remained holding hands. Ariel and Devine stayed relatively back. They were keeping their distance but never taking their eyes off of the two of them while still giving their mistress some private time. "We are in the start of a new war with the Dark."

"Mankind is failing Him," Osiah stated in agreement.

"And you must know we are falling behind on power to stop it. Normally, He would not have initiated a Lite Sentry, but the Darkness is beginning to change the rules. They are tipping the balance."

Osiah stopped in the middle of conversation. "Is this our fault?"

Celestial put her finger on his lip. "No, do not ever think that."

Ariel and Devine approached the two. Devine was the first to speak, "As much as we like to break this up."

"But we are no longer alone," Ariel finished.

Celestial did not hesitate. "Osiah," she said in fear as she looked to the woods.

There was noise coming from the woods of broken branches and red eyes started to appear from nowhere.

Osiah's fists turned to the purple fire mist. His eyes flashed the same color. "Go, get her to the door." He turned to Celestial and gave her a wink. "I got this."

Without hesitation, Ariel and Devine rushed Celestial to the door. The three were gone with the sound of low dark growls approaching closer.

Osiah looked down to Komptin who was on high alert. "Not one can survive."

Komptin's eyes flashed neon blue and as he grew to a purple skinned gargoyle with glowing blue eyes. Komptin's face flattened as four of his teeth grew bigger. His gargoyle ears heightened to the location of the Dark Infiltrators approaching.

Osiah looked to his partner. "Are you ready?"

Komptin growled as his eyes flashed.

***

Alex woke up from her sleep fifteen minutes before her alarm was about to go off. She turned it off thinking she was glad she didn't have to hear that awful sound. She stumbled into her bathroom to grab some Motrin and saw her mom had cleaned her bathroom. Alex needed to do something nice for her, but right now, she was hoping this headache would just go away.

She couldn't remember the last time she woke up with a sinus headache to start her day. She drank some water from the sink and got an Apollo from her little fridge. Her door knocked as her mother walked in with her clean clothes neatly folded.

"Rough night?" her mom asked while putting her laundry.

"Just a sinus headache," she replied. She took a couple of sniffs. "Do you smell that?"

Her mom tried to smell the air. "No. I don't smell anything."

"It's weird, it smells but it smells like nothing," she replied. She opened the window. "It's stronger outside." Her mom joined her at the window and took in a big whiff.

"No, are you on your period?"

"Mom!"

"It's a perfectly legit question. Just before mine starts, my senses and mood are completely out of whack."

"I'm going to shower now." Alex got undressed as she continued to talk to her mom. "Mom, how do you know when you're 'in love' with someone?"

"There's a question that came out of nowhere," her mom mentioned. Her mom came into the bathroom and sat on the closed toilet. "Is this about Kale Moler?"

Alex peeked her head from the shower. "What? No. Gross." Alex continued to shower. "No, I was just wondering."

"Honey," her mom shut the door to the bathroom. "Have you been having sex with the

65

Moler boy?" Alex could tell something serious was on her mom's minds. It was as if she was almost afraid of the answer.

"Mom, that is disgusting," Alex continued. "I have no sexual feelings towards Mole in any way, even though half the school thinks we are doing it."

"Okay honey, I believe you." Her mom got up. "Have you had...?" Alex could see that her mom was having trouble coming up with her words. She didn't know if it was afraid of the answer or just the fact that she was getting embarrassed.

Alex decided to let her mom off the hook before she got too flustered in this conversation. "I have kissed a couple of boys before mom," Alex peeked back out of the shower. "Are you ashamed of me?"

"No honey," her mom replied. "I could never be ashamed of you." She opened up her daughter's medicine cabinet. "It would be hypocritical of me to be ashamed. I was younger than you when I first...kissed a boy." She closed the cabinet. "Just make sure that you are protected in all your decisions. Sometimes two people can get caught up with their emotions."

Alex just nodded as she dried her hair. She looked down at her small hysterectomy scar. She had a pelvic inflammatory disease that caused her to lose the ability to get pregnant. "Mom, are you ever disappointed in me that I can't give you grandchildren?"

Her mom gave her a hug. "Honey, grandchildren are a true blessing from God himself, but so are you." She handed her some clothes for school. "You are a blessing to me, your father, your friends, and the world...don't you ever forget it."

Alex hoped that no matter how old she gets, she would never get tired of hearing her mother tell her how much she loves her. "I'm just worried I would be incapable of love." She got into her dresser to put on clothes. "You know I've made out with some guys, and I liked it, I liked it a lot, but there always seemed to be something missing." Alex could tell her mom was getting a bit uncomfortable. "Are you good with this conversation?"

"Just don't go into detail," she laughed.

"Anyway, but afterwards I really want nothing to do with them," Alex said looking in the mirror. "In fact, they kind of annoy me; sometimes I think I'm incapable of love."

Her mom joined her in front of the mirror. The two of them stared at Alex's reflection. "Honey, you have got more love than anyone I know. You would do anything for the Moler boy and Sara." She put her fingers through her daughter's black woven hair. "And in turn they love you the same."

"How will I know when I'm in love?" Alex asked, staring at herself in the mirror.

"Alex, when you are true to yourself and you act just as you always do, but feel you are overcompensating because of someone in the room...then...you are on the right path." She looked downstairs. "Your father still gives me that feeling."

Alex gave a small force smile. She heard her phone vibrate as she saw Mole was texting her.

"Be careful with the Moler boy," her mom said, spying on her phone.

Alex rolled her eyes. "Is that why he sent him away? Was he worried I would have sex with Mole?"

"Well, that is a conversation we need to have, isn't it?" She turned as she was leaving to look at her daughter. "Alex, just promise me, you will not do anything with him until we talk with your father about it."

Alex looked as if this shouldn't even be a conversation. "Yeah, no problem mom."

"This is serious, promise me," she reiterated. "Promise."

"I promise,. Mom."

***

Sara finished getting ready for school and headed downstairs. Daddy was still passed out on the couch from the night before. The smell of stale beer filled the living room. She opened the window to try to air it out a bit. She shut the TV off and carefully put a blanket over him. Sara softly kissed him on the forehead as she tucked him in. The only thing that was heard was the soft sound of clinging glass bottles as Sara cleaned the living room without disturbing him.

"Did you finish the chores before school?" he grumbled.

"Yes," she quietly answered.

"There's money on the counter." He turned over. "I will be home late tomorrow night."

"Can I sleep over Alex's on Friday night?"

"I don't give a crap. Make sure you do your chores on Friday morning and be back for Saturday night's chores." He could barely be understood. "Your phone is on the counter next to the lunch money."

Sara grabbed her phone and noticed she got a text from Mole asking her if she was going to the game. Oh, how she wanted to go support Alex on the last night of her game. She really wanted to see if Robbie was going to be there as well. She liked him but her dad would never go for it, considering he's Mexican and "they are taking all the work from hard working Americans" as her dad would put it.

She walked outside to wait for Alex to pick her up. She noticed a text from Maria came to her phone. Maria was a code name on her phone to prevent her dad knowing it was from Robbie. This is a nice way to start her day. The air is calm, the dog is quiet, and the birds are in a small morning song. A text from Robbie was just the icing on the cake.

***

Alex sat down for breakfast with her father. He was deep into the paper while drinking his coffee. "Morning, Alex," he said without putting down his paper.

69

"Morning," she grabbed a cup of coffee.

He flipped his paper down as he watched her pour herself a cup of coffee. "Since when do you drink coffee?"

"About two years, Dad," Alex said going through her phone. She texted Sara to let her know she was leaving soon to pick her up. Which was okay because Mole texted her and said he was going to get a ride with Joseph this morning. She let Sara know that they weren't picking up Mole so she could relax a bit before school. "Dad, can we talk about Mole?"

"What about him?"

"Well, I finally got the courage to kiss him last night."

"YOU WHAT?"

"Kidding, Dad, kidding, I swear, I'm kidding." She quickly put her hands up in surrender.

"You're going to give me a heart attack," he said going back to his paper. A message came in on his phone.

Alex was pretty surprised by the reaction she got from her dad. She started drinking her coffee and her mom came from downstairs to give her some toast. The gentleness of her mom's hand on Alex's cheek felt good and heartwarming.

Her dad spoke as he was reading the police reports from the night prior. "Apparently there was a fight last night at Marty's. Know anything about it?"

Alex's heart began to race; she tightened her lips. "Nope."

"It seems the assailant really beat the crap out some poor boy," her dad said,

"Boy?" Alex asked. Alex felt a sense of relief as she continued to drink her coffee.

"Yep, some poor kid smoking meth. Probably a dealer or another user wanting a fix." Her dad looked at his watch. "Looks like this one is going to fall into my lap." He folded the newspaper and drank the rest of his coffee. "I wish I could give personal preference in the punishment."

"Why is that?" Alex asked.

"I'd go for max punishment," her dad replied. "People like that don't belong on the streets."

"Is that why you sent Mole away instead of going for community service?" Alex angrily reminded him. "He made a mistake."

"He could have killed somebody," he reminded her. He closed his eyes trying to calm himself down. "Not having this conversation right now," he said leaving the table. Alex stuck her tongue out at him off behind his back and her father stopped. "And stop sticking tongue out at me."

She slowly stuck her tongue back in her mouth as her mother came up. "How about you let me handle the Moler boy conversation?" She gave Alex some money for lunch. "Now, go to school, and try, if you have time, to look into some colleges. You really need to start thinking on where you want to go."

***

71

Sara just received the text that Alex was on her way to pick her from school. It was about a fifteen minute drive so she found a comfortable place to sit down. She wiped off the morning dew off the lawn furniture. The music from her headphones combined with the morning sun was a perfect way to start her day.

Sara arrived home from school and noticed a white car sitting in the driveway with out-of-state plates. She peeked in the car on her way to the front door but couldn't figure anything out on who the car belonged to. The car was a mess, full of papers and fast food wrappings on the floor. Such a shame for a nice car to be treated so poorly she thought. She walked into the house and saw a little girl about four years old sitting on the floor playing with some dolls.

"Well, who are you? What's your name?" Sara asked the little girl. Sara looked around and noticed a razor blade sitting on the coffee table. She grabbed it to make sure the little girl didn't hurt herself with it. "What's this doing here?"

The little girl looked up and Sara. She placed her finger on her mouth insinuating for Sara to be quiet. She then pointed to the top of the stairs. Sara turned her attention to the top of the stairs. The sound of faint voices came from the master bedroom. Slowly, Sara walked up the stairs as the door opened. A big, long-haired, male walked towards Sara. She quickly backed up to avoid the man. Her heart pounded as she could feel the sweat start to form on top of her forehead. She was pinned

72

in the corner of the landing, frozen with fear. The man, who appeared to be Mexican in origin, sat down on the couch. He sat there looking at the little girl.

Sara didn't feel comfortable with the way he was staring at her. There must be a way to get her away from him. The big man patted his hand on the couch next to him. The little girl got up with her doll and sat next to him. He started to groom her hair. Sara couldn't hear what he was saying to her. Sara had to do something to stop this; she started to walk towards the girl to get her away until she heard someone laughing and giggling in the bedroom upstairs. It was a familiar woman's voice.

"Mom?" Sara continued to walk upstairs. What sounded like laughter as two people trying to keep a secret grew louder and then she heard a man telling her to be quiet as well. Sara quietly whispered as she continued up the stairs, "Mom?"

The door opened. Sara couldn't believe it. Her mom came out of the bedroom in a black miniskirt and holding her pantyhose in her hand. She stumbled down the stairs as she buttoned up a suit jacket.

"Mom," Sara said again. "What are you doing here?"

Her mom tucked her shirt into her skirt and walked over to the Mexican man who gave her a white substance out of his pocket and slipped into her tank top. The door opened again and out walked another man who had brown hair and green eyes.

He came out buckling up his pants as he walked by Sara.

Sara's mom walked into the kitchen and Sara followed her into it. There she took a jar full of money from a cabinet on the top of the refrigerator. She stuffed the money into her purse before dropping it on the floor. The little girl joined Sara by grabbing her hand.

Sara's mom walked over to the little girl and knelt down. "Shhhhh," her mom told the little girl, placing her finger on the child's mouth. The little girl grabbed Sara's hand tight as the two of them watched her mom get into the car with the two men and drove off.

Sara looked down to the child to see she had disappeared. She looked around for the girl and saw her in the reflection in the mirror across the room. Slowly Sara walked towards the mirror as the little girl was mimicking her movements.

Sara approached the mirror and a flash of light startled her. The reflection of the little girl was replaced by the man with the green eyes who then quickly vanished. Sara turned around to the sound of her dad's semi charging up the driveway. The door opened and a dark mystical creature stood in the doorway with red eyes. Sara screamed away into the darkness.

***

"Sara! Sara!" Alex said, trying to wake her friend. "Are you okay?"

Sara leaned over to vomit her breakfast onto the deck. "Alex?" Sara could do nothing but hug her best friend. Sara squeezed her friend so hard she was afraid she was going to break her petite figure.

"It's okay. It's okay," she said, stroking Sara's hair. Alex kissed her on top of the head and placed her own head on top of Sara's, trying to calm her down. "Shhhh, I'm here," Alex said in a soothing voice. "I'm here."

Wiping away tears, Sara choked out, "Don't ever leave me." Sara grabbed Alex's arm as she was holding her.

"I'm not going anywhere," Alex reassured her. "Is your parental figure home?"

Sara wiped her nose and noticed a bit of blood from it. She hid it from Alex because she didn't want to make a big deal of it. "He's in the house."

The two of them walked into the house and Sara's dad was still passed out on the couch. "Mr. Nelson," Alex said walking into the house.

He rolled over. "Take your shoes off before entering the house."

"Mr. Nelson," Alex said in a louder tone. "I think Sara isn't feeling well."

He slowly got up and looked at her from across the room. "She's fine. Go to school."

Alex could feel a tingle sensation in her arms as she was clenching her fist. "Mr. Nelson, get up and check her out."

"Alex! You are really starting to piss me off, you little..." He swung the covers off and approached the two girls in anger.

"You better choose your next word wisely."
Alex stood in front of her friend between the two.
"Now check her out."

Jim and Alex had stared down for a couple
seconds before Sara spoke up. "Alex, I feel fine. It
must have been something I ate," she said. "Daddy,
I feel fine, I swear. I vomited and now I feel fine."
Sara grabbed Alex by the arm. "Let's go."

Alex and Sara got into her car. Alex gave her a
piece of gum. "That will get that nasty taste out of
your mouth."

Sara put the gum in her mouth. She looked to
Alex. "Alex…I …really, I just wanted to say—"

Alex stopped her. "It's okay." The two of them
smiled at each other.

Sara got herself situated. "So, how was the
game last night?"

"Oh, you know, typical night, decided to make
Jeff's night and then got into a fight," she answered
to Sara as she looked out the window of her car and
saw Jim staring at them. She scowled at him and
sped out to class.

**

Vandor came out from behind the deck where
Sara had been laying. Salamor by his side sniffed
the vomit from Sara. "She has much to her."

"Yes," Vandor said. "I would hate to dispose of
such strong force." Vandor looked into house
window where Sara's dad was eating breakfast.
"Such vengeful hate in this one." He looked to

Salamor. "Work on this one. He will be an easy Host."

"To your command." Salamor bowed.

Chapter 4

Anne was having one of the best weeks in her senior year. School spirit was filling the school air. The volleyball team finished their undefeated season and student council was in full swing to ensure school progression was moving forward in their requests. Life was good.

"Hello, Anne," Shawn said behind her in the hallway.

Anne held her books tight to her chest. "Hello. Are you ready for the dance tonight?"

"Only thing that would make it better is if you would go with me," he said to her trying to carry her books for her to class.

Anne pulled the books tighter to her. "This isn't Happy Days. I can carry my own books." Anne stopped at her classroom. "Besides, I have a date."

"Who?" Shawn asked.

Mole came up behind Anne and put his arm around her. "Me, Shawn."

Anne saw the shock on Shawn's face and elbowed Mole in the gut, as she was getting annoyed with the situation. "You wish, now if you will excuse me."

Mole rubbed his stomach. "Noted." He accepted his cue from Anne and sat down in the classroom as Dan started to tease him about getting elbowed. Mole took it in stride and started talking to Kendra next to him.

Anne rolled her eyes. "I'm going with someone from Westington," Anne said. "Besides, I heard you already have a date for the dance." Anne found her seat in the classroom.

Shawn watched her sit down. "Man, that girl is just asking to let loose." He turned around and saw Alex behind him drinking her energy drink. "Oh, Alex, how about round two?"

Alex spit her drink through her nose as she started laughing going into the classroom. She wiped her face as she sat down behind Mole. Shawn didn't take either of those as rejections since he already had a date with Kendra for the dance that night.

He looked over at Anne with pure lust. There was something about her that Shawn couldn't place but he wanted to taste it. He made a personal vow to get with Anne before the year's end.

***

Mole decided to get his bike ride in by going to see his mom at the restaurant before he would make it to the dance. The dinner club was busy as most people came here for a nice Friday night dinner. He sat at the bar in the bike outfit, clearly a fish out of water with the attire that was all around him. He gazed around the dinner club and noticed Anne was there with her date.

The kid was dressed nice but a hint of an "Earthy Hippy" to him, definitely Anne's type. Anne looked over at Mole because he was hard to

79

miss in bright neon spandex. He pointed to the person and gave Anne a thumb's up. Showing her annoyance with Mole, she went back to her conversation with her date.

Down at the end of the bar sat a big man with German Shepard. The man looked familiar, but Mole couldn't really place it. "I take it you weren't injured from your crash." Then it hit Mole, he was the man that helped him that morning he saw that bear.

"Yeah, I was more worried about my bike," he joked. "I never did thank you." Mole paused for a bit. "Ah, thank you."

The man laughed. "No problem." He took a drink of his Jack and Coke.

Mole looked at his drink with envy until something else caught Mole's attention, a very attractive new bartender. Mole took off his helmet and fixed his hair in the mirror in front him. The beautiful girl with light-browned skin came up to Mole. "Can I help you?"

Mole confidently leaned back on the chair. "I just came from riding on the bike and wanted a draft beer to cool the engine down." The bartender looked at him before pouring the drink. Mole couldn't believe he pulled that off without getting checked for identification. Mole grabbed the beer and went to drink it before his mom pulled it from his hand and slapped him in the back of the head.

"Trying to break your sobriety." She turned to the bartender. "Check IDs…on everyone. Especially my seventeen-year-old son." The bartender was embarrassed and apologized to Mole's mom. "It's okay." She sent the bartender off to the other end of the bar and turned her attention back to her alcoholic son. "All that for a girl."

"She's hot, Mom." Mole leaned over the bar checking her out.

His mom gave him an orange juice and a chicken pita. "What do you think Joseph would say if he saw you try that?"

Then a man sat down next to Mole holding a drink. "Yeah, Kale, what would happen if I saw you drinking a beer just to see you hit on my daughter?"

Mole winced as his parole officer sat next to him. "Your daughter? Ah, man."

Joseph situated himself on the bar. "How are you doing, Kate?"

"Just fine. Can I get you another?" she asked.

"Please, Bourbon," he told her, handing the glass. "How's it going, Mole?"

Mole finished his bite of his pita. "Going good. I'm a little sore today for some reason, but other than that, doing good."

"Well, I just wanted to say hi and prevent you from doing anything stupid and of course to see what you were saying to my daughter." He smiled as he patted him on the shoulder. "You are doing well on the training. You told me you were going to do it and stick to our deal, minus this little situation," Joseph said, pointing to his daughter. "Keep your focus, you don't want to fall into a different path."

"Thanks," Mole said. He looked over at Joseph. "I wasn't really going to take a drink of it."

"Don't tempt yourself, especially because you've gone so far," Joseph reminded him.

"You know, I couldn't have done this without you," Mole told him.

"Out of all the kids that came across my desk, I knew you were a guarantee save," Joseph reassured. "Just need to maintain focus." Joseph grabbed his drink Kate put on the bar. He patted him on the shoulder and rejoined his family consisting of his wife and son Robert who should be leaving to join the class for their dance tonight.

"You all done?" Kate picked up his plate.

"Yeah, thanks," Mole answered. He noticed three more people come into the bar. It was Sara, Alex and her mom. He waved over at them. Alex and Sara walked over while Alex's mom went to check on the pizza they were picking up. He gave both girls a quick hug, making sure to give Sara an extra little squeeze.

"Damn you stink," Alex commented, holding her nose.

Mole sniffed his armpits. "That's man sweat."

"It's disgusting," Sara pointed out. Sara's attention was on Robbie, sitting over next to his parents. He motioned for her to sit down next to him. Without hesitation, she just walked over to the table and joined them.

Mole noticed his mother came around the other side of the bar to talk to Alex's mom. The two were in deep conversation. Mole tried to see what was going on but was interrupted by Alex nudging him in the stomach. "Ow, what is it with girls hitting me in the stomach today?"

"Oh quiet, you big ape." She pointed over to Sara who was sitting with Robbie and his parents. Alex and Mole watched Sara smiling. It was nice to see her happy and laugh. "You know her dad would kill her if he saw her talking to him."

Mole nodded. "Yep. She's walking down a dangerous path, but Robbie is a good dude," Mole got up and put his bike helmet on. "I have to get going if I'm going to make the dance on time. Later."

"See you there," Alex gave Mole a quick hug and watched him leave on his bike home. Alex sat at the bar. "Can I get an Apollo?" The bartender gave her the drink with a glass of ice. She couldn't help but notice a strange man with his dog staring at her. "That's one big dog!" she awkwardly said, trying to break the tension.

The man finished his steak and gave a little bit to his dog. "He's a monster all right." He looked over at her. "I apologize for staring. You just reminded me of someone I once knew."

"Once? Did she die?" Alex asked him.

"Yes, she did," Osiah said as he remembered one of the Lite Sentries he came across. Cara was from the early 1400s, or was it 1500s, he couldn't remember, but her death was something he hadn't thought of for quite a while. He grabbed the hair that was woven with a braid of Cara's. He hoped this young Sentry would not have the same fate as hers. He looked down at Komptin. "You can pet him." He swallowed the last of his drink. "He's well trained, I promise you. He won't bite. He's a gentle giant." The dog looked up at him and the man shrugged his shoulders at him. It was almost as the two were having a conversation.

"Dogs really don't like me," Alex nervously said. She looked over at the dog that had a Service Animal garment on. "Oh, I'm sorry. I didn't know he was a PTSD dog."

The man turned to Alex. "It's okay," he patted the dog on his head. "Let me ask you something."

Alex walked over to the man slowly. She cautiously approached the massive dog as she stuck out the back of her hand. She wasn't worried about the strange man, it was more the dog. Alex laughed as the dog licked the back of her hand. "This is the first time a dog licked me on the first meeting." Alex looked up at the man.

"He's a pretty good judge of character. What would you do to protect your friends and family?" he asked her.

Alex looked at him with confusion. "What kind of question is that?" Alex looked at the man who had a sad gentle look to him. "I'm sorry, are you okay?"

The man got up from his seat. "I apologize again if I made you uncomfortable. I just wanted to see if my initial impression of you was correct."

Alex leered at him. "What impression was that?"

"The fact that you have a heart. A heart that has that much caring and equally as strong is rare as blue gold," he said getting up. "And that you will do anything to protect the people you care for." He got up and motioned to the bartender that the money for the bill was on the bar. The strange man looked at her. "Be careful, it's getting dark out there." He left out the back door of the dinner club.

"That was weird," She turned around where Ms. Moler and her mom gave each other a quick hug. "Mrs. Moler, do you know who that was?"

She looked at the end of the bar. "No, he comes in about once a month, just eats, with his dog at his side. He's pleasant and nice, but that's about it."

Her mom turned around and put her arm around Alex. "Thank you, Kate."

Kate replied, "I could not thank you enough. Don't worry about the pizza. It's on the house." The two of them gave each other a look. "I think we do need to do this."

"Yes, long overdue." Alex's mom looked around. "Where's Sara?" Alex pointed over to Sara and Robbie who were holding hands underneath the table. The three of them smiled at Sara. "Oh, let her take her time." She opened up a pizza box and the three of them each had a slice conversing in small talk watching Sara and Robbie talk to his parents.

***

After the dance was over the whole class decided to go over to the lake beach for some unsupervised fun. Some of the classmates had a bon fire ignited to keep them warm during the chilly night. Anne's date was a complete failure. She didn't understand how someone so perfect for her could have no connection. Shawn and his date were partaking in some adult beverages.

Dan and Mole were laughing at each other because Mole had tried dancing but God forgot to give him rhythm. Anne thought he was just being a fool as always. Alex and Sara were talking while Sara was holding hands with Robert who was talking to a group of the guys. Alex had Michael rubbing her shoulders as she wasn't paying any attention to him. Anne immediately looked for Roger who was probably leering in the shadows at her.

She found him doing exactly what she thought. "Creep," she thought. She continued to walk up to the fire trying to find her place and noticed a couple of her friends gossiping about Alex. "What are you talking about?"

"We were just wondering how Alex can go from guy to guy and right in front of Mole," they pondered. "And then when she's done with them, she shows no emotion."

The other chimed in, "Jamie, and don't forget Mole accepts it as if nothing happened. Those two have a weird relationship."

"Well, we all know what happened to Mole last summer," Jamie asked the two of them.

Anne was confused. "No, what happened? I spent the summer with my Grandma going to the college prep courses."

"How boring, anyway. Well, we all know that Mole likes to." She motioned drinking with her hand. "And then, one night he was severely wasted and broke into some guy's garage and stole his car. He crashed the car into the owner's tree, totaling the car."

The other girl continued with the story, "Yeah, the owner who must have been sent from Heaven, didn't even press charges. He just wanted to make sure the Mole was okay and he got help." She took a sip of the beer she was holding. "But Alex's dad had a different idea."

Anne took one of the beers from the cooler. "What did he do?"

"He told the police to arrest Mole and he was going to prosecute him. He sent Mole away for the entire summer to some juvenile detention center down state."

Anne looked over at Mole. "That must have upset her."

"I wasn't happy," Alex said, grabbing an energy drink and a little vile of vodka from her pocket. "Anne, can I talk to you for a second." She walked over to a bench and sat down, patting the seat next to her, motioning her to sit down.

The two girls looked at Anne. "You're dead," they both said at the same time.

Anne took a sip of her beer and began walking towards Alex who was drinking her spiked energy drink. Anne sat down next to Alex who was looking at the crowd. "Look Alex, I didn't mean to gossip about you and Mole."

"Huh? What?" she said, turning her attention to Anne. "I couldn't care less about that. You don't think I know the whole school thinks we're sleeping together, please, I don't care what people think…obviously." She flipped some of her hair and pulled on her studded neck collar.

"Then what did you want to talk to me about?" Anne asked.

"I know you're a smart girl, ambitious, maybe a little too good in the heart department, but that's what I love about you," Alex started off.

Anne didn't know why, but hearing those words made Anne feel really good. She always wondered what Alex thought of her or maybe because she knew she wasn't going to get the crap beaten out of her tonight. "What did you want to talk to me about?"

She leaned over sideways not taking her eyes off the crowd. "Don't trust Shawn. He's only after one thing from you, and it's not a student council position." She took a sip of her drink. "In fact, he only wants you in one position."

"Alex, that's disgusting," Anne said. "But I appreciate the look out."

"I couldn't live with myself if I didn't warn you." She slapped her on the top of the thigh. "Nice talk, we should do this more often." Alex got up and joined the crowd next to Mole.

Anne sat confused and happy at the same time. This thought ended when Roger startled her by sitting next to her in the spot where Alex sat. He rubbed his fingers where she sat and smelled it. "That isn't appropriate."

Roger looked over Alex. "Someday, Anne, someday."

"Well, if you truly care about her, maybe you should change your approach," Anne suggested.

All of sudden, Roger grabbed her hand. "You listen here, you little do goody skank. You have no idea what's coming, I will be at the forefront leading the charge! Then, then she will see."

Anne tensed up and froze. She was literally scared stiff. She could barely get out, "Roger."

"Time for you to go buddy," Mole picked him up out of the bench and kicked him in his backside, stumbling into the woods. "Go join the rest of the group and stay away from Anne and Alex, or go home, or...get your ass kicked." He stood over Anne. "Your choice."

Roger took a step towards Mole and stopped. "See you around." He smirked before turning into the woods.

"What a freak." Mole watched him leave the party. After making sure Roger wasn't going to do anything, he noticed Anne on the log shaking. "You okay?"

"I'm cold."

Mole took off his sweatshirt and gave it to Anne. "Here, why don't you put this on? It will warm you up until you calm down." He sat down next to her. "You'll be fine, besides, for some reason he really hates me, so he'll come after me before you; you'll have time to run," he joked.

"He was so freaky." She rubbed her wrist where Roger grabbed. "I can't stop shivering."

"It's just a very, very, mild form of shock." Mole very cautiously asked, "Is it okay to put my arm around you? It's just to help you warm up, I promise."

Anne smiled with a nod.

Mole slowly put his arm around her in a supporting hug to warm her up. "I remember the first time I got the feeling you got."

"Was that your car accident?" Anne inquired.

"Actually, no." Mole chuckled to himself. "Even though that was a bit of a shock, but the first time I experienced it was waking up from passing out naked on the school football field." Mole thought back. "Worst part was that a bunch of soccer moms found me as they were setting up for their kid's soccer games. There I was laying on my back, buck naked, hungover, and there for every mom to see."

Anne laughed. "That never happened."

Mole stood up. "Yeah, we'll go with that, but I still get free doughnuts every time I go into Mrs. Clark's Bakery."

Anne laughed as she allowed Mole to escort her to the fire to warm her up.

***

Gron stood there looking at Mole after he got kicked by that primate. He knew that now he was Gron he could take on Mole like it was just another day. How he loathed that pitiful excuse for a human. The flare inside him was starting to rise. He could wipe that confident look right off his face and belittle him in front of everyone. Now that Gron was present, nothing was impossible. Anger overtook him as he was about to step out of the dark to destroy him. He took one step forward but was grabbed on the shoulder by Vandor.

"Not yet," he said in a low-whisper. "But you will have your chance."

Gron smirked at Mole as he was comforting Anne on the log. "I'll see you around, rat." He walked into the darkness of the forest.

***

The party was pretty uneventful for the rest of the night. As far as Alex knew, she wasn't going to get into a fight that night. She was happy Roger left. "Thank God."

Everyone was starting to dissipate and head out home. Shawn and Kendra left first, more than likely fulfilling his conquest. That reminded her to see where Anne was. She was sitting on the log talking to Mole, and she was wearing his sweatshirt.

"Wow, now there is something interesting, that I didn't see coming," she caught herself saying out loud.

"What's that?" Sara joined Alex at her side. She saw what Alex was talking about with Mole and Anne. "That's actually kind of sweet. They are total opposites."

Alex turned to Sara who had a smile on her face, but she knew it wasn't from watching Anne and Mole. "Why are you grinning so much?"

"Robbie and I, well, he kissed me," Sara confessed.

Alex hugged her in excitement. "Ooooo. Love it. Is that all?"

Sara shook her head in disbelief. "Yes, Alex. He's such a wonderful guy." She turned in the direction of her house. "I don't know how to tell Daddy this."

"Easy. You don't," Alex bluntly said. "He would flip his lid if he caught the two of you together."

Sara reluctantly agreed. Her dad would go into a fit of rage if he found out she was dating somebody who wasn't white.

Mole, with Anne at his side, came up to Sara and Alex. "Hey were the only ones left. We got five people and one car."

Anne mentioned, "Has anyone not been drinking tonight? I'm feeling a little too buzzed to drive."

Sara and Robbie, who recently joined them, said he couldn't drive. Alex had to confess she too had been drinking a bit this night as well. This was rare for Alex because alcohol makes her sick to her stomach. Everyone looked at Mole.

"What?" He was shocked at what they were about to ask him.

"You have to drive," Alex suggested.

"Yeah, that's not going to happen," he said, looking around for another option. They all still continued to look at him. "I don't even have my license. Hey, and don't forget, I'm not even allowed to drive until I'm eighteen. I really don't feel like going to jail tonight." He didn't see any other choice. "What the Hell! I will illegally drive the car of the daughter of the prosecuting attorney who sent me to juvi, oh and drop off the son of my parole officer at his house; what could possibly go wrong?"

Alex led the group walking to the car and hit Mole in the stomach on the way. "Oh quiet you big ape." They got to the car and noticed Dan passed out from being drunk on the hood of the car. The group just stared and looked at the big man passed out.

"Well, we got ourselves quite a predicament," Mole noticed his large friend passed out.

"No offense to Dan," Anne started to stay, "but this is going to be a very tight fit."

"I'm just worried about how we are going to get him in the car," Robbie was analyzing the situation.

Mole chimed in, "Really? I'm worried if he had Mexican tonight." Mole and Robert walked over to Dan. "Come on buddy, let's get you in the car."

The girls watched the two guys get Dan into the backseat of the car. "Did he vomit in my car?" Alex asked.

"Nope, but we need to get him home before he does." Mole looked over to the car. We're only going to get four more in there."

"I'll stay," Robert offered.

Alex chimed in, "No I will. Mole you take Anne home and drop off Robert, at the end of your driveway, no offense Robbie."

"Understandable," Robbie assured him.

"Then, I'll drop off Anne at her place. Sara and I will come pick you up on the way to your house. I have my bike here and I will ride my bike from your house to mine." The group all agreed it sounded like a good idea. They all squeezed into the car. Mole approached Alex and handed her a knife and bear spray. "It will make me feel better if you have these and stay by the fire."

"Bear spray, really?" Alex started to make fun of him. "You and your fake bears."

"Just humor me," Mole said as he handed it to her. The makeshift taxi went off into the dark.

***

Alex stayed close by the fire overlooking the lake. The dark never scared her and tonight was no exception. She placed the bear spray down and put the knife in her pocket. For some reason, her mind raced to that man at the dinner club with his dog. Then, happiness overcame her as she thought of

94

Sara and Robbie being together. Sara deserved to be happy. There hasn't been happiness in her friend for a long time. What would happen if Mole started dating Anne? She would be good for him, keep him grounded, but Mole never took any love relationship seriously. She doubted if he knew if a girl liked him.

Alex turned around as she heard a stick break in the woods. Something big was out there. A sudden rush of fear was evident as blue glowing eyes were staring at her. "Oh man, I'm going to die." She reached for bear mace. Her arms were starting to tingle; this tingle was getting worse. "Oh, God, I'm having a heart attack and going to get eaten by a bear." The eyes came closer and out walked a massive German Shepherd dog. "I know that dog."

"Komptin," a familiar voice called out.

Alex put her hand on the pocket where the knife was. "I have a knife!" she warned.

"You know, you really don't need a knife," the man called out.

"I have bear spray," she replied.

"You don't need that either," the man said, appearing from the woods.

"Well, I also have," she grabbed the first thing possible. "I have a—" Alex looked. "Apparently I have a small container of vodka."

"Now that is something I need." The man sat down on a log next to the fire and motioned for her to throw the vodka. She tried to throw it at him, but he caught it without even looking. He nonchalantly opened the bottle and chugged it down. "Not a big fan, but it will do." The dog sat down next to the man enjoying the warmth of the fire.

"Are you going to kill me or rape me?" She wouldn't take her eyes off of him. "Because you're going to have to do it in that order and I'm taking Mr. Happy with me."

"Boy, you really are a little spit fire, aren't you?" The man chuckled. "My name is Osiah." He motioned to the dog. "This is Komptin."

Alex greeted the dog and the dog eyes flashed neon blue. Alex stood up stumbling backwards. "What the hell was that?"

"I will explain most of it," Osiah told her. He watched her slowly approach the fire. "Why don't sit down first and tell me your name."

"I'm Alex. Alexandria," she said, slowly sitting down. "But most people call me Alex." She was still on edge as she watched the big man with an orange beard. He had light orange hair with one braided strand with some brown hair woven in. Alex was reminded of a Viking. "Who are you and what the hell is with your dog?"

"Have you ever seen things that you thought you saw but aren't really there?" he asked her.

He watched her agree. "But I just assumed it was just imagination," Alex responded.

"How about a sensation or smell that you can't place?" That question piqued her interest. Osiah picked up a stick and started playing in the sand. "And have you ever had a strange feeling in your arm every time you get anxious or scared?"

"Getting there now," she replied.

"Good," Osiah said. "Why hold back? Let it go."

"Let what go?" Alex asked. "Who the hell are you?"

The same odor came into the air and seemed to be generated from the forest. Komptin was already in an alert stance looking into the woods. The man looked in the direction of the woods. "Oh, perfect timing." The man got up from the log and looked to Komptin. "Protect her." The massive dog got up and stood between her and the woods.

Osiah walked towards the woods as the eyes were getting closer. The man's fists sparked a glowing fire of purple. Alex could feel her arms starting to tingle more. Out of the woods came three dark mists with red eyes. The mists grew into a solid bear-like creature that eyes grew red with more and more hate at every growl. The man cracked his neck and started to fight the beasts. It looked as if the punches thrown by the man were emphasized by the glow.

Alex made sure no more were approaching. The man continued to fight. He jumped on the back of the beasts and formed a purple knife made of Lite that he jammed into the creature's head.

"Ah, what?" Alex said, walking towards the fight.

She walked closer to the fight with her arms tingling more and more. She was completely mesmerized by the actions that have taken place. She didn't realize one of the beasts broke free of the fight. The bearlike creature was stalking with Alex

97

in his sight. His eyes were concentrated pure evil. She started walking backwards until Komptin came between her and the beast.

The German Shepherd started to morph as his fur disappeared. He changed into a four-legged gargoyle creature, which was the only thing Alex could compare it to. Komptin jumped at the beast and they fought before Komptin was able to dig his claws into its chest. The beast growled in pain and disappeared into the ground. Komptin checked back at Alex to check if she was okay. He nudged her towards the fire and stayed near her waiting for another attack.

Osiah was battling the last of the beasts and was on the verge of winning. The beast broke from his clutches, but Osiah shot energy from his hands knocking the beast on the ground.

Osiah walked up to the creature and kneeled on it to prevent it moving. "Komptin, perform a sweep to see if there are any more of them."

As quickly as he said it, Komptin's eyes flashed to agree before he went off in the woods to hunt for more creatures.

"Alex, do you want to see one up close before I kill it?"

Alex started to walk up to the creature.

"Not too close, they have a hunger for Lite Sentries."

Alex stopped in her tracks and looked at the beast trying to swipe at her. "What is it?" she asked.

"Dark Infiltrator," Osiah informed her. "They are used for…"

The creature threw Osiah off his back and he landed on the log hitting his head. The Infiltrator leaped at Alex and a flash of blue came from her fists knocking the creature on the ground. Alex instinctively jumped on the creature's back and stabbed it in the back of the head with a blue mist in the shape of a knife. The creature vanished into the ground.

Osiah ran towards Alex. "Are you okay?" Alex tried to catch her breath as Osiah checked her over. "It's okay to breathe."

"What the hell did I just do?" Alex said looking at her hands. Komptin came back and transformed back to his German Shepard form. Alex patted the dog on his head. "Thanks, Komptin."

"Well, that's really not how I wanted to introduce you to your first lesson, but I will call it a success," Osiah said while checking the back of his head for blood.

Alex looked up. "Lesson, lesson for what?"

Osiah stated, "The darkness has ignited, we've got to diminish it."

Chapter 5

To no surprise, Alex didn't sleep well that night. Sara was fast asleep in the guest room and her parents went to bed immediately after the two of them got home. They were talking in the living room. Her dad was looking like he had a lot on his mind, he always got stressed out when he got assigned a murder case.

It was close to dawn before Alex decided to get out of bed. She took a moment to stare out the window thinking about all that happened last night. In a sense, she was hoping it was all a dream, but in her heart, she knew it wasn't. There was no evidence of that weird stale air when she opened up the window.

She tried to do that thing with her fists again, but her arm wasn't even close to tingling. The house was quiet, causing her to walk quietly downstairs where her dad was drinking a cup of coffee looking out the kitchen window. He was in his bathrobe looking out in the field as if he was in deep thought.

"I can't remember the last time you were up this early," he said, pouring himself another cup of coffee.

"Couldn't sleep," Alex replied, trying to see what he was staring at. As far as she could see he was just looking out the window. "Something on your mind?" Alex stared out the window with him.

Her dad looked at her and poured her a cup of coffee. "Come, let's go sit down on the porch.

There's nothing like the start of a new day by watching the morning come in."

She followed him onto the porch. Alex tightened her robe, accepted her cup of coffee from her father. The two of them simultaneously went to sit down on the bench. Her dad must have landed first because the bench moved causing Alex to fall on the ground. She saved the coffee, but the embarrassment from falling was evident.

Her dad didn't say a word to her. He held out his hand to help her up and steadied the seat so she could sit. It was nice and peaceful, the only sound was her dad separating the newspaper. She rolled her eyes when he handed her the comic section.

"Dad, I'm not a kid any…Oooo, Garfield."

The two of them continued to read the paper together to welcome in the morning.

***

Sara got home a little bit later than she expected but she called her dad to let her know. The house was no more messy than usual. It was odd that her dad wasn't home on Saturday. He worked hard throughout the week and he looked forward to having the weekend off.

She walked upstairs to take a shower before her weekend chores started. She always liked to take her shower before starting them; it made her feel fresh. She walked over to the mirror to fix her hair when she got a text from Robbie.

"Thinking of you this morning."

She could feel the rush of excitement overcome her. She was thinking of a way to answer him back but after several drafts only one seemed appropriate. "Thinking of you too." Sara grabbed some breakfast before heading out to morning chores.

Sara opened the door to see the sun glisten down on her. She took a second to enjoy the nice warmth of the rays while a red cardinal was in the tree branch looking down at her. "Good morning, Mr. Cardinal."

"Sara," a voice came from around the corner of the house.

A startled Sara turned around to see Roger coming up the hill behind her house. "Roger, what are you doing here?"

"Sara, your Alex's best friend." He sat down on the lawn furniture. He rubbed the furniture and sniffed his hand. "When will she see we are meant for each other?"

"Roger, this is a conversation for you and Alex." She opened a metal garbage can that held the dog food. With a scoop full of food, she went to the dog with Roger following her.

"You can make her see how perfect we are for each other," he persisted. "You can see we fit, unlike that preppy jock wannabe Mole."

Sara turned to Roger. "Roger, they are not an item." Buck was barking fiercely through the fence at Roger. "Settle down boy." She turned her attention back to Roger. "I have a lot of work to do."

"Look, if you don't help me to convince her to be with me, I can't be responsible for what will happen," he said grabbing her arm.

Sara tried to pull away. "Roger, that hurts…" And then the sound of the semi came up the driveway. She was never so happy to see that truck come home. Her dad stepped out of the massive truck. He walked up to the two of them.

"Sara, next time you have a boy over, you need to ask me," her dad said. "Mr. Nelson." He extended his arm. "I'm glad to see Sara with a, well, let's just say the right kind of boy."

Roger devilishly grinned at Sara. Sara knew that Roger saw her and Robbie together at the dance and the lake. This could turn bad in an instant. "Daddy, I have to finish my chores." She tried to get away. She just wanted to run in fear of what her daddy would do if he found out she was dating Robbie.

"Sara, don't be rude," her dad said, snapping his fingers at her. "Roger, here, is the type of boy you need to be with."

"Really, Mr. Nelson, I appreciate the kind words that I would be good enough for your daughter, but I'm afraid I'm meant to be with someone else," Roger said. "Sara was just helping me to make sure Alex knows it as well."

"Alex?" Jim busted out with a laugh. "Son, you could do so much better than that little hussy." Her dad started to walk away. "But if you want her that badly, you do what you have to do to make her understand."

"I will, Mr. Nelson." Roger looked down into the woods. "I have to go."

Sara heard the sound of Roger's dirt bike fading away in the distance.

"Creep." Sara shivered. Her dad call for her name and she went into the house. "Yes, Daddy."

"Pull out some meat for dinner tonight," her dad said, putting away his coat.

"What do you want me to make?" she asked while digging in the freezer.

"Anything but Mexican," her dad said, slamming the door.

Slowly Sara closed the freezer door, while a cold shiver traveled down her back.

***

Alex decided to stop at Marty's for a double cheeseburger. Marty's didn't sell Apollos so she had to stop at a convenient store to get one before she went. On her way out, she saw Osiah and Komptin walking across the street. At first, she was hesitant to talk to him until he waved. She quickly ran across the street to greet them. "So, I guess I didn't imagine all that last night."

Osiah was sad at the life she could potentially volunteer into. "Sorry, I'm afraid not."

"I've tried doing that thing with my hands again, but I can't get it," Alex said looking at her hands. "I have so many questions."

"I will answer what I can," Osiah said to her as the two of them walked towards the church. "If you meet me here at the Catholic Church tonight at six, I promise to shed the light on some of this." Osiah gave a gentle smile. "In the meantime, go enjoy being a teenager. There is so much in the world for you." Osiah grabbed the energy drink from her hand and smelled it. "No vodka?"

Alex laughed. "No, actually, alcohol makes me sick to my stomach."

**

Alex just finished ordering her double cheeseburger when Mole rode up on his bicycle with Joseph. He sat down across from Alex while Joseph ordered some lunch him. "Morning, killer," Mole said.

Alex looked up at Mole, and she could feel the blood rush out of her head.

"What?" Mole asked her out of curiosity. "You look paler than usual."

"Oh, never mind." Alex bit into her big burger. "Oh, man that's good." She wiped some ketchup from dripping off the side of her mouth.

Joseph joined the two of them sitting next to Mole. "Good morning, Alex, I see we are eating healthy as always."

She gave him a thumb's up as she was swishing her energy drink mix with soda.

"So, Alex, maybe you can get it out of him; what happened last night that's got him so flustered?"

Alex saw Mole was giving her a short subtle head shake. Alex got the hint. She nodded back and continued to eat her burger. "I don't know," she said, though it was muffled with a mouthful of food.

Joseph laughed at the two of them. "You know, you two have to work on your subtleness." He got up and put his bike helmet on. "Good job today." He patted him on the back and took off. "I'll talk to you later. Nice to see you again, Alex."

"You, too." She waved to him. Alex turned her attention back to Mole. "So, what happened last night with Anne?"

"Nothing," he said, continuing to eat his chicken salad. "We just talked and she was freaked out from Roger bugging her, so I just stayed with her." He looked at Alex. "What about you? When Sara and I returned to pick you up, you looked like you had seen a ghost."

Alex didn't know if they were ghosts, she didn't know anything, all she knew was that something was holding her back from telling Mole what she saw or did. "I was just tired, and my imagination was playing with me." She threw one of her French fries at Mole hitting him in the head. "Now tell me what happened last night."

Mole picked up the French fry and ate it. "Well, I dropped her off and came to pick you up." He noticed Alex giving him a look to tell him that she wanted more. "I mean, it wasn't as cold as that, I assumed Robbie and Sara wanted some—" He finger-quoted. "Alone Time. So, I walked Anne to the door to give them some time together. It was a weird situation. I couldn't go back to the car and then Anne just looked up at me waiting for something; probably wondering why I wasn't leaving. I mean we were talking the whole night and then she didn't really say much when I dropped her off, she just looked up at me. I felt awkward."

Alex closed her eyes and shook her head.

"What?" he asked her.

"Did she give you back your sweatshirt?" She went back to her burger.

Mole looked up to the sky. "No, she didn't. I wonder if I'm going to get that back."

"Doubt it." Alex gave him a wink.

"Bummer, I liked that sweatshirt." He bit into his sandwich. "Should we grab a movie tonight with Robbie and Sara? Try to get those together without her old man knowing," he offered.

"No, I can't." She looked over at him wanting to tell him why but she couldn't. "You started your training program and it inspired me to try something similar." She viewed his facial expression to see if he believed her. Nope.

"Okay, you can tell me when you're ready. Great, now I have to be a third wheel on Rob and Sara's date," he said with annoyance.

Alex rolled her eyes. "You're an idiot."

***

Osiah sat in the bell tower of the church watching out for Alex to arrive. He had about a half an hour before she was supposed to arrive. Osiah didn't know where to begin. He could start with the history, the reasoning, or just jump into it. What he could tell of Alex, he would probably just jump right into before her light overpowered her control. If she accepted the role. Free will, His gift to them to ensure entrance through the gate.

Osiah looked to see where his dog had taken off to. He found Komptin sleeping in the corner. "Show off." A noise of creaking steps alerted Osiah someone was coming. Komptin just rolled over and continued to sleep. The door opened and a priest stood there holding a cup of coffee.

"Joe," Osiah said, grabbing the cup. "Is this Irish?"

"Just like me, Osiah." He smirked. "Black and bitter." The two of them walked together downstairs. "Have you decided how you are going to approach her training?"

"Still debating on that one," Osiah answered, pouring some alcohol in the coffee.

"Make sure you tell her the truth," Father Joe said.

"The truth? I don't even know what that is anymore," he commented to the priest.

"What truth are you looking for?" Malkaroy said out of the shadows. He came up behind him. Komptin looked at Malkaroy and went back to sleep.

"There's something you're not telling me." Osiah continued to stare out the window adding his own little bottle of alcohol to his coffee. He offered some to Malkaroy, but he denied it.

"You know that stuff has been perverted by man," Malkaroy lectured. "Just as they have done with all His gifts." He saw a local boy stumbling from obviously being on some sort of control substance. "Something is off setting the balance."

Osiah turned to Malkaroy. "You think? Last night I approached the Lite Sentry." Malkaroy raised his eyebrow in surprise. "Don't look so shocked."

"I did not think you made up your mind," he commented. "What convinced you?"

"Dark Infiltrators are becoming more abundant. They got awful close to Celestial." The sound of concern animated from his voice.

Malkaroy placed his hand on Osiah. "She is fine. Aerial and Devine would give their lives for her protection."

"They are annoying, but they are loyal," Osiah said, looking over to his dog. "I can relate." There were some headlights coming from the distance.

"It is her?" Malkaroy asked, watching the car pull up in the parking lot across the street.

"Yes," Osiah said. "But there is more. When the Infiltrator took solid form, it didn't lose any power, in fact, he seemed more powerful."

Malkaroy extended his hand. Osiah handed him his little bottle. "This is not the news I was expecting." He viewed a little petite girl dressed up in mostly black with studded skulls and a collar around her neck coming from across the street. Malkaroy could see her pale face glow from the streetlights and her dark make up shadowed her eyes. "This is the Lite Sentry? She is not typical, plus she is really small."

"She took out an Infiltrator last night." Osiah waved to Alex and motioned for her stay there. "Not only that, but there were only three of them and I couldn't hold them. To top it off, one got away from my clutches and almost got to her." Malkaroy looked to his friend, examining his wounds. "I'm fine, I don't feel weak, and they are getting stronger." Osiah chugged the rest of his coffee. "We have to stop this before the balance shifts."

Malkaroy took his hand to his friend's chest. "Do not ever lose faith, my friend. I know I have not always agreed with His choice concerning your involvement, especially with Celestial, but He sees something in you, do not forget that." Malkaroy watched him look to the stars. "Do not forget all that have dissipated in this fight."

Osiah looked to the stars along with Malkaroy. "How could I? I'm reminded about it every night."

Malkaroy leaned over and patted Komptin on the head. "I have to go. "

"Please, tell her…" Osiah looked to the stars.

"She knows," Malkaroy said. "She has got the heart of the world, remember."

Osiah watched his friend disappear into the shadow behind the church bell. Osiah looked to the girl who was about to have her life changed forever.

***

110

Alex opened her energy drink. It tasted so good. She noticed a faint smell in the air, like the one described to her last night. There wasn't anything around that would cause it, maybe it was her car. There was some time to kill so she tried to generate the light from one of her hands while the other held her drink. She started to feel the tingle but it disappeared.

"Don't get frustrated," Osiah explained, coming down the step with Komptin at his side. "It will come naturally to you in time. But first, I think we need to discuss some things that are happening around us and to you."

"I was hoping to get into the glowy things from my hands." Alex studied her hands.

"It will come." Osiah leaned on Alex's car next to her. "But first I need to talk to you about some stuff." Osiah was trying to formulate his words. "How about this? Let's go across the street across from the church." The two of them now faced the red-bricked church. "Close your eyes. What do you feel?"

Alex shut her eyes. "It's something weird in the air. It's cold, but it's not a feeling of cold air."

"Okay, open your eyes," Osiah told her. "That is the normal sense of the world. The world is cold. It is full of people's hate, but it is equal to the love people have. That is why you sense the cold but feel the warmth along with it. It is the feel of constant conflict within it."

"That makes absolutely no sense. Thanks for clarifying that for me," Alex said to her new mentor.

Osiah took a flask from his inside pocket. "You're going to drive me to drink."

"I'm pretty sure you're on cruise control on that one." Alex pointed to the bottle. She chugged her Apollo drink.

Osiah shook his head in disbelief. "Okay, come with me." Osiah walked into the church where a big black man in a priest collar greeted them.

"Am I supposed to bow? Is this… you know… the All Mighty?" she asked.

The priest let out a deep laugh. "My name is Joe."

"God's name is 'Joe'?" Alex's eyes widened.

"I'm the priest here. My role in all this is to make sure this man has a job. I'm leaving for the night." He placed his hand on Alex's head and played with her small weaves. "Youth today. Anyway, I'm going home. Good night, make sure to lock up." He left out the front door.

Osiah waved to his friend before continuing with their lesson. They ended up in the sanctuary and sat in the back pew staring up at the crucifix. Alex sat next to him. "What I'm about to tell you could possibly save your life. So, I need you to listen." Alex made sure to focus on what he was saying. "Extend out those feelings again and tell me what you feel."

Alex closed her eyes. There was a new sensation in the air. It wasn't cold at all. It was warmth, it was as if the sun was directly shining on her. "I feel a warmth," she giggled a little. "I'm sorry, I don't know how to explain it."

"That warmth you feel is only found on His sacred ground. Now I want you to try to generate your Lite."

Here we go! Alex was about to generate it on purpose for the first time. She could feel her heart race into anticipation. Nothing. Not even a little tingle. She looked at her hands. "What the hell!" Osiah looked at her. "Sorry," Alex said, putting her hands over her mouth.

"You will have no power here, but you will be safe. No Dark can hurt you while you are here or any other church, mosque, etc. They are all different, but they all serve Him. It's just that man is confused and latches onto what they think is the best way to serve."

"But why doesn't He just tell them?" Alex asked, looking over to the crucifix.

"Free will," Osiah said. "His greatest gift. He lets man be himself. It is just he perverts it," stealing Malkaroy's description, "and gets lost." He looks down to Alex. "That is when Darkness plays their hand. Normally there is a balance, but it seems the darkness is tipping the scale."

"Why doesn't He just make everyone happy and light?" Alex asked.

"Because then you take away 'free will'," Osiah explained.

"And because the Darkness is tipping the scale, I got 'tapped' as this Lite thing?" Alex said. "Why me?"

"Your caring, strength, and innocence," Osiah explained to her.

"Oh, I'm far from being a virgin."

Osiah rubbed his eyes and sighed. He took another drink from his flask and looked to the ceiling. "Really?" He got up and started walking out of the church. "Let's go."

"What?!" Alex asked, chasing after him.

***

Alex met Osiah and Komptin in an old warehouse across from town. Osiah was placing a bunch of boxes into a pile. Alex was thinking it was some sort of target she was supposed to do something with. He said something to Komptin and his eyes flashed the neon blue. He got up and took off.

"Komptin is just making sure we won't be interrupted," Osiah told her.

"What's with the flash of blue in his eyes and the transformation into that gargoyle looking creature?" Alex finished off her energy drink.

"Komptin is a Guardian. His main goal is protection and hunter from all things Darkness," Osiah explained.

"Why is he attached to you?" Alex asked.

"Protection," Osiah clarified.

114

"It doesn't seem to me you need protection," She looked at his hands.

Osiah didn't answer. "Let's get started. Generating the Lite is kind easy to learn but takes a while to master." Osiah turned on his hands. The purple fire mist generated from his hands. "At first you can use the Lite as an emphasis of your power." He lifted up a cement block with ease. He threw it in the air and punched through it.

"Damn!" Alex said getting the cement pieces out of her hair. "I'm going to be able to do that?"

"And more," Osiah said. "You will be able to generate spears and you will be able to generate enough Lite to 'push'." Osiah lifted his arms towards the boxes. A blast of purple generated from his knocking over the boxes. "But we have to learn to crawl before we run a marathon."

"How can I do this?" Alex enthusiastically asked.

"You have to understand, once you start this path, you are in for a completely different life than you know now," Osiah warned her.

Alex gazed up at Osiah. "As in what? What's the catch?"

Osiah turned and stacked the boxes back up. "Well for starters, you will never sleep again. Even on nights you don't hunt. The Lite energizes your body and you will never sleep. At first you may think it's a benefit, but there will be times you start to miss it and that leads into another thing you will lose. You will lose a portion of your Free Will. You will be sent by the Lite to balance out on what the

115

Dark has done. You will still be you, but you will be sent out on missions, hunts, and be responsible for the wellness of all humans on this planet." Osiah turned to her. "It is dangerous, it is exhausting, and you have to keep it secret from all who you care about."

"Then why do it?" Alex asked looking on the ground. She felt ashamed of being selfish of such a question when God has asked her to do something so important.

"For a Lite Sentry, there is no greater feeling of knowing you are helping the world," Osiah said. "It sounds cheesy, but it's the best way I can put it." Osiah walked up to Alex and put his hand on her shoulder. "I can't promise you that you will enjoy every minute, in fact, you will probably experience much pain throughout the rest of your life, but that is life as a regular person as well. What I need from you, is for you to accept all that I'm about to teach you."

Alex walked towards the boxes. She didn't know what to do. What was she about to get herself into? She picked up portions of the cement block that was punched to pieces by Osiah. Her phone vibrated in her pocket. She got a text from her mom to tell her not to stay out too late. The second text was Mole complaining about being the third wheel on Sara's date with Rob. She understood that she must do what she can do to protect them from harm. She put her phone in her pocket and turned to Osiah. "I will do it," Alex said. Her hands ignited a blue fire mist. She couldn't believe she generated this power.

"Good," Osiah said. "Let's get to work."

Chapter 6

Mole didn't have any trouble getting up in the morning ride at his usual time. This morning was brisk with fog patches throughout the tip of trees. His mom had put out his morning Pop-Tart with a note of encouragement. He texted Alex to let her know that he was going to ride his bike to school today. To his surprise, she answered him as if she was already up. He just gave her a quick little smiley face emoji and then headed off on his bike ride. This wasn't his normal bike ride day; he was just using this opportunity to kill some miles before his swim.

He hopped on his bike and headed down the hill. He made it to the college pool with relative ease. He was quite impressed with his time once he arrived at the college. He's becoming less sore throughout the day and it seemed like he was having more and more energy. Maybe, just maybe, he would be able to complete the race. He locked up his bike and headed into the college to start this portion of the swim training.

The laps were going quick, and the strides were smooth. There was some time he could take for some water. He again looked at his watch to see the time before he had to make it to school. An attractive girl down on the end of the pool was waving to him. He looked around to make sure it was at him. He waved back and finished up his swim. Those final laps seemed to go a little bit better.

He got out of the pool and dried off. The girl who waved to him managed to get down to his pool lane. She obviously went to school here as she was wearing the school's swimsuit. She got out of the pool and stopped to talk to him. "Hello."

Mole wrapped the towel around in fear of being a little too cold. "Hi, there. How was your swim?"

She grabbed a towel as well. "It went relatively well; I'm having trouble with my butterflies. I noticed you have been coming here for quite a while. Do you go to school here?"

Mole was embarrassed because he knew he was going to have to tell her that he was still in high school. "No, I go to high school here." Well, that just came out, he thought. "I just use the pool at the gym because I'm training for an Iron Man competition."

"That's awesome. Seems like training is going well," she said, looking at Mole smiling. She immediately tried to recover herself. "It must have been nice growing up around here." She looked at her watch. "Oh, I have to get to class. Will you be here Saturday?"

Mole was quite happy because Saturday was actually going to be his long swimming day. "Yes, first thing in the morning."

The girl smiled. "Good, my name is Marissa."

"Kale, but my friends call me 'Mole'," he said, shaking her soft hands.

"Well Mole, hopefully I will see you Saturday then," Marissa said, walking away biting her bottom lip.

"Oh yeah, I'm the man!" Mole said to himself. He grabbed his gear and ran off into the locker room. He immediately had to text Alex about what just transpired. He was so excited he could barely text, plus he was putting money down that Alex wouldn't believe him. She then texted him back.

All Alex replied was, "Mole is going to get some."

***

Sara got up that morning. She sat in her bed debating on trying to sleep some more, but she knew she had to get moving to start her day. The birds were chirping loudly when she opened the window. That red cardinal that has been hanging around was in the trees enjoying the sunrise. She grabbed her phone and texted Robbie a picture of the cardinal. She was so excited, even though they never made it official, she believed she had a full out boyfriend.

Why wouldn't Daddy approve if she told him? But she was way too afraid to tell him. She had to delete all his messages from her phone to ensure her dad didn't know it was him she was talking to.

She finished her chores while her dad had already left for work. He left a to-do list on the kitchen table which meant she couldn't go out tonight. What she really wanted to do was meet up with Robbie. Since he was out of town, it their chance to be together.

Alex's car came up the hill with her music vibrating the windows. It was amazing that she has been on time for the past couple of days. She got into her car as Alex was finishing her ritual morning drink. She looked over at Sara. "You look different."

Sara blushed because she knew what it was, but she was afraid to say it aloud. She wanted to deflect the conversation. "How about you? You've actually been on time to school." Sara studied her friend. "You look different as well."

Alex started to drive back to school. "Haven't been sleeping much, so I thought I might as well get to school."

Sara asked, "Do you mind if we stop for coffee?"

Alex didn't skip a beat. "Please, my car is on self-driving mode straight there."

***

Mole was talking to Dan and Robbie when Alex and Sara pulled up to the parking lot. "What's going on?" Alex asked.

"Not much." Dan was eating a fast food breakfast sandwich. "We are just talking about our plans on going out tonight. We were trying to figure out what to do."

"Good, I wanna do something fun tonight," Alex said, finishing her coffee.

Roger walked by Alex. "How about me? I can be something fun."

Alex pretended to throw up in her mouth. "Sorry, a disgusting image just happened to pop in my head."

Sara got on guard at the sound of his voice. "What's wrong, Sara?" Robbie asked her. "You're squeezing my hand awfully tight."

"Roger came over to my house a couple of weeks ago," Sara said. "Really freaked me out." She began to tell them the story.

Robbie was getting quite upset.

"Then he grabbed my arm, wouldn't let me go. If my dad didn't come home, I think he would have really hurt me."

Robbie started to walk over to Roger, but Sara stopped him.

"Don't do anything, it is fine."

Robbie continued to eye up Roger.

"I mean it."

Robbie reluctantly succumbed to Sara's wishes, still watching Roger as he was walking away.

Anne came up to the group next to Alex. "Are you guys going to go out tonight?" She started to dig for papers out of her folder. "Plus I got the weekly Student Council update for you." She handed everyone a sheet. The group read it over and put it in their folders not to be rude. "There's a fundraiser for a food shelter this weekend. We are trying to get the class together this Saturday for a bike ride. We start at the school and head over to Westington, around the lake, and come back to the school for a burger burn sponsored by Marty's." Anne scanned the crowd. "You're all in, right?"

Sara was the first to speak, "I can't. I have chores at that time."

Robbie was next to answer, "I have to go with my dad fishing that morning."

Alex chimed in, "Don't even look at me, I can't even think of a reason to give except.... I'm not going to do it." Sara wasn't surprised at that reaction. Alex didn't really like doing too physical, especially extracurricular, activities.

"I'll do it," Mole was putting the event into his phone "I have to do my long bike ride that day anyway."

"Perfect," Anne said. "It's just $20.00 and some canned goods to enter and you get a free t-shirt at the end!" Anne said with excitement. "Race starts at eight. I have to go and remind everyone about it. See you Saturday," she said as she walked over to Shawn and his friends.

Alex who was giving Mole a surprised look. She mouthed with no words coming out, "What are you doing?" Mole just hid in his phone without making eye contact with Alex and was saved as the bell rang.

***

That night at the town was extra busy for a school night at Marty's. The night was being fun for no particular reason. The air was pleasant and was filled with laughter from class. It was a night that

123

could have lasted forever. Occasionally Alex could feel the tingle sensation come to her arms, but it went away with concentration. She didn't know if it was her imagination or not, but having her fist light up in front of everyone probably wouldn't be the best idea.

Mole and Dan were finishing their milkshakes as Sara and Robbie were talking and laughing with each other. Alex noticed Osiah and Komptin grabbing a to-go bag of burgers at the counter. She gave him a quick wave as she walked up to him to talk. "Checking up on me now?"

"Nope, somebody—" He pointed down at Komptin. "—wanted a burger."

Alex noticed her mom and dad even came out as well for a quick burger. They didn't do it often, sometimes Alex thought they were just here to check up on her. They approached Osiah and Alex.

Her mom tried handing her a bottle of water. "Here honey."

Alex looked at the water in a confusing state. "What is this water you speak of?" They all laughed while her dad just handed her a coffee. "Thanks Dad."

"That's my little girl," he said. She hasn't heard that come from him since she started junior high. She thought she would return the olive branch with a wink. The coffee was disgusting, but she didn't want to hurt her dad's feelings.

"Mom, dad, this is Osiah and his dog Komptin," she introduced.

"Oh, your Alex's boss at the church," her mom said, shaking his hand. "Well, I think it's wonderful how much Alex has changed since working there."

"I would have never thought, you of all people, would work at a church," her dad said. "But I'm glad you are."

Komptin went up to Alex and she started to scratch her ears. Osiah said, "Yes, she is a little spitfire but she is doing some good work for us." Osiah looked around Marty's. "It's nice to have her on board."

"Speaking of which, there is still plenty I need to do," she said looking at her watch.

Mole, Sara, Rob, and Dan walked by Alex. Mole yelled, "Hey, Alex, I'm sure you're hungry. Double cheeseburger on me." The group stopped and Alex introduced everyone to her Osiah and Komptin.

"Go Alex. Go have fun. Be a teenager," Osiah said. "Komptin and I can take care of it."

Her mom had a counteroffer to Osiah. "How about you join Mike and me for a drink at the dinner club?" She looked to her husband who agreed.

"I could go for a drink," Mike said. "Please join us."

"Sounds good to me." Osiah thought he could use a drink. "I will meet you there."

Alex's parents gave Alex some money and took off to the dinner club. Alex turned to Mole. "Ah, where's my burger?"

***

125

Sara was walking out with Robbie to his truck. He was particularly quiet this evening. "What's on your mind?"

"Nothing particular," he told her still being on the quiet side.

She stopped him and grabbed his coat to pull him closer. "Robbie Rodriguez, I know you better." She kissed him. "Now are you going to tell me, or do I have to beat it out of you?"

"Well, I don't want that to happen." He playfully held up his hands. "I was just wondering if we will ever be able to tell your dad were dating, and if he would ever accept it."

Sara didn't know what to say. She wanted to tell him, yes, come over for dinner tomorrow. She wanted to tell him her dad would love to take him hunting or fishing; however, she knew the truth. The only thing she could do was hug him.

***

Gron stood in the shadows smoking a cigarette. Salamor appeared from the darkness of the woods. "Tonight, go, speak, and attack that one from the group. Listen to Salamor, and Vandor will ensure you get her."

Gron finished his cigarette. "What does he want me to do?"

Salamor pointed to Sara and whispered the instructions in his ear. Gron snickered and walked towards the car. Salamor spoke to Vandor who was watching in the shadows. "This should be fun to watch."

Vandor looked up to the sky. "She will become one of us or she will die." Vandor's eyes were black as he leered to the sky.

***

Sara tried everything she could to comfort Robbie. It was evident her dad's views on him were not in his favor. All she could think to do was kiss him and show him that she cared about him regardless of what her dad thought.

"Hey, Sara," Roger yelled across the parking lot. Sara saw the skinny kid dressed in black leather coat approach. "Did you talk to Alex like I asked?" He came up to Robbie and Sara. He smelled of cigarette smoke and death. Sara developed a small lump in the back of her throat. The air suddenly felt dark as he was coming, and she didn't like it. The intensity was growing. She could feel Robbie start to tense up and gently placed Sara behind him. Mole and Dan positioned themselves behind Roger.

"What's going on, Robbie?" Mole making sure everything was okay.

"Nothing I can't handle," Robbie informed him. "Roger, I think it's time for you to go."

Roger was surrounded by all that hated him. "I can see it's time to go." He looked over at Sara. "Maybe I should tell daddy his daughter is a spic's little harlot," Robbie didn't hesitate. He punched Roger across the face. Roger twisted as he fell into

Mole's body. He looked up at Mole who was staring down at him. "Don't worry, I haven't forgotten about you." Mole pushed him off his chest and started to walk towards him.

"NO!" Robbie yelled. "I will take care of him."

Sara screamed, "ROBBIE! He's not worth it."

Roger walked away from the group stumbling all about. He motioned for Robbie to come at him. Robbie punched him again across the face and he fell to the ground. Robbie stood over him trying to calm himself down. "Go home. Leave Sara alone and get the hint, Alex wants nothing to do with you." He turned away to join the group.

Roger got up grinning; he wiped a small amount of blood off his lip. With strength and speed, he grabbed Robbie by the jacket and threw him into a car. Robbie was shocked by the sudden attack and wasn't able to defend himself. Roger punched him in the stomach causing Robbie to keel over to try to catch his breath. Sara screamed in horror. Robbie tried to fight back but was too slow.

Roger kneed him in the face then jerked his chin up with his hand. "Surprise," he grinned as he punched him in the nose, causing blood began to pour.

"ROGER, STOP IT!" Sara screamed.

Mole and Dan went to stop him, but Roger turned to them with a knife. "No, no, no. Three against one really isn't fair." Roger turned back to Robbie. He grabbed his head and bashed it against the car. Rob's head continued to bleed. He stood Robbie up as he could hardly maintain his balance.

Roger gave a devastating blow to Robbie's midsection as he keeled over. Roger pushed Robbie on the back of the head causing him to hit the pavement face first.

"ROGER STOP!" Sara screamed.

***

Alex walked out with Anne out of Marty's, finishing fried mozzarella sticks. "My car is out in the back-parking lot." Alex grabbed an energy drink from her backpack. She opened it up and offered one to Anne.

"Do you know how bad those are for you?" Anne asked Alex who was paying attention to the gang all crowded by Robbie's car. Anne looked over in the direction to see what Alex was. "I wonder what's going on." They went running when they heard Sara's voice screaming across the parking.

There they saw Robbie bleeding on the ground with Sara crying over him. Mole and Dan were almost ready to pounce before Alex showed up with Anne. Roger looked over at Alex with a stone-cold expression. Roger grinned as he turned slowly and winked at Alex as he just lit a cigarette. The whole gang was bent over trying to see if Robbie was okay. Roger turned back around to look at Alex as he blew her a kiss. Alex's sensation in her arms was getting strong. She was just about to charge until Mole grabbed her.

"Alex, he is really messed up." He took out his phone. "I have to call Joseph." He looked over to Dan. "I think you need to call an ambulance."

***

Osiah hasn't had this much of a good time with a human since a century ago. Normally, he found them annoying, beside Father Joe, but these seemed like they were good people. Komptin seemed not to mind as he lay on the ground next to Osiah. They had told him that Mole's mom was actually the owner of this establishment.

"So, not to sound too forward, but are you married?" Jennifer asked.

"Jen." Mike looked at his wife. "I'm sorry, Osiah."

"No, no, it's okay," Osiah motioning to the bartender that he would have another round for the table. "I'm just here temporarily and then I'm hoping to meet up with someone special."

"What's she like?" Jen asked.

Osiah swirled his glass finishing his remaining drink. "She's…she's…well, she's nothing but love for all who come into contact with her."

"The type of woman who is generally sweet; I get that," Mike said grabbing his wife's hand. He paid his attention back to Osiah. "So what does Alex do around the church?"

"Mainly janitorial, cleaning up messes that really no one wants to do," Osiah gave Komptin some beef jerky out of his pocket. "Alex is a very special young lady. She has a big heart and will do anything for the ones she cares about."

"She's a little hellion," her dad said.

"She's really tight with her friends, Sara and Mole," Osiah pointed out. "At first I thought she was dating him."

"Yeah," Jen took a sip of her drink. "We are all worried about that."

"He seems like a good kid," Osiah commented.

Jen and Mike looked at each other. Jen was about to speak until she noticed Kate holding her bartender as she was crying into her shoulder.

"I wonder what happened," Jen said looking over at the commotion.

"I recognize that type of crying," Mike said. He turned his attention back to the table. "Somebody she loves is really hurt or has died."

The young lady grabbed her purse and left the dinner club. Kate came over with the drinks for the table. "Just horrible, her brother got into a bad fight. He's in the hospital."

Jen quickly picked up her phone. "Who are you calling?" Mike asked.

"Alex," Jen said. "That is Sara's boyfriend."

Alex answered her phone.

"Alex, is everything…all." She stopped talking to hear what Alex was saying. "Okay, you stay there as long as you need. Love you." Jen was about to hang up the phone, but Alex must have asked her another question. "Yeah, he's right here." She handed the phone to Osiah.

Osiah was confused why Alex wanted to talk to him. "This is Osiah."

Alex informed him, "He had a strength that I did not expect from him. I didn't know if I should have done something."

"No, you did the right thing," Osiah eased her worry. "I will take care of it," he hung up the phone and handed it back to Jen.

"What was that all about?" Mike asked.

Jen said, "Sara's boyfriend is in the hospital. What did Alex want with you?"

"She couldn't lock up the church tonight. She told Father Joe she would close it but now the church is left open." He got up. "I told her I would take care of it. If you will excuse me." He whistled for Komptin as he got up and followed Osiah out.

***

Alex was in the hospital waiting area sitting next to Sara, trying to reassure her that everything was going to be okay. Mole and Dan talking in the corner about the events that took place. "Do you need anything Sara?"

"I don't want to leave, but I'm supposed to be home soon," Sara told her. "I don't know what I'm going to tell my dad."

Alex didn't know how to answer. All she could muster was, "I will take care of it." Alex hugged her to assure her everything was going to be okay. She walked up to Mole and Dan who stopped talking when Alex came up.

"How is she doing?" Dan asked looking over at Sara.

"She's hanging in there," Alex was worried about her friends. "We need to think of a really good excuse to tell her dad why she's not home."

Mole's face was concerned about Sara. "I don't know."

"Don't know what?" Anne said, returning with coffee for everyone from the cafeteria.

"What to tell Sara's dad why she's not coming home," Mole answered.

Anne was confused, "Just tell him the truth."

"That would not go well," Alex said. "Sara's dad isn't too fond of non-white people and if he found out she was dating Rob…"

Mole continued, "I think he would go off his rocker." He saw Joseph and his wife in the hospital hallway. "I'm going to go see how they are doing."

The three of them watched Mole go over to Joseph and his wife. He was consoling them and then gave them a hug. Alex was watching Mole explain to him what happened. Joseph held his wife and then the doctor came up. Mole took that cue to join back to the group. "I told them mostly what happened."

"Mostly?" Dan said.

"I never liked Roger," Mole said. "But for such a skinny kid, I didn't know he was that strong."

Anne held Mole's arm. "He pulled a knife on you guys. The anger he had, he probably would have killed you." Anne realized she was holding his arm and immediately let go. "I'm going to see if

133

Sara needs anything else." Anne walked over to Sara to comfort her.

"You can never know what a person is capable of," Dan said. "Are we going to take care of this for Robbie?"

"I'm in," Mole said. "Winning a fight is one thing, but he won the fight quickly…he didn't need to continue the way he did."

Alex grabbed Mole by the shirt. "You don't do anything! You hear me!" She looked over at Dan. "You either." Mole and Dan were about to argue with her, but she was in the mood to handle it. She didn't know what Roger had become, what he was capable of. "Promise me, Mole!" She looked at him straight in the eye with intense sincerity. Mole nodded in defeat. She looked over at Dan. "You, too."

Dan hesitantly agreed, "Fine, but under protest."

Alex let go of Mole's shirt. "Now, we need to be there for Sara. Mole, I really need to think of an excuse for her to come home with me for her dad."

Mole assured her, "I got it."

Alex joined Anne to comfort Sara as the stress was getting to her. Her face was almost as pale as Alex's and her eyes started to get bags underneath them. "How are you doing, Sara?"

She sat up from Anne's arms. "I'm okay. Just tired." She looked into the room. "I just wish I knew what was going on."

Alex looked and saw the doctor get done talking to Joseph and his wife. They looked like they had a small amount of relief. Joseph walked over to Sara. "Looks like he's going to be okay."

"What happened?" Sara asked.

"Looks like he had some internal bleeding and they had to rush him to surgery to stop it," he said. "But he's a tough kid. Doctor said he is more than sure he's going to recover." Sara closed her eyes as if a high level of stress was released from her shoulders. "We should be able to go see him soon. I'm going to go home and get some stuff for him. He is going to stay in the hospital for a couple of days."

"Do you need me to come with you?" Mole asked, getting up from the chair.

"No, you should stay here with your friends. I won't be long," Joseph informed the group. Alex watched the concerned father give a fake smile as he walked out of the hospital.

"Alex." Mole pointed to Alex's dad down the hall talking to the cops. Alex's dad didn't appear happy. "This isn't looking good," Mole observed.

Her dad came to the group. "Kale, Dan, Sara, I can't talk to you officially without your parents." He grabbed his phone. "Do you want me to call them?"

"No," Sara perked up out of fear.

Alex petted her friend's hair. "Dad, I think we can all talk here."

He sat down and put his elbows on his knees to address the group. "There is going to be no charge against Roger Somberson."

"WHY THE HELL NOT!" Alex yelled, not caring that she was talking to her father. Sara's mouth dropped out of shock while Mole and Dan bit their lips.

"Look, he was assaulted by Robbie first. Roger claims he defended himself," he explained. "And frankly speaking there is no evidence to say otherwise."

"He pulled a knife on us," Dan pointed out.

"He told the cop he was alone, three huge guys with three girls surrounding him; he feared for his life," Alex's dad explained.

Mole shook his head. "And you believe him?"

"Kale, who do you think the judge or jury is going to believe? A skinny little kid who is 'out-casted' and picked on by his peers or a group of bigger kids which one is a convicted felon," he asked.

Mole got to the point of boiling. "You know, you are really a piece of work!"

"MOLE!" Alex scolded. "Settle down." She was also embarrassed at her dad's actions. "Dad, really? You had to say that?"

Michael stood up to address them with the realism of the situation. "I'm just telling you the facts and how everyone is going to see it." Alex irritation with him was evident. "I'm sorry honey." The group didn't say anything in return, so Michael got up to talk to Robbie's parents. "Stay as long as you want. Just check in with your mother or me once in a while."

136

The group stood quiet before Mole spoke up, who had finally calmed down. "Well that sucked." A much-needed chuckle from the group relieved some of tension.

Alex wasn't fooled though she could tell that her dad bringing up his record wasn't sitting well with him. Mole sat back in the chair with a somber face. She knew he was upset so she placed her head on his arm, giving him the support he needed.

Anne watched Alex's nestle up to Mole. "We are all upset over Robbie," she told them. "We need to focus on his recovery. I need to call my mom, tell her what is going on."

"Oh, damn it," Sara said, grabbing her phone. "Oh God, I'm in trouble!" she said looking at her phone. "I missed a bunch of phone calls from my dad." She went to the corner of the waiting room to call him.

Alex watched her friend nervously call her dad. Osiah's voice was heard down the hall arguing with the nurse about having Komptin with him. "Ma'am, I can vouch, that's his service dog. I know him." Alex walked up to the two of them.

The nurse rolled her eyes and walked away. "Whatever, I have too much work to do to."

"Thanks," Osiah said, turning his attention to Alex. "How is he?"

"Getting out of surgery soon." Alex turned back to her friends in the waiting room. "What are you doing here?"

"I was looking for your classmate, but we lost the trail," Osiah said. "If he is infiltrated the only time you can track them is when they allow the Dark to act on." Komptin walked over to an upset Sara who was still on the phone with her dad and laid down next to her feet.

Alex then said, "She's talking to her dad, that's not going to go well."

Mole came up to Alex's side and shook Osiah's hand. "How ya doing?" He then went to Alex. "Joseph forgot his phone and his wife wants him to have it in case something happens while he is getting Rob's stuff." He showed her the phone. "I'm going to go see if I can reach him before he goes."

Sara came up on the other side of Alex while Komptin returned to Osiah's side. "I have to go home." Sara wiped a tear that was stuck on her cheek. "He's pretty mad."

Alex turned to Osiah. "Can you take her home and hopefully having an adult there will ease the situation?"

Osiah took a deep breath. "Not too comfortable with that." Komptin was at his ready to go. "I don't know, a single male with a sixteen-year old girl at this hour…"

"How about if you take Dan home?" Mole suggested.

Alex begged, "Please?"

Osiah exhaled. "Fine." He grabbed his keys. "Car is this way."

"I gotta go give Joseph his phone. His wife said he's parked on the north side of the hospital." Mole put on a sweatshirt. "Where are you parked?"

"Southside." Osiah scratched the ears of Komptin.

Anne came up to them. "My mom is coming to get me. It's getting pretty late."

Alex gave Anne a sisterly hug. "Thank you, Anne."

Anne returned the hug in kind. "No problem. I just wish there was more I could do." She turned to Mole. "How are you getting home?"

"I guess I could call my mom," he answered.

"My mom and I can give you a ride," she offered.

"Give me the phone," Alex said. "I'll go chase him down to give it to him."

"Are you sure?" Mole asked. He handed her his phone.

"Positive," she said. She walked towards the door into the elevator.

***

Alex walked outside to the parking lot. The hospital parking lot seemed darker than it should be. In fact, the entire parking lot lights were out. Alex thought there was some sort of electrical problem for all the lights to be out. A sea of parked cars flooded the area. An outline of a man could be barely be seen. It looked like Joseph from a distance. She started walking a bit faster to catch him when she heard a crunch underneath her feet. Alex bent over and picked up broken glass that cut the tip of her finger. She winced and sucked on her finger. The parking lot light above her was broken.

"This was a light bulb," she thought.

She walked up the next light; this one was out as well. She hoped it was some kid thinking it would be funny to knock out all the lights, but that familiar stale smell in the air contradicted her thought. Her heart began to race and the tingling sensation in her arms began to arise.

A frightened male scream echoed in the distance. Alex saw a silhouette of a man getting pushed down by a beast like figure. The confirmation of Alex's fear was verified by a flash of glowing red eyes.

Alex couldn't hold back any longer. The quick tingling sensation in her arms resulted in a flash of neon blue covering her hands. The area illuminated with the glow from her Lite. She ran down to wear the Infiltrator stood. The trail led towards the woods.

She prayed that the body which laid by her feet wasn't Joseph, but she knew that prayer was one that couldn't be answered. The light from her hand brightened Joseph's lifeless body. He looked as if he was mauled by a bear or mountain lion. This attack was purely to mangle, purely to destroy.

A necklace holding a crucifix was lying on the ground next to him. Alex looked back at the hospital, she knew there was nothing she could do to help him. All she could do was avenge him. Her eyes flashed blue as she took off into the woods.

Chapter 7

Osiah hated awkward silences in enclosed spaces. Luckily, Dan wouldn't keep quiet. He was obviously venting and compensating for the hate he had for what had happened to his friend Robbie this evening. The part that scared Osiah was that the Infiltrators had already consumed a willing human body. This meant the balance was starting to shift more to the Dark.

Normally, they concentrated in the Holy Land and the South American jungles, but for some reason they have started to arrive in the states. There was sense of the Dark outside the hospital, but it had seemed pretty far away, or a demon was close by. Their scent was much fainter than one of an Infiltrator.

A big problem is that once people become infiltrated, they could walk among the humans at all times. The only humans that could recognize them would be Lite Sentries.

Alex had talent, but she still wasn't able to identify Hosts. Lite Sentries themselves are very rare. Usually just one maybe two walk the planet, but now, there are three. That told Osiah that the Dark was gaining more and more ground. Normally he wouldn't care, but Alex had something to her.

Osiah's train of thought was interrupted by Dan talking about the time he broke the Hell Hot Chicken Wing contest by eating twenty-four wings in under a minute. "And then my ass was burning for a week straight…" he continued to talk.

Komptin was being admired by Sara as he laid on her lap in the back of Osiah's car. "Say, Mr. Osiah, you have a wonderful dog."

"Thank you, Sara," Osiah replied. Komptin was enjoying every moment of being at the mercy of Sara's love.

"How long have you had him?"

"Forever," Osiah tried to remember how long dogs normally live. Considering Osiah has been with him since he banned himself to walk the planet when the primates evolved.

"I've noticed you around town and he doesn't leave your side," Sara said, scratching Komptin's ears.

Osiah knew something was on her mind. Something caught her attention. "Is there anything wrong, Sara?"

Dan looked back at Sara to see what she was getting at.

"I've been around dogs my whole life," Sara said. "I've never seen a German Shepherd like this…not shed and I can't feel him breathe." She tried to pull some hair out of Komptin.

Osiah knew nothing about human dogs, but what he knew about Komptin was nothing a human could fathom. "I guess I could get him checked."

"I wouldn't worry about it," Sara said looking at the window. "He's got a lot of life and love in him." She gave him a big hug. Komptin was enjoying every minute of it. His pointed ears perked when Osiah drove up to Sara's house.

Osiah could feel Sara tense up. It has if the mood in the car went from pleasant to one of fear. "Are you all right, Sara?"

"Yeah, I just know he's going to be mad that I'm coming home this late," Sara informed him, gathering her things. "Thank you for the ride."

"Do you want me to walk you to the door?" Osiah offered.

"No thank you," she said petting Komptin good-bye.

Osiah watched her walk up to the door. The door opened; she turned the light on where her dad's outline was in the window. The body posture was one of anger.

"Man, that guy is a jerk," Dan commented. "We should have walked up to the door with her, but he would just wait until we left."

Osiah could see her dad was starting to yell. The faint yells could be heard coming through to the car. Komptin glared at the house. Osiah turned to Dan. "Give me one of your schoolbooks."

Dan looked at him with confusion. "What?"

"Just give it to me," Osiah commanded. Osiah ripped off the book paper cover Dan spent time drawing on during the U.S. Government class.

"Hey," Dan said looking at his picture of deer. "That picture cost me last week's exam!"

Osiah quickly got out of the vehicle. Komptin jumped from the backseat to the front seat to follow his master to the door. Osiah knocked on the door to the house where Sara's dad was continuing to yell.

"Now what the hell!" An angry voice came from the kitchen. The door opened to a big man, who was balding. The smell of alcohol was evident. "For a second there I thought you were going to be that little spic that she's been sleeping around with."

"Excuse me, but Sara forgot her schoolbook in my car," Osiah handed him Dan's government book. He looked over at Sara who was fighting back tears. "You all right Sara?"

"She's fine," he said, grabbing the book and throwing her feet. "She needs to learn how to follow directions. Directions her dad has set, and not to be giving it to that illegal."

"With all due respect sir," Osiah said. "Sara was making sure the Rodriguez boy was okay. He got pretty messed up today in a school fight."

"Someone beat the hell out of that lettuce picker," he gave an inconsiderate laugh. "Who beat him up?"

"Roger," Sara answered, wiping her tears.

Now he busted out laughing. "That little punk kid? I love it. You know we have to instill in these kids about keeping our race pure." He continued to drink. "I just don't know how to get that through to her. Maybe one of these days I will have to beat it into her for her to learn." He looked at Osiah and laughed, hitting him in the chest with the back of his hand. "You know I'm just kidding. Don't need you to call Child Services on me." He closed the screen door with hate and contentment.

"I guess I should go," Osiah said. "Good night, Sar—" Her dad closed the door before Osiah could finish. Osiah stood there for a second and felt the air. He looked down at Komptin who was on edge from the confrontation. "Did you feel anything?" he asked his fellow hunter. Komptin's eyes grew sad and walked back towards the car. "Yeah, I didn't feel anything either."

***

Alex ran through the woods. The outline of the Infiltrator just ahead of her. She didn't know how far she was going, but all she knew was that there was a clearing up ahead that led to the family park. Focused and determined, this Infiltrator was not getting away.

Osiah taught her the Infiltrators turn corporeal before they can kill, and they can't turn back to their misty state. The only thing they can do is kill or possess someone willing. This black beast was making sounds as he was stepping on twigs and branches so he was easy to follow. He made it to the clearing and Alex wasn't that far behind it.

She was in the full stride; she could feel the wind push against her face and hair flying about. Once she got into the clearing, she felt a force compress on her chest. The Infiltrator had clotheslined her as she entered the clearing. She flipped in the air and landed face down on the ground. A little blood dripped from her nose. Her eyes flashed blue as her fists turned to the blue mystical fire.

"That hurt," she told the creature.

The Infiltrator did a combination of howl growl at Alex as its eyes flashed a fighting red. She slammed her fist on the ground and turned to the creature. "This is going to happen." She ran at him in full force shoulder blocking him and tumbling to the ground.

The Infiltrator howled, trying to claw her but she got out of the way before he could connect. The creature continued to swing as Alex was countering and blocking each one.

Alex finally connected with a punch that caused the creature to stumble back. Alex didn't let up; she continued the attack. She felt the Lite within give her strength. She knocked the creature down on its stomach. She jumped on the back of its neck pounding it in the back of the head.

"Alex," a voice came around in the distance.

Alex stopped her attack to look behind her, but nothing was there. The creature took advantage of this opportunity by grabbing her by the hair flipping her over its own head and her back was on the ground. The creature jumped on top of her and held her arms pinned to the ground. The Infiltrator put its face right next to Alex's and licked her cheek. "Sorry, not really my type, big boy." She managed to break one of her arms free and was able to blast a light from her hands. The creature went flying into a tree. After shaking its head, it snapped its jaw at her and then put itself into a fighting position.

Alex motioned for it to attack. It complied. It charged at full force and Alex timed the punch perfectly to the creature's chin as it fell to the ground. Stunned but still able to move the creature stood back up and started to run towards the kid's playground. Alex sighed out of frustration. "Oh no you don't." She started to pursue it.

***

Anne was down the hall waiting to contact her mom. Mole was still talking to Rob's mother and now his sister. A tap on Anne's shoulder broke her attention and she turned to see Shawn standing close. "What are you doing here?"

"I heard what happened and the team decided to come down and offer support," Shawn said. "What are you doing here?"

"I was there at the fight and wanted to come to ensure Sara would be okay," she replied to him staring out the window. "Now I'm just waiting for my mother to come."

"I can give you a ride home," Shawn said.

"No, thank you," Anne politely declined. "I told Mole I would give him a lift home."

Shawn's face got flustered. "Felon Mole? Is he even allowed to be in a car?"

Anne rolled her eyes. "Yes, he can ride in a car."

Some commotion was going down near the exit of the hospital. There were some alarms going off and security was running down at the end of the hallway. "I wonder what's going on," Shawn spoke.

"I don't know," Anne was trying to see down at the end of the hall with all the commotion.

"Probably some meth head coming off his high," Shawn started to rub Anne's shoulders. "You know you look a little upset, anything you want to talk about?"

"No, I'm fine. Something is really going on." She started walking towards the hectic scene.

Shawn followed her down. "We really should stay out of their way."

"Shhh." She motioned to Shawn to be quiet. "I thought I heard something about an animal attack or something." Anne stopped one of the orderlies that was coming down the hall. "Excuse me sir, can you tell me what happened?"

He looked down the hall. "Someone got messed up by an animal or something in the North Parking Lot. The body was pretty much torn inside out."

Anne ran down the hall towards the body. Shawn grabbed her. "What are you doing?"

She swung her body to get her arm back from Shawn's grasp. "Alex was down there." She stopped the nurse. "Excuse me, can you tell me who got hurt?"

"No, I can't," the nurse sharply told her. "We have a lot to do now, can you please step back?"

"Can you at least tell me if it was a small petite girl with dark eyeliner and weaved in hair?" Anne frantically asked.

"Look, I will tell you, it was a male, Hispanic, in his 40s," the nurse said. "Now please, step out the way."

Anne looked down the hall. "Oh, my God, no."

Shawn took a second to put it together. "You don't think?"

Anne saw the surgeon who informed Robbie's family on his condition. "Doctor, doctor." The doctor was walking down the hall. "Look, your friend is going to be fine. He will be released in a couple of days."

"DOCTOR!" She grabbed his arm.

"What is it young lady?" The doctor was now getting agitated.

"That man that got attacked in the parking lot."

"Yeah, weird having a creature like that this close into town," the doctor commented.

"Robbie's dad was in the North Parking Lot," Anne informed him.

The doctor looked down at Robbie's mom who was still talking to Mole. She gave the doctor a wave of appreciation for all that he had done for her son.

Anne quietly whispered, "Please."

"Hang on, let me check." He turned to the nurse. "Can I get the name of the DOA from the animal attack?" The nurse gave the doctor the initial chart. The doctor gave the chart back to the nurse. "Thank you. I will inform the family." He turned to Anne. "Excuse me, miss." He walked towards Robbie's mom and sister.

"Anne, what do you think we should do," Shawn asked.

She dialed her mom. "I need to stay; this is going to be rough on Kale."

***

Alex walked quietly up to the small buildings that were the restrooms for the park. There was nothing around the building and no trace of the dark beast. She made her way into the front of the building where the entry to the men and women restrooms took place. There was split decision of what bathroom to go into.

"I never saw the men's bathroom before," she convinced herself. She walked into the bathroom where there was toilet paper all over the ground. There was graffiti writing on the wall of symbols and drawings.

She opened the far end of the stall and kicked it open. No creature. She kicked the second, no creature. Something did catch her eye. She looked closely at the writing on the wall next to the toilet in permanent marker.

It read, "Alex Johnson isn't just EASY on the eyes..."

Alex just raised her eyebrows. "Can't really argue on that." She continued to the last stall. Her blue mist fist was in defense in case of an attack. She kicked the door. Nothing was in there. Outside the bathroom she could sense the beast was close.

She quickly glanced all around to make sure she wasn't going to get jumped. When she entered the doorway, the creature grabbed her by the arm and threw her into the mirror cracking it with her head. Her eyes flashed blue and lunged at the creature pushing it into the stall. The creature managed to get Alex off it and attacked her. She stepped to the side and pushed the creature's head into the porcelain sink busting it. A black liquid substance got onto Alex's shirt from the creature's head. "What the hell?" She raised her fist to view the beast that was bleeding on the head. "I hurt it, I hurt it bad." The creature ran outside of the bathroom and Alex chased after it.

Alex walked out trying to get the black blood off her white shirt. She had a mixture of her blood and the creature's blood splattered all over her shirt. Trying to wipe it off caused it to smear all over. "I liked this shirt," she thought. Her nerves shot up as the trail led to the pavilion. The surroundings were quiet. Nothing was making a sound.

She remembered before she got involved in this war how carefree she was. In this very park, she hooked up with one of the seniors last year in that very pavilion after a party one day. He was probably the one who wrote that comment in the bathroom. There was no sign of the Infiltrator near the pavilion. She decided to walk inside to see if it climbed into the fireplace.

The creature dropped from the rafters of the ceiling and grabbed Alex. It wrapped its beastly arms around with Alex coming face to face with the creature. The foul smell animating from the creature fanged mouth was causing Alex was getting sick to her stomach. She was trying to pry free, but her arms were trapped at her side. The hate in the creature intensified as it was about to strike.

Alex wasn't going down like this; she immediately head butted the creature causing it to let her go. It gave her a chance to step back to regain her strength. The creature rushed her, and she ran outside the pavilion. She was still weakened and had to hold herself up on the pole to the swing set. For some reason the creature did not follow her. "It must have left," she thought. The metal swing pole was cold, but she didn't mind. She was hurting.

Then the creature seemed to come out of nowhere and through her into a pile of metal garbage cans. Garbage ended up going down the back of shirt. There was some liquid dripping down her face. It was blood start dripping into her eyes. The blurry image of the Infiltrator was approaching her.

***

Mole dropped to his knees onto the floor. He couldn't breathe and what little air he could get in was being followed by fighting the feeling to vomit. Joseph's wife and sister continued to cry and shout out in the pain of finding out what had happened. Mole got cold and started to shake. He didn't know what to do. He grabbed onto the chair as he tried to pry himself up.

Anne came to his aid. "Kale." Shawn was behind her watching from a distance. She stood in front of him not knowing what to do. A bunch of medical staff rushed over with blankets and wrapped them around Rob's mom, sister, and Mole. "Kale," Anne said again.

Mole looked at Anne who was getting her shoulders rubbed by Shawn. Shawn pulled her away. "We have to let the professionals handle this."

Mole forced himself to get up. The image of Joseph was all he could see. He got up. "I need to, I need to. I need to." He started walking down the hall towards the exit. "I need to…go." He turned around to look at Robbie's mom and sister being consoled. On his way out of the hospital, he physically ran into a big black priest. "Excuse me."

He looked to Mole. "Son, you okay?"

Mole pointed to the broken family. "They need you, father." Mole walked outside of the door and sat on the bench staring into nothingness.

"I need to do something," Anne told Shawn. She gathered her things and headed towards Kale.

"Come on, let me take you home," Shawn offered. "There's nothing you can do, and it doesn't look like he wants your help." He started to guide her to another door. Shawn watched Anne pull out her cell phone to make a call.

She stepped away from Shawn and was talking to someone who he couldn't make out. "Will you still be able to bring me home?"

Shawn's face tried not to smile. "Of course."

"I'm just going to make sure he is taken care of before we go," Anne told him.

Shawn sighed. "This could take all night." He sat down and picked up a magazine to read.

Anne walked out to where Mole was sitting outside and sat down next to him. She didn't say a word. She just sat there with him.

Mole didn't know how long the two of them sat there. Before he knew it, his mom was standing in front of him. She knelt down and spoke with a soft voice. "Honey, you okay?" He looked at her with confusion. "Kale. Come on, Kale." He knew he had to move, but he couldn't. He just felt hopeless and lost.

"Is everything all right?" Father Joe came walking up to the bench. "A grief counselor is with the family right now and I saw this young man still sitting here."

"Father, I need to get him home." Kate was obviously worried about her son. "But I don't know what's wrong."

The priest came up to Kale. "Son, you need to go home with your mother. You need to go home and get some rest." Kale attempted to get up but was feeling too weak. The big priest put Kale's arm around his neck and helped him walk to the car. He put him in the back of his mom's car and shut the door. "There you go, big guy."

"Thank you, Father," Kate said.

"No problem," he answered. "Please call me Father Joe. Do you need anything else?"

Anne got up from the bench and joined the two of them. The priest looked to Anne. "Are you his girlfriend?"

Anne shook her head no.

Kale's mom went over to Anne and gave her a hug. "Thank you for calling me." She turned to the priest. "I hate asking this."

"Go ahead," he insisted.

"Kale is recovering from an alcohol problem. Could you come by and just be there, just until he falls asleep. Priests have helped him in the past during his detention and I hope having you there will make him just feel secure," Kate asked him.

The priest grabbed her hand. "Just give me your address." He smiled and looked at Anne. "Do you have a ride home?"

Shawn came out. "Yeah, I'm giving her a ride."

"Is that okay?" Father Joe asked Anne.

Anne knew Mole had to be left alone with family right now. She shook her head in agreement. "Yes, Father." She went with Shawn to bring her home.

***

Alex grabbed the lid of the garbage can and blocked a swipe from the creature's claws. She got up to distance herself from the Infiltrator. It picked up a garbage can and threw it at Alex. It was easily dodged on her way towards the jungle gym. She ran up the slide and was on a standing on top of it. The

155

both of them took their time determining what the next should be. "Your move," she told him.

The creature's eyes flashed red, and he ran up the slide after her. Just as it reached the top of the slide Alex ran at it grabbing its head. She jumped over the side of the Jungle Gym while holding onto the creature's head. She ended up hanging off the ground while holding the back of the neck of the Infiltrator while the throat was caught on the banister.

The enemies locked eyes. The hate and evil poured from this creature. She let go with one hand and formed a skinny sharp blue spear. It was thrust into the side of its head. The creature's eyes went black and melted before disappearing into the earth.

Alex fell to the ground. "Ow." She got up rubbing her backside. "Oh, the curse of a bony butt." She hoped her future hunts were not this difficult. There was something else on her mind; how was Mole to going to take his mentor being killed?

***

Salamor approached Vandor who was sitting in an empty warehouse surrounded by a bunch of Infiltrators who were eating carcass of a homeless person. "The Virgin Hunt is over my Master."

Vandor finished a drink he took from a local restaurant. He looked at it with confusion. "These are disgusting. Why do the primates like them so much?" He threw down the drink to the Infiltrators.

They sniffed a couple of times and walked away from it. There was a man chained to the wall next to his makeshift throne. "Well, she couldn't have lasted long; he hasn't had that much time with her."

Salamor floated to his master's side as he approached the man chained to the wall. "My master, she had beaten a matured Infiltrator."

Vandor grabbed the man's hair and slammed it against the wall. "What?" He looked into the man's eyes. "How could an immature little primate defeat..." He paused. "She won?" Out of disbelief, he turned to Salamor.

"Yes, my master," he replied.

"Please," the man chained up, ventured to speak. "Please, release me."

"She's got power, which is unusual for someone that young," Vandor put his fist into the chest cavity of the man and pulled out his heart.

The organ was steaming from the cold air. The Infiltrators ran towards the blood on the floor. Vandor scowled at them and then retreated in defeat. Once he made it back to his throne, he motioned for the Infiltrators permission to do what they wished to the body. The Infiltrators tore the body apart like a bunch of hungry wolves attacking a recent kill. "We may need to adjust our strategy," he said biting into the heart like an apple.

Gron came up from the stairs.

"Ah Gron, my newest Host; how's the new power I have given you?" Vandor asked.

"I should have asked for this a long time ago," he replied. "But I still want to taste her. Her scent is so strong to me."

"Patience," Vandor warned. "Her power is raw and undisciplined. She is young, strong, but very inexperienced." He looked over at Gron. "Your seed into her would create something…magnificent." He got up and looked out the window. "All we need is her to be willing." He looked over to his shadowed servant. "I think it's time to speak to an old friend."

Chapter 8

Anne was getting frustrated as she was going through her closet for something to wear. "UGH!" She growled to herself. All her clothes were too happy and nice; she had nothing that was dark and dreary. She turned around and saw her mom looking over at her leaning on her doorframe to her room. Anne got startled from seeing her there looking at her because she didn't see or hear her coming.

"You okay?" her mom asked her, looking at her. "What's wrong?"

Anne started moving her clothes in her dresser and closet to her bed trying to find something. "I can't find anything to wear." She held the darkest colors she could find to her body in front of the mirror. She was disgusted and threw them on the bed.

"Ugh!" she said, sitting on the bed and looking at her clothes. "Everything is so 'cheerful' and 'flowery'." Anne just stopped in her tracks looking in the mirror. "Life isn't so cheerful. It's actually pretty horrible." Anne sat back on her bed looking at her mother for support.

Her mom recognized Anne's cry for help and sat down next to her. "You really think life is so horrible?"

"No," she surrendered. "It's just, I know bad things happen, but for someone to be in the hospital badly beaten and for him to lose his father the same night from some random animal attack seems to be

159

more than what we are seeing," Anne stopped. "And then on top of that, Kale…" Anne stopped herself again wiping a tear from her eye.

"Kale? Honey, is something else bothering you?" Anne's mom asked her.

Anne just shook her head, "I haven't seen…" and then she stopped herself. She went back to her closet to find something to wear.

"Seen what?" Her mom asked.

Anne sat down next to her mom. "Nothing Mom, I don't even know if it's my place," Anne put her head on her mom's shoulders. "Do you have anything in black, Mom?"

"I have something you can wear," she offered. She walked up to Anne's dresser and grabbed a flower. She put it in Anne's hair. "In dark times, a flower can be a powerful gesture." She kissed on the forehead. "Come on, let's get you ready."

***

Sara finished applying her makeup with a final check before she left for the funeral. She couldn't get past the fact that she was applying makeup for such a sad event. The final touches were done, and she headed downstairs, hoping Daddy would still let her go. She looked around the house to make sure she had her chores done.

She paid extra attention to detail to make sure there was nothing preventing her from going to Joseph's funeral. He came into the house from looking outside. The house was ready for his inspection He paid extra attention to it, almost looking for something to prevent her from going to show her support for Robbie and his family.

"Hi, Daddy." She quickly handed him a towel. It seemed he was in a good mood.

"Where are you off to?" he asked, wiping his hands in the sink.

She sat down at the table. "I'm going to a funeral."

He did a half disappointment grin on his face. "Is it that spic's dad?"

"Yes." The ignorance of her dad just made her sick to her stomach. She looked up at him just waiting for him to say she couldn't go.

"Did you get all your chores done?"

"Yes."

He opened up his wallet and handed her twenty dollars. "Don't be too late. That's in case you guys go out for tacos or something afterwards." He walked out the door.

Sara was confused by the nice gesture coming from her daddy. There was something different about him lately. He seemed like he was just going through the motions of his life. He probably had a lot on his mind. Maybe he was warming up to the fact she was dating Robbie. Her dog outside was barking at Alex's car coming up the driveway.

She waved to her daddy who was still working on the truck before jumping into Alex car. They gave each other a quick hug. "How are you doing?" Sara asked her friend who opened another Apollo energy drink.

Alex replied, "I'm fine, considering. A little worried about Mole."

"Have you talked to him?"

"Not really." Alex got a concerned look. "He's been so quiet and withdrawn. I asked Anne if she's talked to him, but he hasn't even talked to her since that night."

"Do you think he's been drinking again?" Sara asked out of worry.

"I hope not." Alex rolled down her window and looked. "We are going to meet him at the funeral."

"What are you doing?"

Alex thought she sensed something, but it was so faint it must have been far from here. "Nothing, thought I smelled something. I don't know how he's going to handle this."

Sara noticed that this might be the first time she's ever been in Alex's car with no music playing. The two of them really didn't say much as they headed towards the Catholic Church to say good-bye to their friend's dad.

***

Anne arrived at the funeral; she saw Kale from a distance with his mom going into the church. A feeling of relief mixed with nerves overfilled her body. She was glad to see he was doing okay, but at the same time, seeing him made her feel nervous. The church was somber and filled with quiet whispers. There weren't many places to sit. She wanted to sit next to Kale to show him that she was

162

there for him, but she thought it wouldn't be appropriate.

One side would be for his mother and the other would probably be for Alex. The best place for her to sit was right behind him, just to let him know that she was there for him.

Alex and Sara arrived at the church. The two of them walked up to Kale and his mom giving them hugs. Alex put her jacket down on the pew next Mole. She motioned for Anne to give her a hug "Do you want to sit up here?" she whispered in her ear.

Anne got a little embarrassed. Was she that transparent? She had to settle down her thinking. This wasn't the time. This was to pay respects to Joseph and be here for his family along with Kale if he needed.

"No, you should be at his side."

Alex nodded with her eyes closed. Anne gave Sara an embracing hug and went to sit down. She placed her hand on Kale's shoulder just to let him know she was there for him if he needed her. He grabbed her hand, squeezed firmly but gently and then he let it go...never looking back. Dan arrived and the two gave each other a quick little hug before the services started.

Father Joe was the residing priest. His very presence seemed to calm the sadness of the room. The tall emotional priest began to try easing the burden of the congregation by starting the prayer. "Lord, God our Father, your power brings us to birth. Your providence guides our lives, and by

163

Your command we return to dust..." he began to pray.

Anne, even though she didn't believe in a particular religion, always felt warmth in a church or even next to a man of the cloth. There were so many different religions, and they pretty much stated the same message. She never understood why people tend to kill each other for the details. The cool air from the air conditioning made Anne get a quick shiver. She quickly regained her focus on the services as the congregation stood to sing a hymn.

***

Osiah looked down at the congregation from the top of the tier of the balcony as Father Joe was finishing the service. The man who died must have been loved because the church was full, and the people were full of tears. The widow was being held by her son and daughter. Osiah noticed the wounds the young man received seemed to be healing well.

There were many reactions to this man's death. He started to feel empathy and guilt due to the demise from the Infiltrator. Komptin, who was curled in the corner of the room, seemed to be at peace. He was clearly relaxed in the church. He knew, as Osiah did, that churches were sanctuaries. No harm could be done to him, nor could he harm anyone while inside. Osiah closed his eyes again and took a sip from his flask.

"There is much sadness down there." Celestial came up beside him. She grabbed his arm. "But no guilt should be put on you."

He leaned his head on to her soft blonde hair and took in the aroma of Lite. A river of peace trickled down his body, filling him with content. "I know, but sometimes I worry."

"Worry about what?"

"I find myself missing it." He looked down at her. "Not all of it, but some of it."

She gazed over the crowd, who now was listening to Joseph's brother speak to the congregation of his lost sibling. "Do not feel guilty; it is important you realize that you miss the correct actions, and not the negative ones."

Osiah looked behind him in Komptin's direction. He was still asleep but now Ariel and Devine were next to him, motionless with heads down. They were obviously taking in the peace of the sanctuary. He knew they didn't like him. How could they? He didn't like himself.

Celestial spoke, "They do not hate you as much as you think."

"But they do hate me?" Osiah turned back to the overlooking position of the church. "I don't blame them. I hate me at times." His attention was drawn to the sound of the widow crying with her children. "Collateral damage never bothered me before, but for some reason for the last 500 years or so, it's been harder and harder to deal with. I must be getting soft."

"No, you are getting stronger," Celestial said, leaning the big man's arm. "What you are feeling is what gives a being strength. Hate is what drives the Dark, but hate will always lose to passion." She looked up at him. "You cannot hold this burden forever," Celestial commented.

"It drives me," he told her. "It drives me to prevent myself from going back." He looked up to the ceiling. "I have constant reminders every night and an executioner on standby at all times." He took out his flask. "I don't know if I'm doing any good."

Celestial held his hand. "What you did way back as man was coming has no explanation. What happened could not have been foreseen by either side," she reassured him. "Look, look down at her."

Osiah saw Alex at her friend's side. Alex turned her head to give her mentor a nonchalant wave accompanied with a quick smile. He returned the wave and found himself smiling back at her before she turned back to the service. "She is a little spitfire," he added. He began to brag as a proud mentor. "She had her first successful hunt all ready," but he quickly recanted, and he looked at the weeping widow saying good-bye to her husband. "Unfortunately, it was too late."

Ariel and Devine came to Celestial's side and she greeted them. "You are a good person. Do not forget that," she told Osiah as she approached her guardians. She ran her fingers through each of their hair. "We all have Lite in us."

"Do you think I should tell her?" Osiah asked her.

Celestial stopped. "It is a gamble. As He gave them an overdose of free will." She looked at him. "We all were made in His image, not just the people below. They are just more swayed by events, emotions, and time." She walked over and kissed Osiah. "Again, no one saw you coming; neither side, especially myself."

"Madam," Ariel interrupted.

"We need to go," Devine finished.

Celestial acknowledged their input. "I have to go."

Osiah wanted to kiss her again, but he refrained. In a church hosting a funeral was not even close to be appropriate. All he could manage to do was give her a wave goodbye. The two maintained eye contact as she disappeared in a doorway.

***

Joseph's wake was packed with people. Stories of Joseph and laughter seemed to be lifting the mood of the room. That seemed to help everybody with their loss. It was being held in the police station's training room. They had a little memorial display of Joseph with his badge, academy graduation, and other photos and trinkets representing his family, friends, and career. Some of the other juvenile parolees came to pay their respects. Alex could tell Mole was uncomfortable to go talk to them, but she saw he managed to stray over there. Anne was at his side holding his hand as he introduced them to her.

"They are cute together." Kate approached Alex handing her a piece of cake. "It's funny that he hasn't really mentioned her."

Alex took a bite. "I don't know if they even know they are together."

"Would you be okay with it if they were?" she asked to study Alex's reaction.

She swallowed her cake. "Of course. Why wouldn't I be?"

"I just know you guys are close," she said. "I didn't know if you were envious."

Alex drank some of her energy drink she was holding. "I love Mole, but as a brother. And honestly speaking." She turned to Ms. Moler. "I've never really talked to Anne until the last couple of months, and she's the real thing. She's not fake, and I hope Mole can see that."

She put her arm around Alex. "He will need you and that girl over there if he is to get through this without starting to drink again." His mom looked over at Joseph's memorial. "He would break his parole and get sent back to the detention center."

"I know my dad would jump at that opportunity," Alex commented. "He wants me to stay away from him."

Ms. Moler hugged her. "Don't be so hard on your dad." She looked over at Mole who was talking to the group of parolees. "I couldn't have asked for a better friend to Kale than you."

Alex watched her walking away wiping tears from her eyes.

"What was that all about?" Sara said with Robbie at her side on crutches.

"Nothing," Alex said, watching Ms. Moler talk to her parents. "How are you doing, Robbie?"

"I'm doing okay," Robbie said, holding his dad's necklace. "Mom and my sister are holding it together. It's hardest when we go home."

Sara squeezed his hand in support. "I was thinking we should all go out to Marty's, just for a relaxing night."

"I shouldn't, I need to go with my family," Robbie replied.

"I understand," Sara said. "Alex?"

"I can't, I need to finish work at the church tonight. Clean up after the funeral and stuff," Alex lied to her friend.

Anne came up to join the group with no sight of Mole. "How are you doing, Robbie?"

"I'm doing okay," Robbie said. "It's really hard, but I will be okay." He tried fighting back tears. "If you will excuse me." He left and Sara joined him trying to console.

Alex looked around the room. "Where did Mole go?"

"He said he had to go to the bathroom," she replied. She looked down the hallway. "He's been gone a while." Alex walked down the hallway with Anne at her side. The two of them waited until a guy came out of the bathroom.

169

"Is there anybody else in there?" Alex asked him.

He replied, "No."

The two of them both looked at each other and walked into the bathroom. Anne looked around. She started opening some of the stalls. "Cleaner than I thought it would be."

"Trust me," Alex said. "Cleaner than the last one I was in."

She looked over at Alex.

"What?" Alex said. "Not my first time in a men's bathroom." She looked in the last stall. "He's not here." She got out her phone and started calling him, but it went straight to voicemail. "Damn it, his phone is off."

They left the bathroom to go find Ms. Moler, both hoping she knew where he went.

"Ms. Moler," Anne asked. "Have you seen Kale?"

"He told me he was going to go for a walk," she said.

"I'm sure he will be fine," Alex said looking at Anne.

Anne stared out the door. "I hope you're right."

***

Alex got to the church early in the evening. She was relieved that she finally got a hold of Mole who was home in bed. It wasn't that she didn't trust him, but in his emotional state, she wanted to make sure. At her request, he video-chatted with her to make

170

sure he was home. She knew time would start to heal his grief, but he did look rough.

Osiah was in the back of the churchyard looking up at the sky. There was a picnic table in the back that she sat on top of. "What are we looking at?"

Osiah continued to look up at the sky taking a sip from his flask. "Just being reminded of something." He sat down on the picnic table the church uses for summer events. "I know it's been a hard week, and there wasn't a good time to say this, but congratulations on your first hunt."

She motioned a high five to him but he didn't return it.

"Do you have a question?" There was confusion in his face.

She lowered her hand. "Never mind." Alex turned to view the over the fence. The town was so different at night. "How can you be so old and not learn a simple thing like giving somebody a 'high five'?"

"I'm just messing with you." He winked at her. "Come on. Let's go for a walk."

They started to walk towards town. By this time, it was dark out and the town was becoming active. They headed into the dangerous part, usually where the homeless stayed, but it was odd because there was none around. Alex could feel a weird sense in the air. "This is creepy."

"There are many Infiltrators about," Osiah scouted the area. "For some reason they are concentrating in this town. They like to prey on the homeless because they tend to be forgotten."

"Excuse me?" Alex was shocked. "Then why the hell are we walking through here?"

Osiah knelt down next to Komptin. He rubbed underneath his chin. "They are growing in numbers. I don't know why. Tell me again the basic rules."

"Well, you can't just kill them with one blow. You have to wear them down first," she said looking around. "Churches are sanctuaries, both sides cannot attack each other, and even though we don't sleep, we cannot sustain a long period of using the Lite."

Osiah looked around. "And if you find yourself in an impossible scenario?" The eyes of Infiltrators surrounded them with low intense growls rumbling in the background.

"Please don't tell me we fight to the death," Alex said as her fist lit up.

Osiah lit his fists as Komptin morphed with a growl. The Infiltrators' bodies approached.

"What lesson is this?"

"RUN!" he said.

***

Sara was glad Anne decided to come with her to Marty's for something to eat. She never really had a chance to get to know her. It seems like she's been becoming more part of the group. Trusting new people was something she wasn't good at, but she always thought Anne was a genuine heart. She

172

just didn't know how she would affect the group dynamic. Although, Alex and Mole accepted Robbie with open arms.

Sara took a bite into her chicken sandwich as Anne was nibbling on her salad. "How's your sandwich?" Anne finally broke the silence.

Sara wiped the mayonnaise from the side of her mouth. "Really good actually." Sara didn't think twice before she asked this next question. "Do you want a bite?"

Anne politely replied, "No thank you." She went on to continue to eat her salad.

"If you don't mind me asking," Sara said. "But are you a vegetarian?" She felt guilty asking that as she bit into her chicken.

"Yes, but it's a personal choice. Not because I'm on some sort of protest or anything. I don't mind if people eat meat," she said looking over Sara's shoulders. "I just never really cared for meat."

Sara turned around to see Shawn and a couple of his friends ordering a couple of burgers. He grabbed his food and asked to join them. Anne surprisingly scooted over as Sara did the same, just to be polite. "And how are you ladies doing tonight?"

"Fine, how are you doing?" Anne continued eating her salad.

"Not bad," Shawn said. "We are just out seeing what's been going on." He put his arm up on the bench behind Anne. "Do any of you have plans?"

"No," Anne said. "We just thought we would come out for a bit."

"I have to be home soon," Sara said. "Plus, I want to see how Robbie is doing."

Shawn had a moment of compassion. "Yeah, it's a bummer what happened to him and his dad." Shawn started to eat some of his fries with his other hand.

Anne quietly said, "Yeah, Kale took it pretty hard as well."

"Mole's got issues," he said. "No offense," he motioned to Sara. He looked to Anne who was finishing her salad. "Rumor has it that you two have been dating."

Anne finished her water. "No, we are not."

Sara almost choked on her water out of sheer shock. "Oh, excuse me," she said as she pounded on her chest. Sara thought for sure those two were dating from how they were acting at the wake. They held hands and didn't really leave each other's side. Then again, Mole and Alex act close around each other as well though.

Shawn adjusted his stance a little bit to get closer to Anne. "His loss," he said. "If he doesn't see how beautiful you are then maybe you should look to someone who knows it." He grazed her wavy brown hair a little bit.

Sara was getting uncomfortable. She knew this was getting awkward and she couldn't tell what Anne was doing. Was she playing Mole to get Shawn jealous this whole time? Should she intervene? It really wasn't her place to get involved with whatever has been going on between Mole and Anne. She knew Mole pretty well, but she thought for sure the two were dating.

Why wasn't Alex here? She would either full out say something to Anne or put Shawn in his place to make him go away. Luckily, a text came in from her dad saying that it was time to come home. "Anne," Sara said, "is there any way you can bring me home?"

"Justin can bring you home. It's on his way," Shawn waved one of his friends over. It kind of caught Justin off guard, but he agreed to it.

Sara was at an impasse. She had a feeling something bad would happen if Anne didn't take her home. "Anne, my dad would go off if he knew some random guy dropped me off." It was all she could think to say.

"I really don't think it would be that bad; just say that it was your only option," Shawn said.

"Please, Anne," Sara pleaded.

Anne went into her purse and grabbed her keys. "Shawn, I did promise to take her home." She reached for her jacket, but Shawn grabbed it and got up offering to put it on her. Anne got out of the booth and let him put it on her. "Thank you," she said.

"No problem," Shawn said. "Drive safe." He rubbed her arms up and down.

Sara wasn't sure, but it did look like that made Anne feel really uncomfortable. Maybe it was because she didn't want Shawn to do that in front of Sara in fear she would tell Mole. Sara walked out with Anne to her car not saying a word. Sara didn't know how to react to the situation. Was she reading into it too much? There was something about the atmosphere she didn't like.

"Are you ready?" Anne said as she started up her car.

"Huh, yah, thanks," Sara said. She got into the car to go home to leave one awkward situation into another.

***

"What in the world are you doing?" Justin asked Shawn. The group walked out of Marty's going to their respective vehicles. "I thought you were dating Cindy."

"Cindy? Cindy is hot and she's got it bad for me," Shawn said. "But there is something about Anne. I don't want to date her. She would drive me nuts with her flower child and goodie two shoe thing she's got going on." He looked over at Roger who was staring at him from across the parking lot. "Creepy," he said to Justin motioning over to Roger.

"She is never going to let you get it," Justin said. "No way."

"Fifty bucks," Shawn said. "Fifty bucks, if I don't get with her by the time of graduation."

"Easiest fifty bucks ever," Justin said, shaking hands. "You're going to need an act of God to get with her."

Shawn looked at his phone. "Cindy just texted me. I guess I will go get my pregame on." The two slapped high fives to each other as they parted ways. The car roared when he started it. He adjusted the mirror when he was startled by a knock on his window. "What the hell man?"

Roger stood outside the door, smoking a cigarette. "God will not act for you; I have a proposition for you."

"Whatever," Shawn replied. "I don't do whatever it is you are selling."

Roger knocked on the window again motioning for him to roll it down. Shawn did just to tell him off, but Roger spoke. "I will cover your bet if you lose but you will need to do exactly what I say."

Shawn took a minute. "What's in it for you?"

"Let's just say I have an agenda of my own," Roger said, finishing his cigarette. "How far are you willing to go?"

"I'm not drugging her or rape," Shawn insisted.

Roger rolled his eyes. "No you putz. It won't work if you do any of that, for either of us. I'm talking about getting rid of the biggest roadblock."

Shawn was trying to think who it was. "You mean the Felon?"

Roger tapped his finger on his head. "Now you're using it."

Shawn's ego started to speak for him, "He's not much of a roadblock."

"You need to open your eyes more," Roger said looking over at a bunch of kids walking by tossing a football to each other.

Shawn looked at Roger. "I'm not going to beat him senseless. Rumor has it you're the one who beat the shit of Robbie."

"Self-defense," Roger pointed out. "No, beating him would only draw her closer to him. We need to pry them apart from each other."

"How do we do that?" Shawn said.

"Rig the game," Roger sneered.

***

Alex was running behind Osiah trying to keep up with him. He moved as if he had run through this before. They made it into woods fending off what Infiltrators were chasing them. Osiah was smooth as he dodged low branches and hopped over fallen trees. Komptin was a brute force busting through whatever was in his way. Alex was having difficulty keeping up, but if she fell behind Komptin would ensure she would not be alone. They made it to a clearing in the woods. Alex took a minute to regain her composure.

Osiah took an assessment of the situation. "I didn't think it was this infested." He looked over at Alex who was actually trying to catch her breath. "You okay?"

"What the hell?" she said looking at her arms. "I can't feel anything."

"Basically, you need to recharge," Osiah said to her. "Don't worry about it, the more you hunt the longer it gets." The growls heard in the background were getting closer. "Komptin and I got this until you are ready."

There was one set of red eyes in the woods as the Infiltrator appeared out of the darkness. They growled and stared at them in a ready stance.

Osiah grabbed his flask and took a sip of his drink before lighting his purple fists. "Looks like there is only one out there."

Komptin flashed his eyes in agreement.

"Stay behind and protect her. Don't let anything harm her, got it?"

Alex dropped to one knee out of weakness.

"You'll be fine. I got this." He winked at her and slowly walked into the woods whistling. The eyes seemed to retreat in fear as Osiah ran into the woods.

Alex scratched Komptin behind the ears. "I'm okay, big guy." Komptin rubbed his big purple head against her body. Alex smiled and tried to stand. The open field was cold with the sky clear view of the stars. The outer trees of the field were illuminated but behind them seemed like death awaiting.

"Erie," Alex pointed out to her four-legged protector. A couple of growls combined with the sound of movement in the woods caught Komptin's attention. He flashed his eyes giving a growling bark, trying to warn off any attacker.

Two Infiltrators jumped from the woods and one of them rushed towards Alex. Komptin leaped and the two met each other in midair. Komptin landed on top of its chest as he started to tear into the Infiltrator's chest. He jumped off the Infiltrator to turn to grab its head with his big mouth.

He flung it back into the woods like a Frisbee. The Infiltrator howled in pain as it slammed into a nearby rock, dissipating into the ground. The second Infiltrator started to sneak up to Alex but Komptin intervened before it reached her. The Infiltrator cautiously backed up towards the woods. Komptin fled after them into the woods leaving Alex alone.

"What a dumb dog," a calm dark voice came behind her. Alex heart raced as her fists lit up with what energy she had. She turned and swung but it was blocked by a dark man with a white face and big black hat. His strength was like none she's ever seen. His long black hair matched the blackness in his eyes. "Tsk, tsk," he said. "Is that anyway to greet someone?"

"If I'm going down, you're coming with me," Alex said gazing into his eyes.

"Settle down," he said. "I just want to have a civilized conversation."

"Why do I have a feeling there's nothing you have to say that I want to hear," Alex swung at the guy. He dodged out of the way and he wrapped his arm around Alex's neck. His black finger grazed the side of her arm cutting it with ease. "Okay, we can talk," she gave in.

The man let her go and licked the blood off his fingernail. "So good," he said.

Alex looked at him with disgust. "Why are all you death creatures disgusting?"

"Allow me to introduce myself, my name is Vandor."

"Okay," Alex replied. She wiped the blood off from her arm. "Wish I could say it was nice meeting you, but I gotta go." Alex turned around to take off and four Infiltrators surrounded her. They were creeping and crawling close to her "Or we can finish our conversation." She quickly turned back to the pale faced demon with a black hat.

Vandor waved them off and then slowly backed away from the two. "Aren't you at least the bit curious on why I haven't spread your organs all over this field?" Vandor asked. "I haven't had a Lite Force heart in quite a while."

"You have some serious issues," Alex replied. "What do you want?"

"All I want is for you to know the whole story," Vandor said. He motioned for the Infiltrator. The Infiltrator came behind Vandor and lay on his stomach. Vandor sat down on its back.

"I have a pretty good idea on what's going on," Alex let him know. "You are trying create an army which you will command; full of torture and torment."

"It's called discipline," Vandor said. "Free will is no good. Look all that it has caused. Heartache, war, fanon, and most of the time you miss out because you want something else." Vandor adjusted his hat. "You could have whatever you want and produce something so powerful, even more powerful than I."

181

"I'm content on where I'm at," Alex sniped back at him. She looked around for a way out of this.

"Sure, you are," Vandor looked down at her hands. "Ever wonder why you're blue?"

"I just assumed it was the source of power for the Lite," She replied looking at her hands.

Vandor seemed surprised, "You are pretty smart for a primate." Vandor looked at the Infiltrator. "Their eyes glow red because of the source of their power; true power, raw power." He stood up. A black mist shaped of a winged person approached and whispered something in his ear. Alex tried to listen but couldn't hear it. He nodded in acknowledgement to whatever was said to him. Alex started looking behind her. "Are you looking for my old friend Osiah?"

Alex snapped her neck around looking at Vandor. "Don't know what you are talking about?" Alex started walking backwards bumping into an Infiltrator. It growled in disgust.

"Oh, my child, I thought he would have told you by now," Vandor said. "Me and him, we had some good times." He looked up at the sky. "Some real good times. Fighting side by side. Angels knew they were doomed when they saw us coming."

"I don't believe you," Alex said. "You will say anything to get what you want."

"True," Vandor said. He got up and walked up to Alex. His hand grazed down the center of her chest lightly touching his sharp nails back up her bare arm. He leaned over. "You need to ask

182

yourself, if your light is blue, and theirs are red…Why is his purple? I have to go my dear." He licked the side of her cheek.

Alex just froze in place. She was certain she wasn't going to make it home as he approached her. He could have easily killed her but he for some reason, he let her live.

"So good." He backed away. "I will see you again."

The Infiltrators joined their master going off to the darkness and Vandor vanished into obscurity. Osiah returned before Komptin. "Where's Komptin? Are you okay?" Komptin soon after came running from the woods with a little of dark blue matter dripping from his side.

Alex stared into Osiah's eyes. "I'm fine, I just want to go home." She got goosebumps on her arms as she tried to warm herself up.

Osiah nodded agreement. "Yes, tonight did not go as I expected."

"Yep, you could say that," she said as the two walked back to town.

Chapter 9

Tomorrow would be a week from Joseph's funeral and Sara was just plain shocked on how close Robbie's family was during this tabulation. She found herself a bit envious on the family bond they shared. Even though she considered Alex and Mole family, her own blood family was distant and cold. Lately, there are two moods to her dad, distant and cold or just plain angry. He'd pushed her into the furniture and threw her to the ground more than usual and then it looks like something is just telling him not to go any further. Scary thing was that it seemed as if he didn't want to, like he wanted to keep on going.

She looked out the window of the kitchen as she grabbed a bowl from the cupboard. She could see her dad carrying the dog's food dish over to him. She thought it was weird that he was feeding him since it was part of her chores.

Maybe he was turning a new leaf. It would be nice; she had always wanted a close-knit relationship with her father. Even though a lot of his views were racist, deep down she thought he had a good heart. She smiled at the thought as she watched her dad approach the dog, who was barking a lot lately. Not just annoyance bark, but a deep growl barks as if something was wrong.

This started to happen a couple of days after Osiah dropped her off and tried to intervene during one of her dad's drunken stints.

Sara remembered being woken up in the middle of the night to the dog barking. Her dad grabbed his gun thinking it was an intruder or animal approaching the house. She started to follow her dad downstairs but he told her to stay in her room. Sara thought she heard a scream, but she couldn't hear over the dog's barking.

Her dad came back into the house and told her to go back to bed. She remembered how cold it got that night and she had to get extra blankets from the linen closet.

The sound of gunshot caused Sara to drop to her bowl. She looked out the window and saw her dad standing over the dog holding a smoking gun with blood dripping down his hand. She ran outside to her dad. "What happened?"

"Damn dog bit me," her dad said. "Now I've to go check to see if I'm rabid."

Sara looked down at her old dog. She was never really close to Buck, but she did enjoy the fact of having him. He was always glad to see her, and she didn't think he was rabid at all. He was actually excited and loving every morning she went to feed him.

"Sara, get in the house and pick up the pieces to this bowl," her dad yelled from inside the house. "NOW!"

Sara instantly ran into the house where her dad was standing on the pieces of the broken bowl washing his hands in the sink. "Do you need any help with that?"

"What I need from you is to pick that damn bowl up," he said, kicking the pieces in Sara's direction. She lifted her leg out of instinct not to be cut from the pieces. "I'm going to the doctor." He walked out the door. "That bowl better be picked up before you go to school."

"Of course," Sara bent over, picking up the pieces of the bowl. She looked down at the pieces that were full of her dad's blood, but then she realized it was from her as her nose started to bleed over the floor.

***

Alex was pulling up Sara's driveway as she saw Jim coming down as well. Alex kindly pulled over so he could get through. As she was waiting for him to pass, she went into her backpack to get an energy drink that she packed for the drive to school. She opened it and at the time Sara's dad was passing. She made eye contact with him as he gave her a face of hatred.

Without hesitation Alex snarled back giving him the same scowl face he had shown her. "Jackass," she said as she pulled up to the house.

Alex was still shocked at Sara's dad. She always knew he was not a fan of Alex, but he hardly ever thwarted anything in her direction. She saw Sara over the kitchen sink trying to stop a bloody nose.

"What happened?"

"I dropped the bowl when my nose started bleeding," she replied. She wiped the blood from her nose with a paper towel.

Alex moved the hair from Sara's face so her hair wouldn't get any blood on it. Alex looked out the window at the dead dog lying on the ground in a pool of blood. "What happened to Buck?"

"Rabies," Sara quickly replied. "Daddy had to shoot him."

"Really?" Alex asked. "Finish getting ready for school and I will pick up the bowl."

"Thanks." Sara walked out of the kitchen and stopped to look at Alex who was picking up the pieces. "Alex."

"Yeah," she said, throwing the pieces in the garbage and grabbing the broom.

Sara walked up to Alex and hugged her. "Thank you. I love you so much."

Alex returned the hug knowing there was much more going on than Sara was telling her. "I love you too. Now, go get your bony butt ready for school." Alex finished cleaning up the pieces of glass and sat down waiting for Sara.

She took out her phone and texted Mole that they would be there soon. Her phone vibrated and Mole returned the message that he was already at school. He said he rode his bike in.

**

Mole finished his shower in the locker room. Even though he wasn't in any sports the coach let

187

him have a spare locker. That made things a lot easier for him when he rode his bike into school. Multiple coaches tried to convince Mole to come out for Track or Football because of his speed and strength, but he was never into the team aspect of the running. He enjoyed the solo sports because he only relied on himself. He finished combing his hair when he was approached by Shawn who seemed to have something on his mind.

"Hey Shawn," Mole said, grabbing his books. "What's going on?'

"Mole," Shawn leaned on the locker. "I'm sorry about your parole officer. Must be hard to lose such a good guy as your parole officer. You'll probably get a real hard ass as a replacement."

"Robbie is the one who needs more attention, he lost his father," he replied. "But thank you."

"Did you get a new one assigned yet?"

Mole looked over at Shawn at that was a weird question. "I'm temporarily reporting to one of the deputies at the police department until a new one is assigned. Would you like to know how my urine tests are going to, the last one was pretty yellow?"

"Hey, don't get mad because you're the felon," Shawn laughed.

Mole said grabbing his book bag. "Is there a point to this conversation?"

"I noticed that you have been trying to hang out with Anne and texting her a bit," Shawn said.

Mole stopped in his tracks. "I want you to note something; it's not any of your business."

"You know, Anne is a special girl and her ending up with a felon is truly beneath her," Shawn commented. "Don't you think you would drag her down with you?"

"What the hell man?!" Mole said slamming his locker shut.

He dropped his bag approaching Shawn who put up his hands. "Hey, hey, I'm not looking for a fight," he said. "I'm just wondering that I think she knows it and she doesn't know how to let you know it."

"We are not dating," Mole said. "She can do what she wants."

"How sweet and innocent she is; do you think she could actually tell you not to contact her anymore. You know we were out last Saturday night…together?"

Mole felt his stomach start to get upset. "You were?"

"Sorry man. I thought she would have told you," Shawn said. "Just do me a favor. Let it go easily. Don't make it dramatic."

"Shawn, somehow I don't believe you," Mole said. "You don't have the greatest reputation among the girls in the school."

"And you don't have the greatest in the town," he came back with. "Don't you think her parents and friends convinced her of that?"

Mole took a second to regain all his thoughts. "Nope, sorry don't believe you." Mole left the locker for class.

"I don't think he believed me," a disappointed Shawn said to Roger.

Roger came from the other side of the lockers. "I'm good with how it went down. Really I just wanted to plant a seed of doubt."

"What next?"

"Show him proof," Roger said.

***

Anne was walking down the hall to her locker. There was so much going on her life right now. She found herself missing Kale. The space she decided to give him for grieving seemed to be doing more harm than good.

Also, she felt she was being a bit selfish for thinking that she should just ask him what she thinks of their relationship or lack of. The other night she caught herself sleeping in Kale's sweatshirt. She even talked to her mom about it, first time admitting it out loud that she had strong feelings for Kale Moler.

The only redeeming feature was the first time in quite a while she didn't have to take her books home. She was all caught up in all her classes. It was probably because she wanted to bury herself in her schoolwork. The passing of Joseph took a toll on Kale. She texted him a couple of times throughout the week but didn't get much of a reply.

She looked at her phone one more time to see maybe if he texted her back or any sign that he was doing okay. There was nothing. She shut the door to her locker where Alex was standing by her locker. Anne jumped because she wasn't expecting her to be there. Her pale white face with dark makeup was looking at her. "Sorry, you startled me," Anne said to her.

Alex moved her small black weaved in hair over her shoulder. "Have you seen Mole?"

Anne replied, "Not as late." The two of them started walking down the hall together. Anne could tell Alex had something on her mind. "Have you?"

"Not really," Alex said with a bit of guilt on her face. "I've been busy with my new job."

"The church job?" Anne asked.

"Yep," Alex answered her.

Sara came up and joined the two girls. "Hi Sara," Anne said. Sara just gave Anne a nonchalant wave. Anne didn't understand the distance Sara gave her. There was something bothering Sara that Anne did. She was hoping she didn't upset Sara in any way. Anne really liked Sara.

"Alex," Sara said. "I don't feel good. Can you give me a ride home?"

"I don't feel like going to the first period anyway," Alex told her.

Anne chimed in, "Is there anything I can do?"

"No thank you," Sara said. "I just need to go home."

The two left for Sara's house. Anne went to class where she ran into Shawn. "Hi Shawn."

"How's it going, Anne?"

"Just going to class," she said, motioning towards the door.

"I'm heading that way," Shawn said as they two walked down the hallway together. "I just wanted to tell you that I had a really good time on Saturday."

"Okay," Anne was confused. "What did you do?"

"We had dinner together," Shawn said.

Anne laughed, "Okay, if that's what you want to tell yourself." Anne continued to walk towards class where Roger was looking in her direction. Anne stepped over to the side running into Shawn. "Sorry, he gives me the creeps." Roger nodded at Anne while giving her a small wink. Anne shivered out of the spine-chilling look he was giving her. Shawn took this opportunity to put his arm around her. "What are you doing?" He reached over to grab the flower in Anne's hair with the arm that was around her.

"I just always love the smell of these," he said. He took a whiff of the flower. "Just emphasize your beauty." He turned her around and placed the flower back in her hair. He then ran his fingers down her face and then down her arm.

"Shawn, please don't do that," Anne said. "You are making me feel uncomfortable."

"Sorry," Shawn said. "I just think you're something really special."

"I'm not interested in you like that," Anne said looking at him with sincerity.

192

"Okay," Shawn said. "I understand. How about a little friendly hug to show there are no hard feelings?"

Anne gave him a hug. Shawn's grip was that of a bear. He squeezed tight and whispered, "Thank you."

Anne walked into the classroom feeling a bit dirty.

***

Shawn took in the smell of Anne's hair during the hug. The smell of her hair was memorizing to him. It made him want her more every time. He watched her go into class and then walked up to Mole who was down at the other end of the hallway. "Mole, I'm sorry you had to see that."

"See what?" Mole said.

Shawn looked at him. "Mole, I know you saw us together. Please, again, for her sake, don't make a big deal of this." The first bell rang meaning that class was about to start. "If you care for her, you will just start backing off." Shawn watched Mole nod in agreement. He put out his hand for a handshake.

"I will."

Shawn shook his hand, which had a surprising strong grip to it. "I'll take good care of her," he informed him. "Just be civil and keep your distance." Mole shook his head in agreement. "If you want Mole, I can set you up with someone, perhaps someone for sure to get your mind off of

Anne? Trust me; I know some girls that will make you forget about anyone."

"I'm good," He was thinking if it wasn't too late to find that girl from the pool.

"Why don't you date Alex? It's not like you two haven't hooked up in the past," Shawn said.

Mole shot him a dirty look. "Alex and I are just friends," Mole said. "No interest whatsoever in her." The weird thing was that Shawn could see it in his face. It was true.

***

Alex came into the church late that night. She felt a little uncomfortable because tonight she was going to ask Osiah about Vandor. This was on her mind all week. The truth was something she was after. She stood outside the church wondering how she was going to approach him. Osiah's light was on in his office. Alex wanted, no, she needed to trust him.

"You are going to confirm what I told you?" Vandor said sitting on the bench in the churchyard. Vandor at the church, giving a snarling look at the crucifix on top of the steeple.

"I know your type," she informed him. "You twist the truth to manipulate your story."

Vandor patted the seat next to him. "Come here and sit next to me. If you paid attention to your mentor, you know I cannot hurt you here or you me." He scooted over. "Come on."

"Still, I'm good keeping my distance from you," Alex said. "You smell really bad."

Vandor almost instantly appeared in front of Alex on the other side of the gate. "You are so full of potential. I could make sure you are showered in power and prestige." He ran his fingers through her hair. "I could give you riches like you would not believe."

The door opened to the church and Vandor turned around. Osiah stood in the doorway looking at Alex and Vandor. Komptin was at his side with his eyes glowing blue. "I think you need to leave."

Vandor stepped away from Alex. Osiah walked up to the two of them. Komptin stood behind Osiah. "Osiah." Vandor stepped away. "I have to go anyway. My future garden needs to get ready for seeding." Vandor jumped over the gate and disappeared into the dark.

"He's a peach," Alex said looking at Osiah. She was about to speak until she was interrupted by Osiah.

"Little Spitfire, there is something I need to tell you," Osiah said, still staring where Vandor had disappeared to. "Something about myself and the dark individual that you had the pleasure to talk to."

Alex got herself situated on the bench where Vandor once sat. She could still smell the foul stench he seemed to put off. "I'm listening."

"Not here," Osiah turned into the church.

Alex got up from the bench and smelled her hand. She tried wiping the stench off her hand on her clothes as she followed Osiah to the balcony of

195

the church. They sat in the church pews overlooking the room of the congregations. Osiah reached into his pocket and pulled out his flask. "Drink," he offered Alex.

"No, I'm good." She got herself situated. "Why do I have a feeling this is going to be a story I don't want to hear?"

"You need to hear it," Osiah insisted. "What you take out of it, let's just say I understand either way." Osiah took a sip of his drink. "Back way before civilization even started, there was war; a war to see who would rule over you, the new primates."

***

Osiah, in battle armor, grabbed the angel and blasted his dark red misting fist under the angel's chest, coming out the other end. The angel screamed in pain as Osiah grinned, pulling his fist out and throwing the angel to the ground where a pile of Infiltrators jumped on the body and started pulling it apart. Osiah then turned around and pulled another angel off his good friend and partner who was starting to fall.

Osiah pulled the first one off and threw him off into the air. The angel regained control in the air and dived after him. Osiah grabbed the angel and tossed him to the other angel who was about to attack his friend. "Vandor," he yelled. "My old friend, we fight until every last one dies!"

The Dark Conduit regained his composure. "Death to blue!" Vandor swung and his sharp fingernails sliced an angel's face.

The angel howled in pain and Osiah jabbed a spear from his dark red mist into that same angel. The angel fell to the ground, lifeless before breaking down to a glowing dust floating to the sky. Osiah took his fist and thrusted it into the angel's chest pulling out a blue glowing heart.

He took a bite of the blue heart as blood dripped from his mouth. He offered a bite to his friend. "Here, this will lift your spirits." They both laughed as they shared the blue heart over the carcasses of angels.

***

Alex was really starting to feel uncomfortable. She started to question Osiah. Was he here to kill her, to convert her, or some evil manipulative plan? She got up from the pew to head towards the door but stopped. She remembered that no matter what, she is safe in the church. She sat on the other side of the room. "I'm assuming there is more to the story."

Osiah got up and walked towards the door. "Come, I will tell you everything." They walked downstairs in the main worship room. "I was fierce, together, Vandor and I were unstoppable! We were ruthless and we loved it." Osiah stopped and looked up at the crucifix. "Then one day, we were called by the Dark."

***

Osiah and Vandor kneeled in front of the Dark. The sounds of torture and screams surrounded the darkness of the ones who had failed the Dark. Vandor was the first to speak, "To your command.'

"There is a new being, a new source of Lite," the Dark informed his executioners.

Osiah spoke, "The Light is desperate to create such a muse."

Vandor finished the thought, "To destroy it, would mean a victory for us."

The Dark spoke, "Kill her and you shall have more power and stature than any of my warriors."

They both bowed. "Consider her distinguished, to your command."

***

Alex was feeling a bit cold. "I can't see you like that, so cold, so heartless."

Osiah couldn't look at her. He was feeling ashamed, he never liked to think about the past, but tonight, he must tell the tale. "I was and possibly still am." Osiah continued the story, "Vandor and I managed to find where the new being was being held up. We had her cornered."

***

The two female warriors were giving Vandor and Osiah more trouble than expected. The green haired one moved with grace as the purple haired one was equally as deadly. Osiah and Vandor called for extra Infiltrators to help distract one of them so Osiah could get into the temple to diminish this new being.

The purple haired female was fending off the Infiltrators. All that was left was the green haired one. Both Osiah and Vandor rushed her, and she maintained her ground between the two. Vandor made it past her but she grabbed him and threw him into the wall. Vandor immediately leaped at her, knocking her through the temple's door.

Osiah didn't hesitate. He ran into the temple to distinguish the new being. The room was white and made of marble. Osiah saw a blonde hair being with her back to him. He slowly approached her, he was getting close, close enough to strike and end this war. Osiah flashed his fists and created a spear, ready to strike. Now the Dark will reign over this new life. Then she turned around.

Her beautiful blonde curly hair was held back by a gold headband. Her misty angel wings were drooped with sadness as glowing lite gold tears rolled down her cheeks. Her white robe was just as elegant as the presence of the being. "Please," she cried. "Stop the hate."

Osiah extinguished the spear from his hands. "I don't know if I can."

She grabbed his hands and put it on her chest where her gold heart laid beating the Lite. "You already made the first step."

"I don't, I don't know if I can help," Osiah said looking into her eyes.

"I believe you truly know who you are," she said holding his hands.

Osiah put his head down in shame. "I can't be forgiven for all the Lite I have diminished," Osiah turned around. "But I promise you this, today is not the day you die." He walked out to the battlefield with his fists blown in a purple brightness.

***

Alex stared at her mentor. "And you have been serving the Lite ever since?"

"More like a self-banishment from both sides," Osiah stated. "I can't trust myself, the hate calls me and I'm afraid of the day where I accept the call." Osiah grabbed a drink. "So, I asked God for an executioner for that day."

Alex felt Komptin come to her side. Her eyes grew big. "You mean—"

"Komptin is a protector against myself, he's under strict orders to execute me if I am to turn," Osiah informed her. He petted Komptin in his gargoyle state. "Without hesitation."

Alex went into her backpack and pulled out an energy drink. "I know it will be a while before you forgive yourself." She stood up and kissed him on his forehead. "But I know I can trust you."

Osiah tried to force a smile at his young apprentice. "Why don't we call it a night? You deserve to take a break for a night."

"Are you going to be all right?" she asked him as she packed up her phone.

Osiah watched her pack her stuff up and smiled. "You are a good person." He got up and headed out to the woods. "I just need to go for a walk."

Chapter 10

Alex came home from being out with Sara and Mole. It was a nice evening, but Mole seemed a little out of it. He didn't really say much, and he mainly sat in the corner of the booth looking at his fries. There were a couple of times Alex was mentioning where Anne was but all Mole said was that he wasn't sure.

Alex opened the door to see her mother and father sitting at the table putting together a jigsaw puzzle while drinking some wine. Alex scooted a cheek over next to her dad. He slid in and offered her a sip of his wine. "That is really sweet."

"Ice wine," her dad told her. "They pick the grapes when they are somewhat frozen. It sweetens the taste," he said, taking another sip.

"How was your night?" her mom asked her to continue to look for pieces of the puzzle.

"It was okay," Alex replied, grabbing some pieces of the puzzle. "Sara is concerned for Robbie and something is eating at Mole, but he won't talk about it."

Her dad and mom looked at each other. "Speaking of which, we are having dinner at the club tomorrow night with Kale and Kate, so don't make any plans."

"I didn't know you were friends with her," Alex pointed out.

Alex's mom answered, "We went to school together. She was in a grade below us in college."

"Sounds like fun," Alex said. She just received a text from Mole telling her that he was just told they are having dinner together tomorrow night. Alex was waiting for some sort of smartass remark but none followed. So, she just texted him back that she couldn't wait.

***

Sara sat in the living room in the dark. The only thing she had for light was a candle she had burning next to her as she read from one her favorite books. It was such a relaxing atmosphere. The candle she thought always added a sense of reading atmosphere. She poured some of her sparkling grape juice into a glass. She didn't dare touch her father's wine. He kept close tides on it and didn't trust her for anything.

She continued to read her book until she heard some growling in the direction of the field. She got up and looked outside the window. She saw some glowing eyes in the field in which she just assumed it was coyotes or a wolf looking for food. She got a cold shiver down her spine and shut the window.

Sara turned around and a weird shadow crossed the living room wall. It made her startle a little bit when she realized nothing was there. "Weird," she said aloud to herself. She took one more glance out the window and then the candle mysteriously blew out. She heard the growling get a little louder. "Who's there?" she asked.

A lump in the back of her throat grew and her stomach was turning in knots. The smell of the burned out candle filled the room. She looked to see if her cell phone was in her back pocket so she could use the light but she remembered she left it on the end table. She walked slowly towards her phone. The air was getting thick as if it was warning her something bad was coming. She started to grab her necklace that held a crucifix for protection.

Lights from her dad's pickup truck brightened the living room. There was a sense of relief to see her dad come home. There was someone else in the vehicle with him. Sara could see a girl that was not going to be a long-term relationship. Sara hurried to put the candle away and put her glass in the dishwasher. She grabbed her book before heading to her room. The door opened and the two of them came inside the house.

"Nice place you have here," the woman with her dad said. "Really homey."

"Don't get used to it," Jim told her. He looked around and then glanced upstairs to see if Sara was in her room. Sara hid back in the shadows hoping her dad didn't see her spying on him.

The strange girl picked up a photo of Sara. "Is this your daughter? She's really pretty."

"Yeah, I'm not really looking to talk about her," he said, putting down the picture on the end table. Her dad grabbed the girl and started nibbling on her neck.

"Hold on there, hero," the girl said. "Before we get any further, I think there is something we need to discuss."

"Whatever," her dad annoyingly said. Her dad went into his wallet and gave her some money. "$500.00?"

She grabbed the money and put it in her purse. "Do you want to go to your bedroom?"

Her dad grabbed the hooker and threw on the couch like a rag doll. The woman laughed out of nervous shock and started removing her nylons. Sara quickly and as quiet as possible got to her bedroom as fast as she could. She gently closed her door and put on her headphones, playing the music as loud as possible so she didn't have to hear what was going on downstairs.

***

Beth just got done with her John. This was one of her worst ones. His breath was foul, he was kind of a jackass. She got off the couch to go to the mirror to fix her hair. She looked at herself not believing the situations she gets herself into. She put her bra on and slipped her shirt on. She couldn't find her nylons or underwear.

"Oh the hell with it," she said, giving up on finding them. "The creep can keep them." She got her skirt on and high heels. She looked outside and realized she didn't know where she was. She didn't know this town.

The clock on the wall said it was passed one in the morning. The guy who brought her here was nowhere to be found. She was kind of hoping she didn't have to stay the night in the creepy place. There was no reception to find a cheap motel to stay at.

"Where the hell am I?"

She gave up trying to figure something out, so she decided to get herself comfortable on the couch.

"You can leave now," her John said from the kitchen.

Beth got up to peer into the darkened room. "Do you mind bringing me to a nearby hotel?" she asked nervously.

He just looked at her.

"Can I at least use your phone?"

He looked over at the phone. "Nope." He just continued to look at her.

"Well, what in the hell do you expect me to do?" she angrily asked.

He just took a sip of his drink and pointed to her feet. He motioned walking with his fingers pointing to the door. The ultimate shock came when he just waved. "Bye-Bye."

"Jerk," she said, grabbing her purse headed out the door.

Beth had been walking about thirty minutes, in high heels, down a road in which had no lights, no houses, and no cars. It was dark, it was cold, and all she wanted was to get into a hot shower and forget this night. She continued to walk as she heard some faint growls behind her. The emptiness of the darkness was all she could see. Her pace quickened, but the growls were getting louder behind her.

She turned right back around. "Crap." The growls were getting closer. Hopefully there was cell reception now. "Oh, thank God," she said aloud. "Service."

A deep growl came from the woods. The phone dropped from her shaking with fear and shattered all over the road.

She started to cry. "Oh God please no."

Another growl was louder, closer.

All that was left was to start running down the street praying that someone would come along. With every step she took, she knew she was closer to some sort of safety. That was the only thing that was keeping her going. She was running out of breath and was starting to lose momentum. She convinced herself to keep going as she was crying aloud for someone to help. There was one more step before she felt claws dig into her back. She screamed and pain as she stumbled on the ground lying on her stomach.

She knew this was it. She cried to mother and father begging them for forgiveness for all trouble she had caused. "Mama, I'm sorry," she yelled. "Daddy! Daddy!!!"

Massive claws rolled her over onto her shredded back. She came face to face with her death. Its glowing red eyes overpowered its blackened body. She attempted to scream but all you could hear was the gargle of blood dripping down her windpipe. The last thing Beth ever saw was a chunk of her throat in the beast's mouth.

***

Alex was getting ready for their dinner with Mole and his mom. She was putting on her dark eyeliner and put on her favorite black miniskirt. A bag with her hunting clothes were ready because she wanted to change into pants after dinner. She was excited for this hunt tonight.

"Alex," her mom yelled. "We are leaving, see you there."

"Okay, Mom," She has been texting Sara all day, trying to get her through the drama of her dad bringing home an escort to vandalize the couch. Alex shivered at the image that popped in her mind. "Burn the couch" Alex texted her. "Or never sit on it again. LOL."

Alex arrived at the dinner club where Robbie's sister showed them to a corner booth. There was an overwhelming compulsion to see how she was doing. It was almost as if Alex felt guilty, like it was her fault Joseph died. "How are you and your family doing?"

"We're getting through this," she said. "Surprisingly, it is bringing us closer together."

Alex nodded. "I get that." A small rub on her arm told her that Alex was there for her. "If you need anything, just let me know."

"Thank you," she showed Alex to the table where she was the last to arrive.

"You're late, shocker," he snickered.

Alex was happy to see Mole was getting back to his old self, but she knew him too well. Something else was still bothering him.

The table ordered drinks and a couple of pizzas. Alex's dad looked as if he had a lot on his mind. Alex wondered if he was going to break some bad news about Mole's new parole officer or worse if he had to go back to juvie.

Kate was the first to talk, "So tragic to hear about that girl."

Alex's dad chimed in, "Yeah, at first the police called me because they thought it was a homicide, but it turned out to be another animal attack."

Alex's curiosity piqued. "Where did it happen?"

Mole chimed in, "Couple of miles from Sara's."

Alex choked on her pizza. "What?"

"Police think it was a prostitute. She had 500 dollars in cash and dressed like a sex worker," her dad said. "I hope they find that animal that is doing this."

"Well, this is just a pleasant conversation to start this night," Kate pointed out. She took a sip of her beer as if something was on her mind.

Alex's mom, Jen, jumped in, "Kids, there is something we needed to talk to you about."

Mole continued to eat as if he didn't really want to be there.

"Kale, you need to listen to this," his mom said, nudging him.

Mole just motioned to go on as he grabbed another slice of pizza.

Mike took a sip of his drink. "So, I'm just going to ask this—"

Alex interrupted him, "Dad, we are not sleeping together!"

Her dad had a dumbfounded look on his face. "Well, that's good. Since incest is illegal in most states."

Mole froze in the mid-bite of pizza.

Alex could only imagine the confused look she must've had as she stared at her mom and dad. "What?"

Alex and Mole moved in closer to each other examining each other like a biology experiment. They looked deep into each other's eyes. The two sat down continuing to look at each other. They just sat there studying each other. Kate couldn't help but continue to look at the both of them, one right after the other. Alex's dad just sat there trying to think of something to say.

Jen finally broke the tension. "I'm sure you have questions."

"Ah, did…but the…ah…how?" Alex asked, going back to at her dad and then Kate.

"You see Alex, when a boy becomes aroused his penis gets…" Mole started to say.

"Kale!" Mole's mom yelled. "You see, a long time ago your father and I…" She motioned with her hands.

210

"In college," Jen continued. "Your father and I were deeply in love...and still are. Anyway, one night your dad proposed to me and I got scared."

"She broke up with me right there," Mike added. "I got drunk, and my buddies took me to a party where..."

"I just happen to be," Kate chimed in. "I had a few in me and next thing I knew..."

"Alex's dad was in you," Mole added in. Kate slapped him on the back of his head.

"A couple months later," Jen continued the story, "Your dad and I talked, and I begged him to propose again."

"That night," her dad said, "was the night we were blessed with you."

"Fast forward three months later, I approached your dad with some startling news," Kate resumed.

"So, the three of us sat down to discuss the situation," Jen smiled at the memory. "Much like we are doing now."

"Surprisingly, the same type of pizza," Mike gave a little detail, grabbing another slice.

"What was discussed?" Mole asked.

"Well." Mike swallowed his bite. "I was just finishing law school and Alex's mom was just finishing her degree with being pregnant."

"And I always wanted to have a child," Kate told them.

"I agreed to give up custody, and in a sense, without sounding harsh, pay your mom child support to help with the raising," Mike told her.

"What?" Alex just shook her head in disbelief.

211

"Honey," Alex's mom said. "Hear us out. It was as if Kate went to a fertility clinic."

"Alex," Kate continued. "Not talking about the money, but your dad gave me the greatest gift I could have ever asked for."

Mole pointed to himself. "And that would be me." He smartly grinned.

Alex rolled her eyes.

Kate continued, "I bought this restaurant, raised a wonderful son, and I have no hard feelings towards your dad." She looked at him. "I could never thank him enough for that." The three adults joined hands in the middle of the table.

"How come you never said anything before?" Alex asked.

"Honestly," Mike was about to be frank. "We really got swept up in our life and didn't think by any chance you two would be as close as you are now."

Mole and Alex looked at each other again. "Hey, wait a minute, you sent my ass to jail!" Mole pointed out.

"Kale, you have a problem," Mole's mom chimed in. "When you got into that wreck, Mike was going to try to sweep it under the table." She looked at Alex's dad. "But I requested a meeting with him and asked what he would do if it was just another case."

"I said I would send you to the juvenile detention center," Mike informed the group. "You were going down a wrong path."

"You can't deny it wasn't the best thing for you." Kate patted her son's hand.

There was a long pause until Mole decided to speak. "So really, let's break this down, logically…it changes nothing. Alex and I still and never will sleep together." He shivered at the thought. "We continue to live the life we are living with no change." Giving Alex a brotherly smile, he said, "I'm good." He grabbed another slice of pizza.

"Yeah, me too," Alex got overjoyed with happiness. One of her best friends was actually her brother. Somehow, she always knew. The feeling of joy got overturned when she saw the blank look on Mole's face as he faced in the direction of the door.

Alex turned around to see what he was looking at. Anne was up at the bar picking up some dinner to go. The two of them met in eye contact. It was almost as if Anne was equally as concerned on seeing him. There was a brief moment of time standing still before she forced a smile with a wave like. It was obvious she wanted to talk to him.

Mike took a gander over in her direction. "She looks like a nice girl."

Mole just nodded in agreement. "She's the best."

Alex could tell that Anne wanted to come over to talk. So, being the little sister she is to Mole, she yelled, "Hi, Anne!" The restaurant looked over in Alex's direction as she was waving like a fan at a basketball game.

Anne shyly came up to the table. "Hi. I was just picking up dinner for my mom tonight." She politely greeted everyone at the table. "How's everyone doing?" Everyone answered positively, even Mole who was obviously lying through his teeth. "How've you been Kale? I haven't heard from you lately."

"Just a lot of training. The race is in a couple of weeks," he reminded her. "My training is getting longer and longer."

Anne nodded. "I get that. I know how important it is." She and Kale had words they wanted to say but nothing came out. "I've gotta get going." She put her hand on Alex's shoulder. "Call me."

Alex nodded in agreement. Mole was playing with a green pepper on his plate. His mood changed from happy to one of gloom. She texted him, "We are going to talk."

* * *

After dinner Mole and Alex went to Marty's for a milkshake. Mole wanted a chocolate shake and he ordered Alex a vanilla because he knew she was going to mix it with an Apollo energy drink. It was quiet as they sat across from each other. There was tension as when they walked in they saw Roger sitting in the corner. Alex was thinking she should find out right here if he was infiltrated. There was no way to do that though. There was no sense she could tell unless he used the Dark.

Her thought was interrupted by Mole. "What do you think about this, sis?"

Alex smirked when Mole called her "sis" gave her a sense of happy completion. "I don't know, but it is as if we always knew."

Mole nodded in agreement. They sat for a bit while Alex mixed her vanilla shake with her energy drink. There was a sound of plastic rubbing together started as Kale moved the straw up and down staring at the chocolate as it came up with the straw.

"Are you going to tell me about it?" Alex flat out asked.

"What's there to tell?"

"Well for instance, you've been keeping your distance away from her. Did you guys have a fight or something?" She inquired.

"No," Mole turned around and noticed Roger was sitting on the other side of the restaurant listening to music and eating a sandwich. He was also reading some magazine, but Mole couldn't make it out. "It's just that Shawn told me that he and Anne were starting to date. He wanted me to keep away from her."

Alex almost choked on her shake. "Anne and Shawn…nope. Can't see it."

"I saw them in the hallway," Mole said. "It was pretty obvious."

"I think you are over imagining what you saw," Alex didn't believe what he was saying. "Why don't you just man up and go talk to her? The way she came to our table suggested otherwise."

"I don't know," Mole said. "I would hate to lose any friendship we developed over this. I would rather have that than nothing at all."

Alex took her straw out full of milkshake and blew it all over Mole's face.

"What the hell was that for?!" Mole asked.

"Are we still close even though you're mad at me?" she asked him, halfway giggling.

"I'm actually pretty pissed," he half-jokingly said, wiping his face off.

"Are we not friends anymore?" she asked Mole.

Mole knew exactly what she was going at. The relationship he had with Anne could withstand this. Alex went back to her drink. "You know you're right. I think we need to clear the air one way or the other. I miss her. I really do. Tomorrow I will swing by her house while on my bike ride after she gets back from church and talk to her."

"Good for you," Alex said, looking at her phone. They finished their drinks and headed out the door. "Do you want me to bring you home?"

"Nah, I think I will just walk," Mole said. "The walk will let me clear my head on what I'm going to say."

Alex wasn't comfortable with that idea since that girl got killed last night by an Infiltrator. She did know that he needed to walk to clear his head. The two got up and gave each other a quick hug before going their separate ways.

***

Gron took off his headphones and watched Alex and Mole leave Marty's. How he was tempted just to eliminate him, but he wanted Mole to suffer; he wanted him to pay for keeping him away from his conquest.

He walked outside and he could still smell Alex and the Lite she produces. He closed his eyes to soak it all in. He grabbed his phone and called Shawn. "You have somewhere to be tomorrow morning."

***

Osiah walked outside with Komptin faithfully at his side. The Infiltrators were growing stronger. He put his flask inside his inside coat pocket before he started his walk. There was a sense to join Alex on her hunt tonight, but it was time she did one herself. Even though she was young, she was very powerful. That didn't stop him from worrying, though.

Osiah saw that her friend was walking towards his house. It wasn't too late, but it was getting there. He received a quick wave and he returned one back to him. "Komptin." The massive dog looked up at Osiah. "Make sure he gets home all right, okay?" Komptin flashed his eyes and took off into the woods to ensure not to be seen by the boy.

Osiah walked towards a local park. He caught himself thinking of how he wished he was able to have a family. He and Celestial would have little kids running around, going to school, going to PTA meetings, arguing over if they should have pizza or burgers on Friday night. He smiled at the thought of normal life. A life he found himself envious of.

A chill came up from the back of his spine. There was a powerful sense of the Dark. Without turning around, he acknowledged his former partner in evil. "Vandor."

"I'm tired of waiting."

Osiah faced him but giving himself some distance in case he attacked. "Waiting for what?"

"The Lite Sentry, I want her," Vandor said. "Convert her to my side."

"Why the hell should I do that?" Osiah got on the defensive.

"You convert her, and I will stop my hunt on Celestial."

Osiah looked at him in confusion. "What?"

"You convert her to red, and I will not hunt for Celestial…permanently," he proposed.

Osiah put his arms down. Vandor's eyes were dark, opaque with blackness. Infiltrators in their corporal form now surrounded him. "Your army is growing powerful."

"And ready to attack at my command," he replied proudly.

He reached into his pocket and grabbed his flask. "May I have one last drink before I die?"

Vandor patted his old companion on the shoulder. "Of course, enjoy it."

Osiah took a sip of flask and put in his pocket. He ignited his hands for preparation of the inevitable attack. Vandor motioned to his dominions to attack as he disappeared into the shadows.

**

Alex followed the trail of the Dark to a howling of Infiltrators being diminished. There was only person that she knew of that could destroy those beasts. Infiltrators surrounded a man with glowing purple fists. Osiah was in pure defensive posture.

Alex's eyes flashed blue as her hands lit, and now she was in full attack mode. By the time she got there Osiah was down to one knee as the biggest Infiltrator approached him with his claws raised for the kill. Osiah's hands were barely sparking as Alex could tell he was struggling to ignite them.

Osiah closed his eyes for the anticipated the blow. Just as the beast was about the swipe Alex came and jumped on the beast's back pounding her fists into his head. The surrounding Infiltrators howled as another grabbed Alex and threw her onto the ground.

The beast jumped into the air as Alex kicked it to prevent it from landing on her. The beast went flying into the group of other Infiltrators knocking them over.

Osiah got up and was able to ignite his hands once more. The two of them stood back-to-back. Alex who gave him a quick smile and a wink. The two attacked the Infiltrators in a life and death handicap match.

They flowed together in the fight; each of them knowing what the other was capable. Osiah grabbed one of the Infiltrator by the arms and flung it into

219

Alex's direction. Her ignited hands formed a blade and decapitated the Infiltrator. "Hot damn!" she yelled. She didn't have time to celebrate as another Infiltrator grabbed her from behind squeezing the life out of her. Osiah quickly ran up and formed a spear with the hands jabbing it into its eye.

The remaining Infiltrators regained their fight positions as five more joined from the shadows. "Looks like it is going to be a long night," Osiah said with blood dripping from nose and forehead.

Alex cracked her neck. "If I go tonight, I'm not going without a couple of these bastards."

The Infiltrators howled and growled as they came in for the attack. Osiah and Alex were holding their own. One Infiltrator broke through Osiah's defense and sliced his arm causing him to spin around knocking him into Alex. Alex lost her balance and fell over onto the ground hitting her head on a wooden sandbox. An Infiltrator slowly crawled up on top of Alex growling with deep red eyes gazing into her.

The Infiltrator was just about to pounce when Komptin pounced on the side of the Infiltrator knocking him down on its side. Komptin grabbed the Infiltrator's head with his mouth and ripped it with ease. Komptin spit out the head as it disappeared and veered in the direction of the others. The Infiltrators analyzed their situation and decided to retreat into the shadows.

Osiah tried to get up but only had enough energy to lean against a big tractor tire the kids played on. He reached into his pocket and pulled out his flask. He noticed the flask was cut open from one of the Infiltrators claws and all his drink had leaked out. He checked the blood dripping from his nose. Komptin came over to check on Osiah. He patted him on his head as the massive gargoyle creature walked over to check on Alex.

"I'm good," Alex said to Komptin as she used him to get up and crawl to sit next to Osiah.

She checked her weave as she felt one of them missing. "Bastards ripped one of them out." She checked the spot where one of them was missing. Blood was its replacement.

"Ah man." She looked at her fingers when she checked her lip, as that too was bleeding. She walked over to Osiah and grabbed his flask tipping up for a drink and nothing came out. She shook it a couple of times. Osiah grabbed the flask and turned it around showing her the hole in the flask. Komptin jumped on top of the tire keeping guard as the two of them rested.

***

Anne got back from church before her parents because they had to run to the store for some gardening supplies. In the driveway she could see Shawn's car with him sitting on the hood like some 80's movie cliché.

Anne shut the car off as she wondered what he wanted. "What are you doing here, Shawn?"

"I just wanted to see if you wanted to go swimming with a bunch of us down at the beach."

Anne looked at the temperature for it was already hot for a late morning. The idea of running into the lake on a day like this sounded appealing.

"I don't have a problem with that," she told him. "I wouldn't mind getting together with the class before we graduate." She walked into the house and Shawn followed her in. "Wait here, you can grab something to drink." She halfway expected him to follow her into her bedroom to watch her change.

Once she put on her swimsuit, she grabbed an oversized t-shirt and slipped on over her. Now if she only could find her shorts.

***

Mole rode into Anne's driveway on his bike and noticed Shawn's car was there. He didn't know what he was going to say to Anne. He just convinced himself that he was just going to clear the air. He wanted to see where he stood in Anne's life. His gut feeling was that this was going to go in his direction. Things were going to go right.

***

Shawn saw Mole coming up on his bike just as Roger predicted from the window. He looked in the direction of Anne's room and could hear her stumbling around. If Anne came out right away, she would ruin his plan to keep the felon away forever. He only had one shot at this if it was going to work.

Mole came to knock on the door. He hurried to take off his shirt, shoes, and socks as he headed to the door. He quickly unbuckled his belt and opened his fly to show as if he just put them on before opening the door. "What are you doing here, Mole?"

"I just wanted to talk to Anne," he replied.

Shawn put his arm up so Mole couldn't walk in. "She can't come to the door right now," he said motioning over to their bedroom. "Besides, I thought we agreed you wouldn't come around her anymore."

"I just…" Mole tried to say when he heard Anne's voice.

"Who is at the door?" Anne yelled from her room.

Shawn cringed because she was going to ruin this moment for him. Anne came to the other side of the room with a large t-shirt on. It looked as if she had nothing else on. Shawn looked up to the ceiling. "Thank you."

"Kale," Anne said in surprise.

Mole closed his eyes and tried for something to say. He just nodded "Okay, Shawn." He buckled his helmet and jumped on his bike down the driveway.

***

Mole wanted to make sure he was clear out of sight before he pulled over. He got off his bike went to tree as he felt he was going to vomit. He continued to dry heave a couple of other times, but

223

nothing came up. He looked around to make sure no one was around before spitting on the ground. He thought, "How could he be so stupid?"

Roger leaned against a tree overlooking all that has happened. He walked up to the tree where Mole leaned against. There was nothing but satisfaction of what just transpired. The plan was falling into place.

Chapter 11

It was Friday morning; Mole didn't sleep well throughout the night. His nerves were on overload. All he has trained for the last year and half was about to come to head. This was the final weekend. His mom gave him permission to skip school today so they could leave for the race. He had a two mile swim, 120 mile bike ride, and a twenty-six mile run to do Sunday and less than seventeen hours to finish it. The suitcase was triple checked to be placed in the car. The bike was securely fastened to the rack, but a couple more checks wouldn't hurt. He leaned over on it and took a deep sigh. The neighborhood seemed different. All the memories of him getting up so early to run or bike are hopefully about to pay off.

"Getting nervous?" his mom asked, putting her suitcase in the car.

"You have no idea," he said. "I just wish Joseph was here."

His mom saw a bird sitting in the tree. "Look, he's seeing you off."

Kale smiled at his mom's attempt to ease his nerves.

"No matter what happens, I just want to tell you that I'm proud of you." She slapped him lovingly on the face and checked her watch.

"We should get going." Mole got into the car. "Check-In is the first thing tomorrow."

Down the driveway, they turned the corner of the street and there was a huge banner "GOOD LUCK MOLE!!!! YOU CAN DO IT!!!" There under the banner was Robbie and Sara, Alex with her parents, and Dan cheering and screaming. Mole's mom pulled over with tears running down her face.

Mole looked over at his mom. He quickly wiped a tear from his face before he stepped out of the car. Robbie and Sara were the first to come to Mole. Sara gave him a hug and Robbie patted him on the back. Dan and Mole screamed at each other as the two bumped chests and grasped each other in a hug. Alex's mom and dad approached Mole giving him a small box.

"This is just a small gift," Jen said.

Mike put his arm on his shoulder. "I know it hasn't been easy and I couldn't ask for a better gift for my daughter than to have a brother like you." He smiled at him.

Mole shook his hand and gave him a quick hug. Mole opened the box and it was the top of line model GPS watch which only the top elite triathletes wear. Mole's eyes grew big and fought back more tears. "I...I...I don't know what to say."

"There's a first," Alex chimed in, punching him in the arm.

"You don't have to say anything," Mike said. "Just kill it."

Mole grinned. "I'll try."

Alex pulled Mole to the side. "So, how are you feeling?"

"Nervous," Mole said. "But now, I know I'm going to complete it."

"You got this." She looked over to the crowd. "Sorry, I didn't know if I should have invited Anne or not."

He verified Anne wasn't there. "It's best that she wasn't here."

Alex hugged Mole and kissed him on the cheek. "I know something happened last Sunday, but if you don't want to tell me, you don't have to."

Mole took a deep breath. "Actually, it might clear my head for the race if I tell you." He began to tell her how Shawn answered the door with his pants unbuckled and Anne coming out in nothing but a large t-shirt.

***

Alex could feel her arms start to tingle as she heard the hurt coming from Mole's voice. She quickly gave him a hug and buried her head into his chest to prevent the flash of blue from showing to anyone. "You just concentrate on the race and finish it upright. You hear me."

Mole gave her a quick squeeze. "I will."

Mole and his mom said their good-byes and then drove off. He worked so hard. Alex just prayed this situation wouldn't distract him from completing his goal. Everyone screamed and hollered as they drove off. Alex continued to wave as her mind was racing on what her next move was going to be.

Sara came up to Alex. "You look upset."

Alex turned to Sara. "Is it possible for Robbie to bring you home?"

Sara nodded. "My dad is out of town this weekend. Why?"

"I have to go pick a flower," Alex said, getting into her car.

**

Anne has never been so mad at anyone before than at Shawn. All week she was thinking of ways to make this right with Kale. She was not a dumb girl, she knew what happened. Shawn made it look like they were sleeping together. His pants were unbuckled when talking to Kale. Then she just had to come out in a t-shirt that made her look like she was naked underneath. There was fury just thinking about it. Poor Kale, what he must think of her.

Anne was finishing getting ready for school when she looked at her phone. She knew Kale left for his race today. She started to text him but didn't know how that would go. The two of them avoided each other all week. If she was Kale, there was no way she would believe it. Many drafts went on her phone before she just decided to give up. She placed her flower in her hair when she heard someone pulling into the driveway.

"Shawn, if that is you..." She was going tell him once and for all to leave her alone. There was a bit of shock that it wasn't. "What's Alex doing here?"

228

Anne opened the door just in time to witness Alex forcefully opened her car door just to shut it in anger. Anne's urge to run increased as fear overcame her body when she started to approach. A pit in her stomach formed. Anne knew where this was going. "This is not going to end well," she cried to herself. "Alex," Anne pleaded. "Alex, now wait a second." She held her hands up. "Alex."

Alex grabbed her by the shirt and swung. Anne saw a flash of blue before she slipped on the stairs before Alex was about to connect. Anne grabbed the back of her head because she hit her head on a flowerpot on the way down. Debris from the siding of the house covered Anne's head.

Alex towered over her even though she was smaller than Anne was. She stood panting with her fists clenched. "Why did you lead him on?" She huffed. "Was it just to make Shawn jealous? You like playing people like that?"

Anne just stayed down covering her in fear that Alex was going to start kicking her. Alex just hovered over Anne like a barbarian over a kill. Alex slowed her breathing down. Anne thought she had no defense. She had never been in a fight before. To Anne's surprise, Alex gently picked up to set her on the porch stairs. Anne wiped her tears.

"I thought we were friends," Alex scolded her. She then screamed pointing in Mole's direction. "You hurt him!"

Anne started crying. "Alex, I swear, Shawn and I aren't anything, never was. I would never hurt Kale, I…" Anne stopped herself.

Alex stopped her initial attack on Anne and studied her. "You really care for Mole, don't you?" Anne looked up at Alex with tears running down her eyes as she nodded. Alex sat down next to Anne, picking out some of the siding from the house out of Anne's hair. The two of them stared out to the field. They just sat there for a couple of minutes before Alex spoke, "First fight?"

"If you want to call it that." Anne blew her nose from a tissue Alex gave her. "This is new territory for me."

Alex put her hand on the back of Anne's head. "I'm glad you're not bleeding." She looked at Anne. "Sorry about that." She picked up the flower that was Anne's hair to place it back where she normally puts it.

"In a sense, I knew this would be coming." Anne brushed off her pants. "He must have told you what happened that morning."

Alex nodded. "Why didn't you come to me and tell me what happened?"

"Shame, trust, I didn't think you would believe me," Anne admitted.

"What happened then?" Alex asked.

"He told me there was some group picnic at the lake and he just came to tell me about it," Anne picked up a chunk of the house and looked at the corner of the house that was missing. Anne looked on in wonderment. "Then next thing I know, Kale is at the door while I was changing into my swimsuit." Anne could tell Alex's mind was racing thinking about something. "What is it?"

"Sounds too perfect of a situation to be a coincidence," Alex stood up and held her hand out. "Come on, I'll buy you a coffee and bring you to school."

***

Alex and Anne both walked into school together. The two of them were joined by Robbie and Sara who walked behind them. Alex saw Shawn talking to his friends, making some sexual innuendos.

Anne asked Alex, "Did Kale leave this morning then?"

"Yeah, we were all there wishing him luck," She showed her some of the pictures she took wishing him off.

Anne put her head down in shame. "I'm sorry I missed it."

Alex rubbed her back. "Just talk to him when he returns. Just don't text him or call him prior to finishing the race. He's worked too hard to get his mind all jacked up."

"I get that." She wondered how she was going to approach him. She could have Alex warn him, but she felt like this was something she needed to do herself.

Shawn came over to the group of them. "Hey, ladies." Shawn went over to Anne. "I can't get last weekend out of my mind. Seeing you in nothing but a t-shirt," he said, grabbing the flower from Anne's hair.

231

Anne didn't hesitate. Her knee quickly came into contact with Shawn's groin. He crashed to the ground holding his crotch as the bell rang. Anne picked up her flower and put it back in her hair. "This does not belong to you." She stepped over him and walked to class.

Alex's eyes grew big in shock as Robbie and Sara stood frozen in disbelief. The bell rang and the crowd dispersed leaving Alex looking over Shawn on the ground. "You guys go to class. Shawn and I are going to have a little talk." She dug her fingernails into his ear as she dragged him into the girl's bathroom.

***

"That was so awesome," Alex said to Anne. "All day the school has been talking about you kneeing Shawn in the nuts, but in all seriousness, I'm so glad to witness it," she laughed while drinking her energy drink.

Anne wasn't too proud of the way she acted. All day girls came up to her thanking her for doing that. Sara, Alex, and Anne sat outside on the school bleachers watching the band practice for graduation. Alex was sipping on her typical energy drink while Sara and Anne shared big water.

"Do you think he will make it across the finish line?" Sara asked.

"No doubt about it," Anne said, going to her phone.

Alex continued to look around the football field.

Sara asked, "What are you doing?"

"It's weird, in a couple of weeks, we will never have reason to come back to this field again. A lot of making out with guys under the bleachers during the games," Alex recalled.

"How many times…?" Anne asked.

"Don't ask questions which you don't want the answers to, but if you go underneath where we are sitting, I think it's the spot where Bill and I were making-out during the Homecoming game," Alex pointed. "As I recall, the only score of the night."

The three of them laughed.

"You know what would be neat," Sara suggested. "We all watch Mole cross the finish line on Sunday night."

Anne perked up and glanced over at Alex.

Alex grabbed her keys. "I'll drive. Just let me ask my parents." Alex picked up her phone ask her parents.

"I gotta do the same." Anne got up to call her parents.

Sara called her dad and surprisingly he said she could go. The other two girls came over with both the same answer.

"Where are we going to stay for the night?" Anne asked.

"Mole's mom said we can stay with her and Mole in their hotel room."

Sara clapped. "Yippee. Girls' trip."

233

***

Robbie brought Sara home after their date on Friday night. They had gone out to a movie. It was so nice being just the two of them. They ended up at Marty's for a burger to meet up with Alex and Anne. She kind of felt sorry for Robbie because the three of them just started making plans for the girls' trip. Robbie was a trooper though because he just suffered through it with a smile on his face.

"Sorry about all the girl trip talk." The two of them sat in the truck in the driveway.

"I enjoyed it," Robbie said. "I've never seen you this excited about something for yourself."

Sara just smiled and gave him a kiss. "Do you want to come inside for a second?" She motioned to the house. "It's probably going to be your only chance to see what the inside of my house looks like since my dad is out of town."

Robbie shut the truck off. "Sure, I have to use the restroom if you don't mind."

"Not at all," Sara said, opening the truck door.

The two of them went into the house together. "Nice place," Robbie told her. "Really clean. I like the glass coffee table."

Sara cringed on the inside as he said that. "It's a pain to keep clean. There's a bathroom off on the other side of the kitchen."

Robbie went into the bathroom. As he came out, he walked through the kitchen and Sara was standing in the living room with her shirt and pants

234

off. Robbie just stood there with a surprise look on his face.

"I hope you are not disappointed," she said motioning to her body.

Robbie just shook his head, he tried to speak but nothing came out. "I have protection."

"Good," Sara said. "I've never really done this before."

Robbie walked slowly up to her and embraced her firmly, giving her a caring kiss to make this as special as he could. He started moving her towards the couch.

Sara stopped. "No,"

"You wanna stop?" Robbie said lifting his hands off of her. "We can wait, I just need a quick cold shower."

"Huh? Oh no, I still want to, but I will never sit on that couch again," Sara said. She grabbed his hand and guided him upstairs to her bedroom.

***

Alex's little side effect of being a Lite Sentry was starting to take effect. It was two in the morning and she wasn't even coming close from being tired. She started flipping through the TV in her room and stopped at an infomercial about a mop. She caught herself thinking it would be a good investment in the long run. She quickly dropped the remote when she shut off the TV. "Oh God, it's starting." She looked down at her phone and got a text from Sara. She texted Alex what had just transpired.

"You go girl!" Alex replied. "Details on the trip. I have questions!!! Luv ya!!"

She went through her phone. "I can't sleep," she texted Osiah.

He replied, "I just saw this great commercial about a mop."

Alex shook her head. "Nope, not happening." She grabbed her phone to tell Osiah she was leaving town on Sunday.

"Have fun," was his reply.

***

Vandor called for Salamor. "To your command," he answered his master.

Vandor sat on the throne of human flesh and bones. He got up and looked outside the window. "We need to separate her from her support," Vandor mentioned. "We need to break her down, so she has no choice but to join us." He turned to Salamor. "Go fetch me Gron."

***

It was Saturday, Sara was making sure all her chores were done so she could get ready to pack for her trip. She had no idea what to wear. There was something about herself. She was happy. After Robbie left for home Friday night, Sara realized that she needed to leave. Her current home life was far from being healthy. She was going to have to leave home for college or the military or something to get away from her dad. He would never let her have a life outside of him and this town.

"What's that smell in here?" Her dad's voice came behind her.

Sara screamed from being startled. "Dad." She grabbed her heart. "You almost gave me a heart-attack."

Her dad walked in smelling the air. "I know that smell." He walked closely up her sniffing.

"Dad, you're kind of freaking me out," she said backing away from him. "I thought you were out of town this weekend?"

"The load got pushed back," he said looking around the room. "How come you're so nervous?"

"I just wasn't expecting you home so soon," she admitted. "I didn't get my chores done yet." It was all that she thought of that he would believe.

"Was there a boy in here?" He flat out asked her. "How come it smells like sex?"

"I have no idea." She couldn't see any proof Robbie was in this room.

"Well, okay, then." He turned around heading out the door. The sound of him walking down the stairs in anger echoed through the house.

Sara sighed. "Oh thank God." She continued to pack for her trip.

"GET DOWN HERE!!!"

Sara's heart dropped to the bottom of her stomach. She slowly walked downstairs into the kitchen. "Yes."

"You didn't take out the trash on Friday. Friday was garbage day…now we have a week to smell of trash around this place."

"Dad, I will take it outside right now and put it in the garbage can. You won't smell it in the house," she told him, lifting up the garbage.

He grabbed the garbage bag from her hands and dumped it all over the kitchen floor. "Pick this up and clean the kitchen."

Sara accidentally let it slip out. "You didn't have to do that."

Her dad's hand came across her face knocking her into the kitchen chairs. "Don't ever tell me what to do." Her nose started bleeding as the welt from her eye started to swell. Her dad just walked out of the room and yelled, "I don't know what you're hiding, but your little trip is off." He grabbed her phone. "You tell that little goth bitch that you're not going and then give me your phone."

***

Alex slammed her phone on the kitchen table. "Jackass!"

"Alex," her mom said, giving her something to eat. "Language."

"Sorry, Mom, but Sara's dad is a real piece of sh...crap," Alex declared.

Her dad chimed in, "Yeah, there were rumors about him but nothing ever substantial to look into."

"Can't you send him to jail for just being a jerk?"

238

He looked at Alex while holding his coffee. "Really?"

"What happened?" her mom asked.

"All of a sudden he told Sara that she can't go on this trip because she didn't do all her chores."

"Maybe she neglected what she was supposed to do," her dad pointed out.

"It was probably something stupid like not taking out the trash or something. He's just a...jackass," she said out of anger. Alex couldn't help but think that Sara needed to get out of her house and start her life.

***

Anne couldn't believe that Sara wasn't coming. Anne knew she was excited about the trip and for her not to go, something must have come up. "What do you think happened?" Anne asked Alex as they were pulling away out of town.

"I don't know if everything was fine until Saturday," Alex said, opening up her can of energy. She handed Anne water.

"Something must have happened between Friday night and Saturday," Anne mentioned opening the water. "Thank you."

Alex's eyes grew big. "I wonder if that jackass found out."

"Found out what?" Anne wiped her face from water that spilled as Alex hit a bump in the road.

"You can't tell anyone," Alex decided to confide to Anne.

She confirmed with her motioning it on her chest. "Cross my heart."

"Robbie and Sara had sex Friday night…in her bedroom." For some reason, Alex was whispering. "And if he found out."

"There would be no way he would let her go with us," she finished Alex's sentence. "That poor girl."

Alex noticed Anne kept looking at her phone. "Why do you keep you looking at the app on your phone?"

"It's a tracker, I'm watching to see where Kale is on the race," Anne said. "I'm kind of stalking him."

Alex laughed. "Where is he?"

"Just transitioned out of the water," Anne commented. "His swim time was one hour twelve minutes."

"At least he didn't drown," Alex said as they continued to drive.

They made it to the hotel where Mole's mom met them in the lobby with their hotel keys. "Hello girls," she gave them all hugs. "Where's Sara?"

"She couldn't make it." Alex was getting worried about her friend.

"Well, I'm glad you are here." She looked at Anne. "Does Kale know you are here?"

She shook her head no. "Ms. Moler, I…"

"Kale's face lights up when he sees you, or even talks about you," she told Anne.

"He's talked about me?" she asked her.

"Constantly. He'll never admit, but there is no doubt in my mind that he's got it bad for you."

Anne's face blushed as she looked down on the ground.

"Where is he now?" Alex asked.

"Well, he's around mile fifty on the bike, so we got a while. When do you plan on seeing him?" his mom asked.

"Not until the finish line. We don't want to make him lose his concentration by seeing us," Alex said.

"Not a bad idea. Well, here are your hotel keys. We are in H303," she handed them the keys. "I would recommend the pool. I'm off to run some errands while I'm here. I have a meeting with my food distributor. Always working." She hugged the girls again. "Enjoy the pool."

***

Anne was enjoying the sun beating on her body by the poolside. Alex went and got something to drink for the two of them. It was bliss until the sun was being blocked by something. She opened her eyes to see two guys hovering over her. "Can I help you?" She politely asked.

"Just wanted to come over and say 'hi'," one of them said.

Anne acknowledged her with a simple, "Hi." She continued to put her head back on the pillow. "If you don't mind, I'm trying to enjoy the sun."

She adjusted herself and tried to close her eyes, but she could feel the two boys standing there.

"Can we join you? Looks like you are all alone over here," the other one said.

"I'm also in high school," Anne said, hoping to scare them away.

"Cool, we just graduated from high school last year," the blonde one said. "Looks like you're burning on your shoulders; do you want me to get those hard to reach areas?" The two of them laughed.

"You gotta be kidding me?" Alex said holding two drinks. "That's the dumbest line I ever heard. I wouldn't even give in to that." She sat down in her black bikini. "Here's your drink." She handed it to Anne. Alex looked to the two boys and shooed them away with her hand. "Bye, bye."

"Damn, you don't have to be such a bitch about it," one of them said.

Anne only moved her hand to take Alex's drink. She walked over to the blonde one to push him into the pool simultaneously grabbing the one who insulted her. She twisted his arm and threw into the wall. "What did you call me?" She pressed his face into the wall harder. "What did you call me?"

"A bi...ahhhhhhh," he screamed.

"That's not nice," she informed him. "Apologize."

"Ahhhh, I'm sorry, I'm sorry," the man quickly said, trying to get out of her hold.

The other man got out of the pool and Alex swung his friend around. The two collided with each other both falling into the pool. The remaining people around the pool applauded. Alex just waved to them and calmly sat down.

"What is it with you anyway?" Anne asked, handing back her drink.

"What do you mean?" Alex said watching the two guys climb out of the pool in shame.

"How are you so strong when you must weigh 100 pounds?"

"I'm 116." She waved at the boys. "You be nice now," she said in a really fake southern accent. Alex quickly changed the subject. "Where's Mole now?"

"Mile ninety of the bike," Anne checked her phone. "At this rate he should be done around eleven o'clock tonight."

"We'll leave about an hour before he is finished, so let me know when he hits mile twenty of the run," Alex requested.

Anne rolled over to look at Alex. "Can I ask you something?"

Alex followed suit. "Yeah what's up?"

"What is with the two of you?" Anne asked, almost afraid of the answer.

"He's my brother," Alex said, rolling back on the cot.

"You mean he's like a brother?" Anne asked.

"Nope, flesh and blood," Alex corrected her.

Anne rolled over on her back. "Like brother?"

"Yep, brother."

***

Mole was hurting, there was no question about it. Even though it was about an hour before the race closed, he was still calculating how much time he needed to run three miles. There was a sense of relief as he thought he could finish walking. This was a sense of completion. He did it. He went from a teenager with a drinking problem to a, well, still a teenager with a drinking problem, but now he knew that he could overcome it. He was just about to complete an Ironman race.

Aches from muscle fatigue was evident. He actually had no energy in his body left. He was starting to get passed by competitors who he had passed on the bike portion quite a bit ago. Still, he wasn't going to give up. Over the next block he started to hear the cheer of the crowd; this gave him a little boost of energy. The feeling of such an accomplishment was just under a mile away.

He was now in a full out stride. Crowds were getting bigger, people cheering were bringing a sense of overwhelming feeling over him. He just passed the sign stating only half a mile left...ten more minutes and all would be completed.

"Just one foot over the other," he thought to himself. His stomach was turning in knots. He didn't know if it was anxiety or the fact his body was breaking down. All he knew was he now only had a quarter mile left to go. Only one lap around the track as it related to.

The crowd, the music, the look of the finish line was just moments away. Over the loudspeaker he heard his name being spoken by the announcer. "Kale Moler is now an Iron Man!"

He did it. He fought back tears as a lady put the Iron Man medal around his neck. Another young college kid quickly wrapped a plastic blanket around him and kept on asking if he was okay. Mole just nodded and kept on walking. His legs were starting to feel like jelly as he peeled a banana to eat.

He walked over to the meeting area where his mom was waiting for him. He fought back the tears as she was in full out crying. "I'm so proud of you," she said as she hugged him.

"Thanks, Mom," Mole started to walk towards the leaving area when he noticed his mom wasn't moving. "Are you coming?"

She shook her head as she pointed in the direction behind him. Mole turned around to see Alex standing there with a huge grin on her face. Her pale skin seemed to glow in the lights. He couldn't hold it in any longer, a tear started to roll down his cheek as he gave her a big hug. "I can't believe you are here!"

"I wouldn't have missed it," she gave him a hug. "I'm so proud of you."

"Thank you," he returned.

"Oh, someone else wants to say congratulations to you," Alex informed him. "Right behind you."

Mole turned around expected to see her parents or Sara, but when he did turn, he saw Anne looking at him. She had a big smile on her face with a tear running out of her eyes. She pulled out the flower out of her hair and held it out.

Without hesitation, Mole just placed his hands on the cheeks of her face and kissed her. Anne wrapped her arms around Kale's sweaty neck and returned the kiss. It was a moment Mole never wanted to end.

Mole finished the kiss and looked at her in the eyes with a smile.

"Kale, I…" Anne tried to say but Kale stopped her by kissing her again. She just wrapped her arms around him tighter to bask in the moment.

"Okay guys," Alex said. "You know we are sleeping in the same room, right?"

Kate joined Alex by her side just watching the happiness Mole was protruding. On the back of Mole's running shirt was a sign reading, "This is for Joseph."

Chapter 12

Osiah and Komptin just came back from another hunt with no sense of the Infiltrators, not even a scent. They both were on edge from the sudden lack of Dark presence. Osiah came back to the church and stopped right outside church grounds. He pulled out his flask from his coat pocket that had been damaged from the last attack.

Osiah took a drink from his flask that he had to weld back together. He examined his work and was quite happy with it. Komptin joined him in his office that was being lit by the morning sun. He put his feet up on the desk pulling out a bottle of rum.

"Anything?" Father Joe came up to him handing him a cup of coffee.

"Nothing," Osiah replied. He veered towards the window. "Not a frog croaking, not a cricket chirping." Osiah took a sip of his drink. "It's almost as if every living thing is in hiding."

Komptin, who normally would rest after a hunt, sat down at Osiah's side, on point with his ears perked. The three of them ventured to the window staring at the woods. The forest was in complete silence. Osiah couldn't help but think how particularly dark they seemed.

***

Sara was glad Alex and Anne weren't in school yesterday, they were still returning back from Mole's race. Her bruise on her eye was healing rather quickly. She managed to keep Robbie calm by saying she tripped on while out on a nature walk, but she knew he didn't believe her. She winced from touching her sensitive eye. This bruise was just another representation of why she had to get out of there.

From what was in her room, there wasn't much in there she would take after graduation. It would be rough, but anything would be better than living with her dad. She started to think who she could stay with while she got situated with her life. She didn't have much money and she needed to get away far from this place, never to return.

Sara had it made up in her mind that she was going to ask Robbie what his final plans were after he graduated. She didn't want to live with him; she just wanted to be near him. There were no ties here. Alex and Mole wouldn't stick around. The vibrating windows from music meant Alex was there to pick her up.

She ran downstairs and grabbed her bag. She looked everywhere for her phone hoping her dad left it there for her, but it was still hidden. Sara jumped into the car and consciously tried to prevent Alex from seeing her bruise on her eye. She gave Alex a quick hug. "How was the trip?"

"So sweet," Alex said, drinking her energy drink. "As soon as Mole crossed the finish line, he kissed Anne so…the only word I can come up with is passionately." Alex looked over at Sara. "But enough with that, tell me about your little night of naughtiness."

Sara could feel her face blush. "I want to say it was nothing, but it was so wonderful." She thought back on that night being in Robbie's arms.

Alex raised her arm to put her hand on the back of Sara's head and Sara flinched. "Easy girl."

"Sorry," Sara said trying to cover her tracks. "Just caught me off guard."

Alex just smiled at her. "Where's daddy?" she asked as she put the car in gear and started driving away.

"I don't know," she said. "He took off early this morning." The music in the car blasted as they drove to start their day.

***

Gron approached Vandor and Salamor. Vandor was drinking blood from a demonic chalice. He looked around for a body but didn't see any. The Infiltrators probably devoured what was left of the carcass.

"To your command," Gron bowed to Vandor.

Vandor picked up what seemed to be a severed finger and took a bite off from it. "Choices. Choices got to be had." He looked to Gron. "Who's your first choice?"

"But of course, you are. Above all else," he reassured his master.

"Good to hear," Vandor said. "Life is full of tests. This particular test will be difficult for you."

Gron with a straight face, locked with Vandor's dead eyes. "No choice is hard to make when it comes to you."

Vandor stood up as Sara's father walked into the room. "She joins us or dies."

Gron said, "What must I do?"

"Fulfill a desire you have wanted to do for quite a while," Vandor said.

Gron nodded and walked out the door.

***

Osiah sat down in his office with his feet on the desk shopping on his computer. Komptin was lying down in the corner in his bed fast asleep. Osiah was on a website for a carpet cleaner he saw last night on TV that he was really interested in. He pulled out his credit card and purchased it.

When he hit purchase, he found out he got a free portable steam cleaner with it. He was quite happy with his recent victory. He got up and walked out the door where Father Joe was about to knock on his door.

"That was weird," Father Joe laughed. "What's going on, Osiah?"

"Just purchased this neat carpet cleaner that I saw on an infomercial," Osiah said excitingly. "It takes out over ninety-eight percent more germs and stains than the leading competitor."

Father Joe put his hand on Osiah's shoulder. "I'm glad you are happy with your recent finding," he laughed.

"Please have a seat," Osiah said sitting behind his desk.

Father Joe followed him and sat down. "I got some news"

"What's up?"

"I got transferred to Moscow," he said. "I'm not too happy with it but the Council wants me up there to get ready to replace a priest who is getting ready to retire in Washington D.C."

"That is ridiculous!" Osiah said. "There are very few Council Priests left in the church. Is your replacement part of the organization?"

"Unfortunately, no, that is what I argued, but it didn't matter to the Council," he said. "I have to leave by the end of the week."

"End of the week!" Osiah said louder. Osiah's voice woke up Komptin who looked up at his friend. "Don't they know what is about to go down here?" Osiah argued. "It's almost as if it is the calm before the storm." He looked at a picture of Alex and himself she made him take after one of their training sessions with Komptin between them.

"She's a good kid," Father Joe said. "She's strong and she's got one hell of a mentor. She'll be fine with you."

Osiah put the picture down on his desk. "Who's your replacement?"

"Father George Hanley," he replied. "He has no idea what's going on here or what your roll is in the

251

church." He looked at the picture he took of Osiah and Alex. "As far as he knows you are the head groundskeeper and Alex is a troubled teen trying to get her life in order."

Osiah laughed. "My little spitfire's mouth will validate that." Osiah got up and gave his good friend a hug. "I will come see you every chance I got."

"I look forward to it," Father Joe said. "Let's go get some dinner before Alex gets here."

***

Alex was glad it was Wednesday. Even though she didn't go to school on Monday, it seemed like it was a long week. Last night's training session wasn't really productive. There were no signs of Infiltrators and Osiah's mind was off somewhere else. The only highlight of the night was that she got a piece of pizza he saved for her and saw a neat carpet cleaner that Osiah had coming in the mail.

Robbie and Sara were talking about something serious as far as Alex could see. She saw the two of them were in deep discussion. Alex just stood there for a minute to let them finish their discussion before she brought Sara home.

Anne came up on Alex's side. "Hey, what are you looking at?"

"Robbie and Sara."

Anne watched them as well. "Robbie got accepted to the University of Minnesota."

"Really?" Alex said. "Good for him. It's what he wanted." Alex looked around. "Where's Mole?"

Anne smiled. "He's having dinner with my parents tonight."

Alex raised her eyebrows at her. "And you're not there?"

"His idea," she said. "He wanted to go into the lion's den alone." Anne went to her phone where she had a picture of the Mole on the night he earned his Iron Man medal. "He said that he wanted to clear the air about his past to them."

"Wow. Mole doesn't like talking about that," Alex was paying attention over to Sara and Robbie. She watched them hug as Sara was fighting back tears. Alex approached the two of them with Anne at her side. "Congrats on Minnesota."

"Thanks," Robbie said.

"You okay, Sara?" Alex said.

Sara smiled. "Couldn't be better."

Alex was almost afraid to ask. "Not the answer I was expecting."

"Robbie's sister is moving out of her apartment and her roommate said I could stay there," Sara said. "She said not to worry about rent until I get situated with a job and get into a school of some sort." Sara was crying. "She is so nice. I talked to her for about an hour. Denise, that's her name, talked to her family about my situation and they agreed." Sara looked to Robbie. "Robbie's dorm will only be about a 30 minute bus ride from the apartment."

Alex screamed with happiness and hugged her. "When do you get to go?"

"I'm leaving right after we graduate. I will pack when he leaves for work," Sara said. "He will never hit me again."

"Excuse me," Alex said out of shock.

"I thought you knew," Robbie said. "When you left town last weekend, he knocked the hell out of her."

Alex had to hold back the tingling in her arm. She didn't really feel like explaining why her fist would be glowing blue. She calmed herself down. "Just because you are getting the hell out of there, I'm not going to do anything." She hugged Sara. "I'm sorry I wasn't there for you."

"Is your dad going to be home tonight?" Robbie asked.

Sara shook her head.

"Good, come over to dinner with my mom and sister," Robbie suggested. "You could use a good meal."

"Sounds good," Sara said.

"I just have to go to my locker and get my keys. I'll be right back," Robbie said as he went over on the other side of the school to his locker.

Sara watched as he walked away. "Alex, I am so happy. First time that I ever feel like I'm free."

Alex said, "I'm so happy for you." The three girls hugged each other.

Anne said, "Let's make it a point to keep in touch once graduation is over. I love you like you were my own sisters."

Alex and Sara both said at the same time, "Agreed," as they continued to embrace each other.

***

Mole sat across from the dinner table of Anne's parents. It seemed they just stared at him. "You know, our little girl is very special to us," Anne's dad said, swirling his drink. Mole could tell that it was Crown Royale with ice. It was funny because Mole still could identify any form of alcohol that someone was drinking.

"Yes sir," was all Mole could think of saying. "She is very special to me. This year hasn't been easy and Anne helped me through a lot of it."

"She's all heart," her mom said, serving up the pot roast.

Mole waited to eat until Anne's mother sat down and was ready to eat. He was waiting for the dad and mom to start eating before he started. Once they started to eat, Mole went to town. A home cooked meal was something he cherished because he didn't get it very often. He looked up and just Anne's parents were looking at him in shock.

"Hungry?" Anne's dad asked laughing.

Mole looked down and he just realized he ate almost half his meal before they even put a dent in the meal. "Sorry. I guess I didn't realize how hungry I've been since the race. Even my mom was telling me she couldn't keep up with the food in the house."

255

"I didn't know the school had a race last weekend," her mom said, dishing him more food.

"It wasn't a school event," Mole said. "It was something I needed to prove to myself."

"Oh, what was that?" Her dad asked cutting into his meat.

Mole knew he wanted to address his past but was still unsure when to bring it up. "I wanted to prove to myself I could complete an Ironman."

"Really?" Her dad said. It looked like the first time that night he was involved in the conversation. "How'd you do?"

"Just over fifteen hours," Mole answered. For the rest of the meal Mole was actively engaged with Anne's parents regarding the details of the race and listening to the stories of their past athletic competitions.

***

Osiah sat in the bell tower overlooking the town covered in the trees. It was so pretty at night, so peaceful, but he knew somewhere out there were Infiltrators waiting to pounce. He looked down at Komptin. "What do you think?" Komptin turned his head to see Celestial joining Osiah.

"Osiah, training is going well. He is quite satisfied with everything," she said. Ariel and Devine sat outside the doorway. They both were wearing jeans and the same style shirts but different colors. The color of their shirts was the color of the other's hair. Celestial was in what Osiah would say

256

as a woman's power suit of some sort. Osiah thought the new steam cleaner he bought could remove any wrinkles she may have gotten.

"It is," Osiah agreed. "When she graduates high school, I was hoping to follow her to her choice in college to continue to help in the fight."

"If that is what you wish but you have kept yourself here long enough, I was really hoping you would come home," Celestial grabbed his hands.

Osiah knew she was serious. This was the first time she had come out to say she wanted him to go with her. She truly felt it was time. The feeling was true, in his heart he knew, it was time.

Ariel and Devine walked into the room. Ariel was the first to speak, "Now I am not happy, I bet against you…"

Devine finished her sentence, "And now she owes us dinner."

Celestial smiled. "Will you be able to join us?"

Osiah so wished he could. "I am expecting Alex. I will have to tell her the news. She will not be too happy."

Celestial kissed Osiah. "That is why I love you." She turned around kneeling to Komptin who laid his head on her lap. "You two have earned the right to come home and rest."

After Celestial left, he walked downstairs to a bench outside the church. Komptin followed and jumped on the bench next to him. Osiah scratched his longtime companion's head. "My old friend, you have been with me for a long time. You saved my life, and I the same to you. I know you are tired, but there is something I must ask of you."

***

Mole was invited into the basement of the McClure's house. Anne's parents had converted their basement into a type of game room. In the middle was a pool table and what Mole could see was a nice stereo and theatre station.

"This is my relaxation," Anne's dad said. "How about a couple of games of 301?"

Mole agreed. He looked at the darts and chose his set. Anne's dad got a nice dart case from behind the bar. "I play in a league every year." He showed Mole where the mark was. "Now the point of the game is to hit points down to 301 without busting. The outer markings are double and the middle of the numbers are triple. The outer bull is twenty-five and the inner bull is fifty. Any questions?"

Mole shook his head. "I think I got it."

"I'll let you go first," Anne's dad suggested.

Mole set up his feet. "Just like this?"

"Yep, that's good."

Mole took the dart and put three darts straight into the triple twenty. The computer deducted a quick 180 points from the score.

"Damn," her dad said out of shock.

Mole shrugged his shoulders. "My mom owns a dinner club. I spend a lot of time there."

Anne's dad walked over to the bar and poured himself a drink. "Do you want a drink?"

"No, I'm good," Mole said, grabbing his darts off the board.

"I know you're still in high school, so I understand." Her dad gave him a wink. "It was a little test."

Mole stepped to the side of the dart board. "Well, a year ago I probably would have taken you up on that." This was the window he was looking for. "Just something I've been meaning to talk to you about," Mole said, taking a drink of his Iced Tea. "I'm sure you have heard of my past."

"Rumors, Anne wouldn't go into it," he acknowledged.

Mole continued to tell him the generalization of his drinking problem and being sent to a juvenile detention center for the summer. "So, I'm legally allowed to get my license after graduation."

"And that is why you rode your bike here today?"

"Yes, sir."

He put his hand on Mole's shoulder. "Thank you for telling me this."

"To tell you the truth, if I hadn't cleaned myself up, I would have never had the privilege of getting to know your daughter, who is unlike anyone I have ever met," Mole confessed.

"She is something," her dad said. The two of them continued to play darts for the rest of the night discussing Mole's plans for the future.

***

Sara got dropped off at her house by Robbie after having dinner at his house. She never realized how nervous she got every time she drove up the driveway. There was no evidence that her dad was home. The truck wasn't in the driveway. She wanted to stay in the truck, she felt safe in there.

"Doesn't look like he's around," Robbie said, getting out of the vehicle.

Sara came out of Robbie's truck. The two held hands as they approached the door to her house. It was quiet in the yard. "Robbie, I just want to say, I don't know where I would be without you."

Robbie held her hand. "Sara, no matter where life brings us, I promise you, we will remain together, even if it is just friends…which I pray will never come." He kissed her.

"Do you want to come inside?" Sara said. "He won't be home for quite a while."

"I have to get home," Robbie said. "There is a lot to plan for with graduation happening in a couple of weeks."

"Yes, I'm looking forward to it," Sara said. "I just applied to a small college in Minneapolis. Talking to the counselor she said that there is a good chance I could help with tuition on a track scholarship."

"That's great!" Robbie said. "When will you find out?"

"She said sometime in June," Sara said. "And I got a job with my roommate's parent's law firm as a receptionist. They are going to work around my school schedule."

"See, it's all coming together," Robbie sounding more excited than Sara.

Sara opened the door to the house. "I'm getting the hell out of here the day after graduation." She hugged and kissed Robbie. "See you tomorrow in school."

"See you tomorrow," Robbie said, pulling slowly away.

"I love you!" Sara screamed at him.

"I love you, too!" Robbie returned slapping the hood of his truck. He honked the horn and drove away.

Sara could not help herself but laugh as she turned the lights on. Her dad was standing in the dark with an expressionless face staring at her.

***

Alex and Anne pulled into Anne's driveway from having dinner at Marty's. Alex was happy to see Mole's bike was still here. Dinner must have gone well if he was still here. The two girls walked into the house where all you heard was music and laughing from the basement. Downstairs, Mole was laughing with Anne's parents while shooting pool.

"What's going on here?" Anne said as she walked up to Mole to give him a hug.

"We're just talking about life, movies, races, and different stories…" Anne's mom said. "You picked a good one Anne."

Alex raised her eyebrows at Mole and smirked. Mole returned with a grin.

"And who is this?" Anne's dad asked, referring to Alex.

"This is my sister, Alex," Mole naturally said.

"Hi, Alex," Anne's mom said. "Do you care for anything to drink?"

"No, thank you," Alex replied. "I have to get to the church. Mole, do you want a ride home?"

"Actually, I'm kind of in the mood to ride home," Mole said. "Do you happen to have any of my riding gear in your car?"

"Surprisingly, I do," Alex said. "It's in the trunk."

"Do you mind if I change into my gear in your bathroom?" Mole asked Anne's parents.

"Be our guest," Anne's dad said.

Alex watched Mole slowly let go of Anne's hand as he walked upstairs.

"Seemed like that was going well," Anne said to her parents.

Alex heard Mole coming running downstairs. Alex just threw her keys behind her as Mole caught them and walked back upstairs.

Anne's mom said to Alex, "So Alex, are you getting ready for graduation?"

"Looking forward to it," Alex said. "I know it will be challenging but yet rewarding."

"College normally is," Anne's dad said.

Anne looked up as she heard Mole close the door to the bathroom to change upstairs. Alex watched her smile as Anne was embarrassed because her parents were staring at her. "What?" she said.

"He's a fine young man," Anne's mom told her.

Anne's dad walked up to her. "I don't know why we even questioned your judgement; we should have known better. He is a good guy and cares for you a lot."

Anne hugged her dad. "Thank you." Her dad let her go. "Let's go see him off."

The four of them walked upstairs and out to the porch. Mole joined them getting his bike situated. "Do you mind taking my clothes?" He handed Alex his folded clothes.

"I'm not doing your laundry," Alex told him as she threw them in the trunk slamming it shut.

Mole walked up to Anne's dad and shook his hand. "Thank you, sir, for inviting me into your home." Anne's dad returned the handshake. Mole then turned to Anne's mom. "Thank you for the delicious dinner."

Anne's mom gave him a hug. "You are always welcome."

Mole turned to Anne as the two just stared at each other.

"Come on, hon, let's give them some privacy," Anne's dad said as they turned towards the door. He stopped to check the chunk of the side of the house missing. He rubbed his hands over it and looked at the pieces on the ground. Alex looked at Anne and the two smiled at each other.

"I'll text you when I get home," Mole said, looking over at Anne.

Anne replied, "How long?"

"Should take me about just under an hour; I'm still pretty sore," Mole said. The two of them just stared at each other. Alex turned around to give them some privacy.

Mole kissed Anne. "I'll talk to you soon." Mole got on his bike and Alex approached him.

Alex teasingly mocked him, "I'll talk to you soon."

"Shut up," Mole teased back.

Alex lovingly punched his arm as he rode away. "He's got it bad for you."

Anne smiled. "It's amazing what this year has brought. A year ago, I would have never thought Kale Moler and myself would be dating."

"You two complement each other," Alex said. "And I'm glad I got to know you better." Alex looked at her phone. "I gotta get to the church."

Anne looked at her watch. "At this hour?"

Alex tried to think of an excuse but all she could come up with was, "Midnight Mass prep. I gotta go. See you tomorrow." She got into her car and drove off.

Chapter 13

Osiah opened his desk drawer to refill his flask. There really wasn't a need for it anymore. For some reason he didn't feel like having any. He looked through all his belongings; he didn't know what he was going to do with all his stuff. He was going to let Alex pick whatever she wanted. The rest would probably be dropped off at the shelter. There was guilt over leaving her, but he knows she could do it. Once he goes, he's not allowed frequent trips back like Celestial. He would be there, in the Lite. Out the window he could hear Alex's music coming from down the road.

"Ready," he said to Komptin. He answered Osiah by flashing his eyes and followed Osiah down the stairs to greet Alex. Before he approached Alex, he turned to his four-legged companion. "I hope you know I can never repay you for this."

Komptin put his head on Osiah's shoulders and nestled into him.

"What is going on, Old Man?" she said as Osiah walked down the stairs with Komptin at his side.

"Hello, Alex," Osiah was trying to capture this moment with his little apprentice.

"Hey, how old are you actually?" Alex asked him out of curiosity.

"Old enough. I think I stopped counting after the second ice age or was it the third?" he thought back.

Alex jumped over the fence and playfully fought Osiah. "What's the plan tonight? I haven't sensed anything all week. They're off hiding from being scared. We're such badasses." She was joking around.

"Yeah, it's been pretty quiet," Osiah replied. "What do you think we should do?"

"How about I mock hunt you and Komptin?"

"Could do that, but how would you feel about hunting with Komptin?" Osiah asked her.

The massive German Shepherd sat next to her. "We could do that, might be fun for a quick change."

"How about permanently?"

Alex stopped moving around. "What are you talking about?"

"After you graduate, I'm leaving with Celestial. I'm going home," Osiah dropped the news to her.

"What do you mean you're going home?" Alex asked. "How the hell am I supposed to take on the Dark alone?"

"Little Spitfire," Osiah stopped her. "There is nothing more I can teach you." He grabbed her by the arms. "You are the most talented Lite Sentry I know. You have an equal amount of fire and heart, which is rare." Osiah continued, "You are strong, smart, and a beautiful young woman with her future ahead of her."

"But—" Alex tried to say.

"Trust me, you are much more advanced than you think," Osiah said. "Besides, I will be able to come see you occasionally. If you need some guidance, I will make sure to show up."

"Awesome! You're going to be my Obi-Wan," Alex laughed.

"More like Yoda," Osiah knelt down to Komptin.

Alex looked at her in shock. "Really, you watch Star Wars?"

"My favorite movies." He turned and knelt down to his dog. "Komptin my ol' friend." He looked up at Alex. "Komptin will be yours." He looked back at his dog. "You promise me you will protect her, listen to her, nothing, I repeat, nothing will happen to her that's within your control." Komptin eyes flashed as he transformed into his gargoyle form with a vicious roar as Vandor approached the church gate.

***

Mole was making good time considering he was coming off his post-race. He was about ten miles from his house. The soreness from his legs disappeared and it felt as if he could ride all night. The natural high he had from such a good night also helped. Anne's parents seemed to like him, he had confirmation of a wonderful sister who was his best friend, and a perfect girlfriend that made him feel special. He just realized for the first time he was ready for whatever the future was going to throw at him.

He made it to the hill where he always had trouble climbing. Tonight is the night he was going to make it full throttle up the other side. He picked up the pace and was reaching top speeds. He leaned over the handlebars to gain speed.

The air hit his face with a biting sting as it started to intensify. On the corner of his eyes, he saw a red light which caught his attention, he looked but nothing was there. He turned to the front of him where he saw Roger which startled him causing him to swerve his bike into the ditch. Mole went flying over the handlebars and landed in the ditch. "What the hell, Roger?!"

Roger slowly walked up to Mole as he laid there to look over his body. "The fall didn't break anything, did it?" He almost sound concerned.

"No," Mole said, trying to get up. "But it sure hurt like hell."

"It didn't break anything?" Roger helped him get up.

Mole hesitantly answered him back, "No."

"Good," Roger eyed his body up and down.

"Roger," Mole tried to start moving backwards trying to get away from Roger.

Roger took a baseball bat out from inside his trench coat. "You know Mole," he said tapping the bat on his hand. "You took away something that belonged to me, and now it's my turn to take something from you." He swung and smashed Mole's knee with the bat. He never felt such pain as he grabbed his knee. "Shhh, quiet Mole. People are trying to sleep." He pushed Mole's hand off his knee with the bat. "Come on, come on, get up."

Mole managed to get up and limp off into the woods trying to get away. Roger followed Mole into the woods. Easily catching up to him, Roger swung the bat again this time hitting Mole's arm. Mole screamed again as he fell to the ground.

"Oh, how I am enjoying this." He stepped on Mole's chest as he walked over him.

"Anne," was all that Mole could muster to say.

***

Anne looked out the window; she thought she heard Kale's voice. She knew that Kale said that he would call in an hour, but she felt something was wrong. She walked outside to the porch with phone trying to call him. "Come on, Kale. Answer your phone." She looked at the time again. She got a weird feeling as she looked down her driveway. "I'm coming, Kale." She went back inside and grabbed her keys. She took off down the driveway headed towards Kale's house to make sure he got home okay.

***

Osiah instinctively put himself between Alex and Vandor. "What are you doing here?"

"I am a patient entity, but even I have my limits," he watched Alex. "I'm tired of waiting for you to make choices. Join me, or someone dies."

"Kiss my ass," Alex said behind Osiah.

Osiah looked down at his young former mentee shaking his head. There was small smirk Osiah showed due to his Little Spitfire's confidence. That quickly disappeared as he turned to Vandor. "I think you got your answer."

Vandor leered with hatred towards his former partner of the Dark. "Rumor has it you're going home. Good for you." His attention turned to Alex. "Young little dark mistress, whatever shall you do? So hard for someone you love, as a sibling, to die such a horrible death."

Alex just happened to get a text from Anne saying she hasn't heard from Mole and she is going to go out to look for him. Then it just clicked what Vandor said. "What did you say?" Alex said walking up to Vandor with no fear. "Say that again."

"You heard me," Vandor's face turned cold. "Such happiness is about to be extinguished."

Alex jumped over the fence and her eyes flared blue with her fists raging a fire flame. "You piece of dark, skin-rotting, smelling, son of a bitch!"

"We can fight where you will waste valuable time and lose, or you can go be a hero," Vandor informed her.

Alex wanted to hit him. "I swear you black hearted bastard." Alex turned to Komptin. "Can you find Mole?" Komptin flashed his and sniffed the air. He growled and barked towards the direction to find Mole. Alex looked to Osiah for permission.

"GO!" Osiah yelled. "I'll catch up."

Alex nodded. Komptin took off in full sprint as Alex followed. The glow of her light disappeared into the dark.

"Why?" Osiah asked Vandor.

"Why?" Vandor shouted back. "You know the reason. The Dark was always present until the Lite invaded. This world was ours, we were here first." Vandor opened the gate inviting Osiah to step off church property.

Osiah stepped off property and lit his fist with a purple haze. "Not exactly how I wanted to spend my evening." He cracked his neck looking at his former partner in evil.

"Yes, just think, you could be at dinner tonight," Vandor told him.

"What?" Osiah asked as he stared at him.

"Do you think you could do it again?" Vandor asked him sneeringly. "I don't think her guardians can defend her from that many Infiltrators and Hosts."

"There is no way you could get that many through," Osiah stated out of fear.

"Willing to bet her life on that?" Vandor sneered.

Osiah turned and ran, trying to find Celestial.

Vandor turned to the church as he spat on the ground. "No matter what, I win tonight."

***

Anne was frantic. Kale wasn't answering his phone. Now she was more worried than angry. Now

271

she knew something was wrong. She was no sign of him in a ditch or anything. In this distance she saw what seemed to be a small blinking red light. Anne sped up and as she got closer, her fear had come true. Kale's bike was on the side of the road. She slammed on the brakes and ran to the bike but there was no sign of Kale. There was no sign of him, he didn't answer when she yelled for him. She grabbed her crucifix around her neck and said a prayer. She opened her eyes when she heard a faint scream in the woods. Anne ran into the woods after what she heard. There was a figure standing in a small opening in the woods. She got closer and saw it was Roger with a baseball bat in his hands.

He turned to her. "Anne, what are you doing here?"

"Roger, what are you doing?" Anne asked. "Have you seen Kale?"

He put his finger to his lip. "Shhhh…" He pointed down. "I think he is trying to say something."

"Anne," Kale moaned out. "Run, get out of here."

Anne looked down to see Kale on the ground with blood dripping from his nose and several cuts on his face. "KALE!" Anne screamed as she ran up to him. "What have you done?!"

"Anne." Roger didn't know what to do. "You were always way too innocent. You should have stayed away."

Anne dropped to her knees to tend to Kale and kissed him. "I'm here, I'm here," Anne nurtured.

"Roger." She looked up at him. "Please stop. Please, I beg of you."

Roger took a minute to think about the situation. He looked to Anne, then Mole, and then back at Anne. "Wait a minute. You two?" He made a circle with his left hand and he put his right finger in the hole, motioning it up and down. "Huh, didn't see that coming." He shrugged it off. "Oh well, gotta finish what I started." Roger raised the bat to hit Kale for a final blow and stopped. "Just kidding," he said playfully kicking him. He put the bat down to help pick up Kale. "Damn, you're a heavy guy."

Anne was on the other side of Kale helping him up. "Hang on, Kale, I'll get you to a hospital."

Roger placed Kale on a tree hanging his arms over two branches to support him leaning forward on the tree. Anne could see Kale's knee was broken as he could hardly stand. Anne hurried to find her phone. She grabbed her phone and tried to call 911.

Roger grabbed the phone and threw it in the air smashing it with his bat. "No, Anne, bad."

"Roger," Mole said from hanging on the tree.

He walked up to him. "Speak up there, buddy, can't quite hear you."

"Roger," Mole said. "You're still a pathetic little man."

For a second there, Anne thought she saw a flash of red come from his eyes as he grabbed Mole's head and hit it against the tree. Anne screamed and started advancing towards him. Roger went to swing his bat. "Nope," he said to her. "Not one more step."

Anne stepped forward. "You're going to kill me anyway."

"Not necessarily," Roger said.

"He's suffered enough!!" Anne screamed.

"Nope," Roger pushed Anne out of the way. He swung the bat and smashed it against Mole's back. Kale went crashing down to the ground.

"ROGER!!" Anne screamed. She ran up to Mole as he dropped down again. She placed his head on her lap and stroked his hair. "Shhhh, Kale. Save your strength. Just concentrate on not falling asleep. Whatever you do, don't fall asleep," Anne was fearful if he closed his eyes, it would be for the last time.

Roger walked up to Mole. "You kept Alex away from me by leading her on, keeping her blind on what I can do for her. In turn, I will make sure you will never walk again." Anne's eyes grew big as she hugged Mole's face. She prayed for something to stop Roger. She watched as Roger raised the bat ready to strike and then he was tackled by a big purple creature. Anne's eyes were now even bigger. This towering, massive gargoyle looking creature stood in front of Anne and Mole almost as if he was protecting them.

"Oh my God," Anne said looking at the creature. It turned to Anne and flashed its big neon blue eyes. It slowly walked over to the two of them, almost checking to see if they were all right. Anne saw the creature look back at Roger who was knocked out lying on the ground.

Anne covered Mole's eyes. "Don't look," she said. "Easy, boy." Anne stared at the creature.

"Komptin," a familiar voice yelled in the distance.

Alex came running up behind the massive creature.

Roger stood up from being knocked down. His eyes glowing red as his fists were starting to do the same. "Alex, what are you doing here?"

Alex's fist lit blue as she flew in the air and punched Roger down. He stood back up from Alex's attack and returned the same with a demonic growl. He leaped at Alex and she managed to throw him into a nearby tree breaking it in half.

"What...the...hell?" Anne asked, looking at Alex and the massive creature.

Alex walked up to the creature she called Komptin and patted him on the back. "Good boy," she said. She bent down to Mole. "I...I...I don't know what to do," Alex said, fighting back tears. "Oh Mole, hang in there."

"Alex," Anne said. "I don't think we should move him." She continued to hold him. "And what was all that?"

"I will tell you later, long story," Alex said. "Do you trust me?"

"Of course," Anne was trying to figure out all what was going on.

Roger seemed to float up on his feet as he wiped the bark off his jacket. "You're not supposed to be here."

Alex's eyes flashed blue as she got up from kneeling next to Mole and Anne. Alex stood up facing Roger. "What do you mean?"

"Vandor said you would be on the other side of town," he explained wiping the brush off his leather trench coat. "You are kind of messing things up."

Alex took a minute to try to figure out what Roger meant. "Vandor said, 'So hard for someone you love, as a sibling, to die such a horrible death.'"

Roger laughed. "Oh, my dear, it is unfortunate you are not as smart as you are pretty." He sat down on a stump in the forest. He reached in his pocket and lit a cigarette. "Someone you love as a sibling, and you chose Mole, why? Anyway, bad call on your part," Roger informed her. He looked down at his watch. "All these years, you knew but did nothing to help, well tonight, daddy is going to start his punishment."

Alex turned to Anne. "Sara!"

"Took you long enough," Roger said, tapping his head.

Alex nonchalantly lifted her arm and blasted a neon blue energy force from her arm knocking Roger into the next tree breaking it on top of him.

She knelt down next to Anne. Alex placed her hand on Mole's chest. "Look, I don't know how much time I have. I have to get to Sara's." She turned to Komptin who was looking around the forest. "Komptin?" He turned his attention back to

Alex. "Will you look after the two of them? Make sure nothing happens to them." Komptin shook his head in disagreement. "Komptin, look at me. Promise me you will protect them with your life."

Komptin flashed his eyes and snuggled up to Alex with his big gargoyle head. Alex kissed him on his forehead and turned to Anne and Mole.

"Komptin will make sure nothing will happen to you."

Alex nodded to Komptin.

"Alex, what is going on?" Thunder and lightning started to show itself in the distance.

"I promise I will tell you," Alex said. She kissed Mole on his hand, got up and hugged Anne tightly as she was still holding onto Mole's head on her lap. "If I make it back."

She got up and started to run to Sara's house.

Komptin started to growl and barked in the direction of Roger who was just getting up from being knocked down. "Damn, I think I want her more now," he laughed.

Anne looked at Roger with a serious scowl.

"Don't get mad at me, you're just collateral damage, and your boyfriend was, well, perks of the job," he said picking up his cigarette off the ground. Roger turned his head and nodded as if someone was talking to him. "I have to go now, but we had a change of plans. You gotta die."

Anne looked to the woods and three sets of red eyes appeared in the dark. Sounds of low growls filled the cold dark air. Komptin turned and faced them with a growl flashing his eyes and offered a loud growling howl in preparation for a fight.

***

"Dad," Sara said. "You scared me." Sara turned to lock the door behind. She tried to control the trembling in her hands, but she couldn't stop it. "Are you hungry?"

"Where do you think you're going?" he said to her in an eerily calm voice.

"The kitchen, I'm a little hungry." She walked into the kitchen for her phone but couldn't find it. The refrigerator seemed to be a focus to find something for her dad, hoping to God he didn't hear any of what she and Robbie were talking about. "How about some cake?" When she closed the door, she turned to find her dad was standing right beside her.

A little startled scream seemed to echo in the house. "You scared me. Are you hungry?" Sara heard a far distant thunder rumble outside. "Sounds like rain is coming." She was trembling when she sat down on the table with the cake in front her.

Her dad seemed to be quite larger than she remembered. Even the comfort of cake didn't seem to help her nerves.

"This piece is just too big." She got up and went to the knife block to cup a steak knife in her to slide it in her pocket as she grabbed a knife to cut the cake. The sound of her taking a couple deep breaths before turning around couldn't be hidden.

"Dad—"

But he was gone.

Sara walked out of the kitchen and into the living room still holding the knife in her hand. "Dad," she softly said as the thunder was getting a little bit louder.

Sara didn't know what to do. The only thing she thought of was, she wasn't going to wait until after graduation. It's time to get the hell out of there. With the knife in her hand, she walked upstairs to her bedroom. It was quiet, she was trying to listen to hear any sound of her dad. The door creaked as she opened the door to her bedroom.

"Dad?"

She hurried, looked around and quickly grabbed her suitcase from underneath her bed. She grabbed what she thought she could survive on and what little money she had stored.

Sara ran downstairs and headed towards the door as lightning flashed. She turned around half expecting to see her dad standing there again. He wasn't there but the lightning flashed again, and she saw her cell phone sitting on the kitchen cabinet. There was no sign of her father. As calm as she could, she put her suitcase down before carefully going for her phone. The sounds of thunder were not doing her any favors in keeping calm. She peeked in the kitchen to see if he was in there.

She quickly snatched the phone and tapped the screen. "Come on, come on." She hoped for a little bit hope of getting out of here.

It was shut off. She fumbled with the phone trying to turn it on. The startup screen came on and a loud thunderous noise came from outside with a flash of lightning. Sara ran out the door. The instant she stepped onto the porch, she was grabbed by her dad. He forcefully carried her into the living room throwing her onto the couch.

"No, no," her dad said. "I don't think you are having Mexican tonight."

"Dad," she pleaded. "You are scaring me."

"Oh, I haven't even begun to scare you." His dark eyes flashed red, and he grinned showing his animal-like teeth.

Sara screamed and jumped off the couch. She headed into the kitchen to get out the back door, but her dad grabbed her, dragged her by the hair, and threw her down into the coffee table. Pieces of wood and glass shattered. Sara felt weak and all she could see was the outline of her dad approach her with his glowing red eyes.

He knelt beside her; Sara decided she wasn't going down without a fight. She grabbed the steak knife she had placed in her pocket. She screamed as she shoved the knife into her dad's stomach.

Her dad got up and sighed when he saw what she did. As if it didn't even hurt, he pulled it out of his stomach. He dropped it on the floor like a comedian dropping his microphone. Sara saw a small hole in the storm's cloud from the window where she saw a star peer through.

"Please forgive me for…." Sara screamed from the pain as her body was torn into by her father.

After a flash of light, an essence of peace came over to Sara as she slipped away.

**

Alex ran as fast as she could through the woods. The speed and agility was as if she was almost flying through the air. All she could think of was Sara. How could Alex be so stupid? How could she let her guard down? She will never forgive herself if anything happened to Sara.

She appeared out of the woods to Sara's driveway. Alex ran to the house and jumped over the stairs of the porch as she lit her fists. The doors open with a blast from her fist, busting off its hinges with debris flying across the living room.

The room was dark. Alex's fists lit the room enough to see Alex's fear had come true, she was too late. Sara's lifeless body laid in the shattered coffee table. Alex picked up Sara's torn body carefully placing it on the couch.

Alex moved the bloody hair out of Sara's face. Alex fought back the tears as she placed her head on Sara's chest. "I'm so sorry," Alex cried. "I'm so sorry."

Alex turned to the window behind her and saw Sara's dad staring at her with blood dripping from his mouth. He flashed his red eyes and grinned at Alex. She didn't hesitate as she jumped out the window grabbing him and throwing him into a tree.

He growled when he got up from the ground. "You know I always hated you."

"Wasn't too fond of you either," Alex said, lighting her fists.

She swung as he ducked out of the way. A chunk of the tree landed on the ground. Alex instinctively swung and kicked Jim knocking him to the ground.

He looked up and growled and charged Alex. The wind got knocked off her as she got tackled by the Demon. Alex head butted him and slithered out from underneath him just as he tried to stomp her head in with his boot.

Alex got up and punched him in the back kidneys. Sara's dad swung behind him as Alex ducked out of the way and she nailed him with a blue lighted uppercut. He fell to the ground.

He regained his composure and stood up.

"Sara never hurt anyone," Alex said, looking to her father. "Why?"

"Because nothing tastes better than human meat that has been affected with fear," he replied, licking his lips. "And she was the best I've ever tasted."

Alex fist burst as she was about to attack but Jim took off running. Alex took a couple of steps to chase him but stopped. She didn't know if she was going to survive the night and if it was to be her last night, she needed to make sure she was going to do it right.

Chapter 14

Alex walked into the living room where her friend laid lifelessly still. Alex took a minute to reminisce on all the good times the two of them had together. Alex knew this was no way for her friend to die. She should have stopped him. She was a Sentry, she was supposed to protect.

Her failures caused Alex to break her promise to her best friend. Sara's hand felt cold when Alex grabbed it. "I'm sorry." She kissed her on the forehead. "Be at peace." She wiped a tear from her eyes to follow her murderer into the woods.

She could feel what route Jim had taken. There were some stars showing in between the clouds. Alex dropped to her knees and folded her hands.

"For some reason that I cannot think of, You chose me to be a Lite Sentry. At first, I thought it was something pretty cool, but I now know what it entails. I know why I am, what I am." She wiped another tear from her eye. "Please ensure Sara is at peace, she deserves the break." Alex stood up, brushed off her knees of the dirt and looked to her fists. "If I don't make it through the night, take care of my parents, Mole and Anne, and tell Osiah...send a message to him that I appreciate everything he has done for me." She lit her fists while her eyes had a continuous blue glow. "One of us will not see morning."

Alex ran off into the woods.

Anne still didn't know what to think of this massive, purple-skinned creature sitting in front her. All she knew was that he did not like those red eyes looking at them through the night woods. She could hear the growl from Komptin anticipating the attack. Anne picked up a rock that was lying next to her. She didn't know what this rock would do, but it was the only thing she had.

Mole started moving around trying to get up. "Stay down, Kale," Anne said stroking his hair. She was fighting back tears as she wiped the blood from Kale's head on her clothes. "Shh…we're going to be okay." She looked up at Komptin. "Aren't we?"

Multiple crashes through the woods meant it was starting. Anne was almost afraid to look up. Komptin quickly gazed upon Anne to see where they were at. He nodded at Anne, assuring she was going to be okay. Anne caught herself smiling at the little assurance from this gargoyle.

The first creature that was all black broke through the wooded darkness and Komptin greeted him with a force to take down a mountain. Anne's eyes grew big as Komptin took down the creature. Komptin grabbed its head and swung the body around flinging it like a Frisbee into a set of trees, breaking them in half.

A second creature came charging and jumped onto Komptin's back digging its claws in as far as they could. Komptin screamed. He bucked him around like a bull kicking off a rider. The creature

284

fell on the ground. The giant gargoyle puts his massive claw on the creature's head. He opened his massive mouth and tore out the creature's throat. The creature choked on its own blood as it disintegrated into the ground.

Komptin then charged the creature he threw into the trees. He jumped and landed on the creature. All Anne could see were the two shadows wrestling.

"What's going on?" Kale asked, trying to look.

"Stay down, Kale," Anne said. "And just look at me."

Kale looked at Anne and smiled. "That's easy." He lifted his hand to her face. "You look like an angel."

Anne smiled back at him. "Kale, you're going to be fine."

"Anne," Kale said. "I feel funky."

Anne's stomach dropped. "You stay with me, you hear me. You are not allowed to leave me!"

Kale heard some commotion in the woods. He looked back at Anne. "Leave you? I don't think I'm in the condition to leave anywhere." Kale tried to look at his body. "Oh man, you think I will make my morning run tomorrow?"

Anne laughed. "Stop scaring me like that."

"I'm either lying in a mud or I think I made a mess in my pants," Kale laughed.

"If it makes you feel better, you are lying in some pretty stinky mud," Anne pointed out.

Kale smirked. "Well I may need help washing it off?" He choked as he was laughing, wincing in pain.

Anne playfully slapped him. "I can get that big male nurse from the hospital."

"I bet he's got soft hands." Kale started to laugh. "Anne, I really hurt."

Anne looked down at Kale smiling. She leaned down and kissed him. "Kale, I just wanted to let you know…"

The sound of a tree branch cracking made Anne look up and she was face to face with one of those black creatures with its mouth opened.

***

Alex was running through the woods and came across to the backside of the parking lot of the junkyard. Alex could faintly make out the figure that must have been Sara's dad. Alex could feel her eyes tear up and she started getting angrier. Her body was bursting with anger. The images of Sara and her lifeless body lying on the couch raced through her mind. She started breathing heavier and heavier and the emotions were starting to become overrun.

She turned a corner and was grabbed by two twin girls before Alex had run into a beautiful blonde girl. "Child, what is your hurry?" She motioned for the other two to put her down.

Alex just dropped to her knees and uncontrollably started to weep. The two girls, one

286

with green hair the other purple stayed by Alex's side. "I...I...I...failed her," Alex cried.

"No, no you did not." She wiped Alex's tears off to the side. She knelt to meet Alex face to face. "She is safe now and her dad will not hurt her anymore. She will no longer know what pain is. She is so proud to be your friend."

The two girls turned to the blonde girl, the green-haired one spoke, "We need to leave..."

The purple-haired angel finished the rest of the sentence, "Before it is too late."

The two twins both looked in the direction with a look of deep concern. "We are not alone."

"No, no you're not," a familiar voice came out from the darkness.

Alex looked to see Vandor approach the four of them with Infiltrators and their glowing eyes slowly surrounding them.

***

Anne embraced Kale. "Don't look," she said. She covered Kale's head with her body anticipating the attack.

The creature lunged forward at Anne and Kale but Komptin jumped onto the creature's back and bit into the back of its neck. The creature howled in pain. Komptin tossed the creature off to the side like a rag doll. Anne got excited and threw the rock accidentally hit Komptin in the head. "Sorry," Anne embarrassingly apologized.

Komptin turned his attention back to the creature. The creature started to circle around and lunged at him. Komptin returned the assault by overpowering the creature. The bear-like creature landed on its back with Komptin standing on its chest. Komptin bit into the creature's neck, grabbing the bottom half of its jaw ripping it off. The creature disappeared into the ground as Komptin spit out the remains of the black creature. Their massive protector walked over them to ensure they were safe.

"Kale," her dad's voice came from the roadway.

"Dad?" Anne yelled. "Dad we're over here!"

"Anne?" Her dad was coming into the woods. "Is that you?"

"Dad! Please hurry," Anne cried out. "Kale is hurt, he's hurt really bad!"

"What happened?" Her dad asked the two of them.

"Kale got jumped by someone and I found his bike, I came running to help him, my phone got busted, my car got stolen, and this creature came and different creatures, Alex came with this gargoyle looking thing," Anne cried out.

"Anne, are you okay?"

"Dad, I'm telling you, look at this…" Anne turned to Komptin who now a German Shepard was sitting down licking his paw.

"Whose dog is this?" Anne's dad asked.

"I don't know," Anne said. "What about Kale?"

"I can't get any reception in the woods, let me get to the car because I had a few bars out there. Stay here, keep him conscious," her dad said, running to the car.

Anne looked down at Kale. "Don't worry, help is coming." She stroked his hair. Anne viewed over at Komptin who continued to lick his paws.

Anne's dad came running back into the woods. "Anne, the ambulance is on its way." He looked down at Kale. "Hang in there, Kale. Can he talk?"

"This kind of hurts," Kale told Anne's dad.

He had a worried look in his face as he rendered Kale first aid. "I'm going to grab my jacket from the car to use as a blanket for Kale."

Anne looked to Komptin who was still licking his paw. "Did I imagine all that?" Komptin stopped licking his paw as something had grabbed his attention. He looked to the distance and back over at Anne, flashed his eyes before he ran into the woods.

***

Alex jumped to her feet. The two girls pushed Alex out of the way surrounding the blonde girl. The two girls' clothes disintegrated showing off their angelic battle armor. The glowing misty wings were set to a fighting position. The green haired one pulled out a lighted sword as the purple one showed off her skills with a lighted bow staff with a pointed end. Alex peered over at the blonde girl who was backed against the wall. She grabbed Alex pulling her towards her like a lioness protecting her cub.

Vandor looked up to the dark clouded sky with silent rumbling in the distance. "Nice night," he said with an evil grin.

"It would be highly suggested…" the green haired girl said.

"If you left," the purple haired girl finished.

Vandor showed the Infiltrators started to show their presence. "Please, bluffing is the last form of desperation. You two are scared, almost as scared as that one night." He looked at the two bodyguards. "You know you are outnumbered and overpowered." He gazed upon the blonde girl. "Celestial, it's been a long time."

Alex had to do a double take. "You're Celestial?"

"Vandor," Celestial spoke. "What you are about to do will do neither side any good."

"Good? I will make sure good does not exist," Vandor said. "Hate is what drives humanity." Vandor looked to Alex. "My little girl over there is oozing with it."

"Kiss my ass!" Alex yelled.

Vandor looked over to Roger as he appeared from the herd of Infiltrators. "Now, now, I promised that to Gron."

Roger looked over to Alex licking his lips as he flashed his red eyes. "Hey Alex, all of this could be avoided if you just realize what we could do together." He blew her a kiss.

Alex cringed at the thought. "I'd rather die."

"That may be the case after tonight," Vandor said. He gazed upon Celestial. "I'll give you a deal.

Either you give me the Lite Sentry or be eliminated."

"Give him the girl," the purple haired girl said.

Alex gave her a dirty look. "Excuse me?"

"She is expendable," the green haired girl continued.

"You are out of your damn mind," Alex said to the girls. Alex broke away lighting her fists. "It will be a cold day Hell before I let you take me."

"Either way," Vandor said. "I'm going to have one of you." He walked closer over to three of them.

The two girls cracked their necks and got into a battle stance.

"VANDOR!" a scream came from the woods.

Alex saw Osiah coming from the woods. Alex looked to the sky. "Thank God."

Vandor got Alex's attention. "He had nothing to do with it." He turned his attention over to Osiah. "Ah, my old friend. Seems like we are revisiting our last night together so many years ago."

The Infiltrators cleared a path for Osiah to get through. They growled and snapped as Osiah walked up between Vandor and the girls. He nodded over at Alex. "You all right, Little Spitfire."

Alex nodded. "I'm okay."

He walked to the purple and green haired girls. The two of them parted for him to get through to the blonde girl.

The blonde angel spoke with fear in her voice. "Osiah." She reached out her hands. The two locked eyes.

"Celestial," he returned.

"How touching." Vandor was showing signs of growing impatient. "So nice for you all to die together."

Osiah looked around his surroundings. Alex could tell he was calculating the battle plan. He met eyes with Alex and gave her a small wink and a grin. Alex prevented herself from laughing because she knew he had a plan to get out of this. He turned back to Celestial. "How far are you from a gate?" he whispered over to her.

"A bit far, east," Celestial spoke.

Osiah gazed to the left quickly. "Okay."

He turned to the Dark Conduit. "Vandor, I have a proposition for you."

Vandor interest piqued. "I'm listening."

Osiah patted Celestial's hand and kissed her. "You're going to be okay." He squeezed Alex's shoulders as he walked passed. Alex knew something was going to happen. He turned his attention to Vandor. "You let them go and I will come with you."

"NO!" Alex and Celestial both shouted.

Osiah turned and motioned to them that it was going to be okay.

"And why would I do that?" Vandor said looking at the girls.

"If you kill me, I will never be, I disappear," Osiah said. "But, if I choose to come with you, you will have me for eternity."

Vandor looked interested. "Go on."

292

"Think of what the Dark Master would say if you brought me back down for eternity. Think of the gratitude he would have for you bringing back the one who betrayed him. You'll have other shots at Celestial, you know this, but you'll never have a shot at bringing me back."

Vandor walked up to Osiah. This was truly an opportunity. He grazed his hands across Osiah's face then grabbed his orange-hair, pulling it back. "You are really going to regret this proposal."

"Will you let me say good-bye?" Osiah asked. "Least you could do for an eternity at your command."

Vandor let him go. "You may, only because it will be more torturous for you knowing it will be the last you see of them."

Osiah turned to the purple and green haired girls. "Ariel and Devine, how I am going to miss you, please one last group hug before I go." Ariel and Devine looked at each other and came in for a hug. The three of them hugged each other tightly. They let go each other and Osiah walked over to Alex. He knelt down. "My Little Spitfire."

"Don't go, we can fight out of this," Alex pleaded, fighting back tears.

"This is not the time for that," Osiah said, wiping the tears off her cheek. He placed his hand on her heart. "I will always be with you. Keep your faith and stay strong." He got up and kissed her on the forehead. He tapped her on her heart. "Rare as Blue Gold."

Osiah and Celestial looked at each other and then embraced each other in a last kiss. Celestial whispered, "You do not have to do this."

"You know I do," Osiah replied. "I love you."

"I love you, too," Celestial replied, wiping golden tears from her eyes.

"Are you done?" Vandor impatiently asked.

Osiah patted her on the hands again and turned around. "Yeah, let's do this." He sadly walked over to Vandor.

"NO!" Alex screamed breaking free from Celestial. Devine quickly grabbed Alex holding her in a bear hug. Alex continued to scream as she was kicking and swinging about.

"Alexandria, you must stop," Devine whispered in her ear.

Ariel came to the other side of Alex, "It is the only way."

Osiah raised his arm towards the Infiltrators. "See you on the other side."

Vandor walked up to Osiah and put his arm around him. "Come on ol' friend. I know someone who would like to see you." Osiah started to walk towards the woods when Vandor stopped in his tracks. "On second thought."

Vandor punched Osiah in the back going through to the outside of his chest. His demon-clawed hand pulling out Osiah's glowing purple heart. "I'd rather see you die."

Vandor turned to the Infiltrators. "Kill them."

Osiah turned to look at Celestial and Alex who were screaming. Osiah dropped to his knees catching himself with his hands on the ground. He coughed blood and looked to the four of them as he disappeared into the air.

Devine let go Alex. "It is time, Alex."

Ariel added, "To put your training to use."

Alex slammed her fists on the ground lighting them up. "For Osiah, you will not touch her."

Vandor walked through the Infiltrators towards the woods. "Have fun." He walked into the woods and disappeared.

The surrounding Infiltrators attacked. Alex gave a massive uppercut to the first Infiltrator of the group which sent it flying into four others knocking them over. Ariel grabbed her sword and sliced open the fence to the junkyard and then swung around hitting an Infiltrator across the face, knocking it to the ground.

Devine jabbed her bow staff upwards to an Infiltrator leaped into the air. She then jumped into the air swinging her bow staff to the other side. She forced the Infiltrator's head into the ground. Once she landed, she swung her staff around, knocking another across the face, tossing it into two other Infiltrators.

Two more Infiltrators lunged at Alex; she quickly stepped to the side, but a third Infiltrator tackled her to the ground. Devine quickly jumped on the Infiltrator's back. She put her bow staff around the Infiltrator's neck and pulled back as hard as she could. Another Infiltrator sprang at Devine to knock her off, but Ariel met it with a kick sending it flying into a pile of wood that was stacked up.

"We have to pull back," Ariel cried.

"Into the junkyard," Devine said.

"Alex! Take Celestial into the junkyard," Ariel commanded.

"We will buy you time," Devine screamed as an Infiltrator scratched her arm. She instinctively kicked the Infiltrator giving her some room to maneuver. She spun her bow staff to the pointed end and jabbed it into the chest of the Infiltrator. It screamed in pain as it disappeared into the ground.

Alex acknowledged. An Infiltrator swung and sent Alex flying into the wall landing next Celestial. "Oh, there you are," Alex said. Celestial helped Alex up. "We need to go."

Alex grabbed her hand and led her into the junkyard. Ariel and Devine continued to fend off the Infiltrators. Alex was hoping they wouldn't get overwhelmed because if they did that meant she was on her own.

She didn't think Celestial was the type to get her hands dirty. "Are you scared?"

Celestial turned around. "Are you?" She turned her back around to look at an old car.

"Extremely," Alex said looking around. The faint sounds of battles were dissipating as they dug deeper into the junkyard. Alex could see she was sad, but not for the fear of death, it wasn't even for the loss of Osiah. It was something else. "I will die before anything happens to you." Alex walked towards Celestial. "Osiah has trained me well, hell, I even…" Alex tripped over a muffler lying on the ground. She had fallen face first into the dirt. She sprung right up, hoping Celestial didn't see that.

"If I am to disappear into the night, the human race will become enslaved in what they will perceive as a living Hell," Celestial stated.

"What do you mean?" Alex asked.

"Ever hear the quote 'better to reign in Hell, then serve in Heaven'? You cannot reign if you have no one to maintain power over; mankind is the 'someone' that demons will reign over," Celestial pointed out.

"And you were created to ensure the balance couldn't ever be tipped," Alex concluded.

Celestial turned to Alex, "I am the conduit for the Lite; for it to reach mankind, I must be mortal because mankind is mortal."

"Then why are you here?" Alex asked looking around.

"A conduit is represented on both sides; I leave this plane to, as your generation would put it, 'recharge', and then I must return to Earth to disperse the Lite," Celestial said. "I go where Dark has the most potential influence."

"Influence?" Alex inquired.

"The draw of a potential Lite Sentry has led them here," Celestial taught her. "If they were to turn you, it would damage the Lite chances to keep the Dark at balance."

"This whole thing is to turn me to the Dark?" Alex asked.

"With my death as a grand prize," Celestial said. "If they do not turn you, they will kill you."

297

"Nope, not going to happen," Alex said. "I'm going to get you out of here, I'm going to college, and I really, really, really, could go for an Apollo right now."

Celestial walked over to Alex and put her hand on Alex's cheek. "I can see why Osiah treasured you."

Alex heard a crash and turned around to see Sara's dad looking at her. His glowing red eyes and fingers now had claws were aimed at Alex. She turned around with her fists lit. "Go." She turned her head to Celestial,

Celestial stayed behind a car surrounded by piles of old cars. She crouched down watching out for potential Infiltrators to find her. "Alex," Celestial called out to her. "Hosts, or what you call Demons, are a lot stronger than Infiltrators," she warned. "Be careful."

"Don't worry, I got this," she said as she winked at her. She turned around as was instantly met with the most powerful punch she had felt. It swung her around knocking her to the ground. "Ow," was all she could muster to say.

"Last chance," Sara's dad said. "Join with Gron or die a horrible, miserable, painful death…for you." Sara's dad stepped forward. "I really hope you choose death."

Alex stood back up brushing the dirt off her shirt. "Sara didn't deserve to have a father like you," She told him, circling around.

"She was a horrible daughter to have. She wouldn't listen, she defied my every word, and she ruined my life just like her whore mother," Jim said. "And when I was offered to get rid of her on that night, I took it."

Alex screamed and charged Sara's dad. He stepped out of the way as he scratched her on her back. Alex could feel blood drip from her back. She quickly got up to face her opponent. "That was my favorite shirt."

Sara's dad hissed as his eyes flashed red. Alex ran towards him. He swung as Alex ducked while simultaneously punching him in the stomach. He bent over from the blow. This gave Alex the opportunity to grab the back of his head and kneed him in the face multiple times before he picked her up.

He flipped her over his back, causing the Lite Sentry to be slammed into the earth. She coughed up some dust she had inhaled from the ground. Quick reflexes prevented Jim's boots from smashing onto her face. She grabbed that muffler which tripped her before and stood up swinging it, crashing it up on the chin of Sara's dad. He howled in pain as he staggered back to gather his bearings. Alex watched Jim flex his body as he grew, tearing some of his clothes.

"Oh crap." Alex ran over to Sara's Dad at full sprint.

He swung as she slid underneath his legs. She got up and jumped on his back, punching him on the back of this head. He ran backwards slamming her into a wall of cars. Alex screamed in pain. He stepped forward and then slammed backwards again.

Alex broke her hold and fell to the ground. She stood up and was met with an elbow her in the face. It caused her to be swung around. She was then punched her across the face. Alex staggered away from Jim, falling on the ground. He aggressively kicked her in the side which sent her flying into a car. Jim walked over as she tried to get up and he punched her in the face again knocking her down. She spit out blood as she tried to stand.

A crash of cars falling distracted Jim for a moment. It was just enough for Alex to catch her breath, but it wasn't enough to do anything. So, she tried to sneak off but was grabbed by Jim. He lifted her up with two hands on her throat. Her feet dangled in the air as she tried prying his hands off her throat.

"Now you little Goth Bitch, you die." He then was holding her with one hand on her throat. He took his other hand and slowed jabbed his clawed finger into Alex's neck.

Alex screamed in agonizing pain. She spat in the face of the Host and a mixture of blood and saliva dripped from his face. He threw Alex out of anger into a deep pool of murky water near one of the cars.

Jim took a moment to see if Alex was going to get up. He started walking over to her when he realized that Celestial was unprotected. This was the opportunity to get rid of her. He flipped over pieces of junk that covered the location where Celestial was hiding. Celestial was not there. She was nowhere to be found. He checked his surroundings and noticed something broke through a pile of metal where Celestial escaped. Screams of anger over losing such an opportunity to gain the advantage echoed.

A glow of blue caught Jim's eyes. He turned and saw the pool of water lighting up. Alex rose out of the water with one hand on the ground and other one had her fist glowing. Her body was covered in waves of blue lite. She lifted her head slowly as water dripped from her face that had a few strands of her black weave. Her eyes glowing neon blue were vibrant. She now stood up on both feet. She confidently walked out of the pool breathing heavy. She headed towards Jim with this intent; one of them was going to die.

Sara's dad growled and charged Alex. She dodged out of the way and she punched him across the face. With a kick to his stomach, Jim staggered a bit. This didn't prevent him from landing a punch on Alex's face; she staggered back but quickly gained composure. Determined and wanting to avenge Sara, she confidently walked back up to him, he swung again landing another across her face, and she returned the punch as he staggered.

They exchanged a one-for-one punch until Alex gained the advantage. Sara's dad tried lifting his arms for protection, but Alex's punches kept breaking through. Alex then ran around Jim and climbed the car. She jumped over to the demon's shoulders grabbing his head on her way to the ground.

His head smashed into the hard surface. Alex formed a sharp spearhead on her fist. She bent back his head and thrusted the pointed end into the ear of the Host. It poked out on the other end as he howled in pain. It disappeared into the ground and air.

"I'm Industrial." Alex got up to gather her thoughts.

Then, she remembered about Celestial. She ran over to a spot where she knew she was hiding but she was nowhere to be found. All she saw was a busted path leading to the outside of the junkyard.

"Oh no," Alex said, dropping to her knees. "They got her anyway."

She started to cry. She failed to protect Mole, failed to protect Sara, and now failed Osiah from not being able to protect the one he loved. All she could think about was how she was supposed to fight the Dark that will fall upon the world. Will it come all at once? Will it come slowly? How will she be able to fight such a force by herself? She leaned against the car, realizing all hope was now lost.

A battered Ariel and Devine came up to the hole in the junkyard. They sat and stared looking at the hole, each of them had their share of cuts oozing out glowing blue blood. Alex couldn't bring herself to look at them. Ariel grabbed the flannel shirt that Sara's dad was wearing and tore it. She wrapped it around a cut on her leg, wincing in pain. "We should go," she said.

Devine checked some wounds on her arm and head in the car mirror. "We do not have much time." The two of them went through the hole where Celestial was taken. Devine looked back at Alex, "Are you coming?"

Ariel continued, "Or do you want to just sit there?" She vanished her swords walking into the woods.

Alex hopped off the car and followed them into the dark forest. She swore she was going to right by making up for her failures.

Chapter 15

Alex walked through the woods with Ariel and Devine who really didn't say much. They didn't even acknowledge she was present. They too must have felt horrible for failing to protect Celestial. Alex didn't want to bring it up because she knew it was a sore subject for herself let alone for Ariel and Devine who spent eternity protecting her.

Devine stopped in her tracks. Ariel looked off into the woods. A white light appeared in the distance. Celestial was seen walking up from within the forest.

"Celestial," Alex whispered. "But…how?

A flash of blue eyes came up alongside Celestial. Komptin walked up beside her. Celestial petted him behind the ears. Ariel and Devine did a quick bow. She walked up to her guardians to check their wounds. "Are you alright?"

"They got a couple of good hits in," Ariel said.

"But nothing that a dip in the Golden Water will not heal," Devine pointed out.

Celestial smiled, placing her hand on their shoulders. "Thank you."

"Are you alright?" Devine asked.

"We are sorry about Osiah," Ariel said.

Celestial looked to the sky smiling. "I know what he did, he did for us. I will always remember him every time I look to the sky."

Alex looked to the sky but couldn't see the star that appeared when Osiah was killed. Alex fought back tears as she remembered her mentor. She turned to Komptin. "Mole and Anne, are they okay?"

"Komptin did not leave their side until he knew they were safe," Celestial said. "Your brother and friend are at the hospital now under care." Celestial walked over to Alex. "Your friend will need you; he has a rough recovery ahead of him. He is a good man, and he has a strong pure heart at his side right now."

Alex smiled. "I hope they make it."

Celestial turned around and headed towards the woods. "Their love for each other is strong, more than usual for such a young couple." Celestial gave Alex a concerned note of advice. "You have a rough life ahead of you." She knelt down to let Komptin lick her on the face. "Try to keep faith, we cannot afford to lose a Lite Sentry to the Dark."

"I will try," Alex said. She motioned for Komptin to join her at her side. He gave Celestial one final show of affection before joining Alex at her side. She waved to Celestial.

"I will come see you now and again, just remember you are not alone," Celestial pointed out. She motioned to Ariel and Devine. "Are you ready to go home?"

"You have no idea," Ariel said.

"Yes, she does," Devine pointed out.

They walked up to Alex.

"You did good kid," Devine mentioned.

"Almost as good as us," Ariel said.

"Almost," they simultaneously said with a small grin. A small light appeared in the darkness of the woods. It stretched to a doorway where Celestial and her guardians disappeared. Alex tried to peak on the other side, but it was too bright for her to see anything.

Alex took a minute to gather her thoughts. She knelt, petting Komptin as he licked on her face. "I need to go and check on Mole."

***

Alex stood outside the church gate in a long black coat. The Lite Sentry powers healed her wounds quick enough not to show by the time of her friend's funeral. She looked up at the bell tower where Osiah liked to overlook the town. She caught herself thinking about the hunts and on how he tried to prepare her for all her future encounters with the Dark. Also, he drank a lot. She pulled out an energy drink and chugged it down. "Some people have no self-control," she said to herself.

"He will be missed," a voice said beside him.

Alex turned around to see Celestial standing beside her. She gave her a big hug. "I don't know if I can do this," she cried into her chest.

She hugged her back. "It will be okay," she comforted her. "You will never forgive yourself if you do not go inside."

She looked up at her with tears running down her face. "Will I be forgiven?" she asked.

"For what?" She inquired.

"Failing."

"You did not fail," Celestial informed her as they both looked toward the sky. "Failure is not trying, failure is falling to Dark." She wiped the tears from her face. "You were nowhere near any of those." She opened the gate to the church. "Go, be strong."

Alex nodded and walked into church. The organ was playing, and the congregation was in small whispers. Alex sat in the front pew with Robbie on one side and Mole with Anne on the other, where she saw the coffin where her best friend was laying to rest. Father Joe got up in front of the church and addressed the congregation to begin the service.

***

After the service Alex, Mole, Anne, and Robbie, next to Dan, sat down at a table eating Sara's favorite kind of cake. No one really said anything. They all kind of looked at each other. Mole was first to speak, "This is really good."

"It is," Robbie agreed.

Alex snuck a piece of cake and fed it to Komptin.

Mole pulled out from the table with his wheelchair. Alex did everything she could do to prevent herself from crying at the sight of her hurt brother. "Well, look on the bright side, when I actually get my license, I will have great parking." The table laughed.

307

"What did the doctor say?" Robbie asked.

"It will be rough, but I will be able to walk again with a lot of PT, but my racing days are pretty much over," Mole informed them.

Anne rubbed his back affectionately giving him a loving smile. Mole's mom came over and put her hands on Anne's shoulders giving them an affectionate squeeze before giving her son a loving hug.

"All of you come on over to the restaurant tonight," she said. "Dinner will be on the house."

"Sounds like fun," Alex said.

Mole silently confirmed with Anne, "We're in."

"I'll be there," Robbie said.

Dan chimed in, "I never pass up the opportunity for free food."

Alex gave a loving pat on Komptin's head.

Robbie pointed out, "That dog hasn't left your side for about a week now."

Alex smiled down at Komptin who fell asleep. Alex found herself being jealous of him because she hasn't slept for over five days. She knew the Lite Sentry had taken its full effect on her. She even caught herself ordering a set of kitchen knives. "The church helped me get the paperwork through. He's my service dog and pretty much he goes where I go."

Anne looked to Komptin. "He's good dog." She scratched him behind the ears.

Father Joe came up to the table. "So, Alex, I got some news for you."

"What's that?" Alex said.

"You got a full scholarship to a college," Father Joe informed her.

"What?!" Alex asked, confused. "I didn't even apply to any."

Father Joe pulled out a pamphlet. "I took the liberty of applying to a college for you. You got a full ride. Congratulations," he said, smiling. "It's a Catholic college up north, St. Michaels."

The table all congratulated Alex. She was still confused but got excited at the same time. "What's the catch?"

Father Joe gave her the pamphlet.

"Are you serious?" Alex asked him.

"Enjoy college," Father Joe said, snickering.

"What's the catch?" Robbie asked.

Alex turned the pamphlet around and showed all the students in the school uniforms; a plaid skirt with a white shirt wearing a blazer. The table busted out laughing so hard they had to catch their breath.

Mole was starting to get anxious. He rolled back and started balancing his wheelchair on two wheels. "I'm in the mood for some fresh air before dinner." He glanced over at Anne. "Wanna ride?" Anne smiled and jumped into his lap as Mole moved towards the door. "See you guys tonight." Mole stopped at the elevator. Anne jumped off and hit the button to go up. Mole quickly wheeled himself backwards to Alex. "Hey, Alex." Alex looked over at him. "I love you, sis." He leaned over to give her a hug and she returned it in kind.

"I love you, too, bro!" Alex said. "I'll see you tonight at dinner."

***

After dinner, Alex walked into the church. Alex knew where the lights were, but she felt more comfortable in the dark. She strolled toward the altar to say a quick prayer. She gazed around the empty church before heading up to unlock the door to Osiah's office. She sat down in his chair. She opened up his desk drawer and saw his flask. Her fingers raked across the welding spots where the Infiltrator had shredded it. She opened it up and smelled it.

It made her sick to her stomach.

"Gross," Alex said.

The sound of opening an Apollo caused Komptin to look up at her. There was sadness to his eyes as he missed his former master.

"I miss him, too." She put the flask down.

They both headed downstairs to go outside. She took a sip of drinking her energy drink while staring at the lights of the town.

"I can feel them out there," she said aloud to Komptin. She looked to the sky. "I hope I do him proud, wherever he is."

"My child, he is proud of you," Celestial said coming up behind her.

Alex turned around and saw a fresh Ariel and Devine standing next to Celestial. She gave them a quick wave and they returned with a head nod. "I know what happened to him when he died." She looked up to the sky. "I'm just really nervous of doing this alone."

Celestial walked behind Alex and covered her eyes. She whispered something that Alex couldn't make out. She uncovered her eyes. "There."

"What did you do?" Alex asked.

"Look up," she insisted. Alex saw a purple star brighter than all the others. She smiled as she knew, but she still wanted confirmation from Celestial. "There is Osiah. Use it as a reminder of what he stood for. I know he was proud of you, he told me himself." She placed her hand on Alex's shoulders. "Be sure to never forget."

Alex turned around and Celestial had disappeared. The night had a stale fowl feel to it. Komptin walked up to Alex. "I'm kind of in the mood for a hunt." Komptin flashed his eyes in agreeance and transformed as a gargoyle. He gave out a tremendous roar. Alex flashed her eyes with her fists lighting up. "Lead the way." She motioned to Komptin. He easily jumped the fence and took off into the woods. "Show off," Alex said as she too jumped over the fence with ease to follow him.

***

In the shadows, Vandor and Salamor watched Alex take off into the dark forest. "She has great strength."

"Yes," Vandor commented.

311

"What is it that you wish?" the shadowed figure asked.

Vandor took a sniff of the air. He picked up some dirt and tasted it with his tongue. "Gron is off in the capital preparing a secondary front." Vandor turned to his dark misty servant. "I need you to go to college," Vandor turned around. "Don't fail."

Salamor bowed to his master. "To your command."

END OF PART 1